AN IRISH MYSTERY

Murder, Mayhem, and Scandal in an Irish Village

By

R. Dutton White

To Konstantine with heartfelt regards

An Irish Mystery
Published through Harpeth Editions

Interior Book Design and Layout by
www.integrativeink.com

ISBN: 978-1-63443-989-3

AUTHOR'S PREFACE

In the spring of the year 1816, I felt that I must take a respite from my work as a reporter for one of London's respected daily newspapers. The tasks assigned to me had been most demanding for several months previous and I was fatigued. Accordingly, I determined to make a leisurely trip through the south-western counties. The seventh of June found me in the village of Chawton in Hampshire where I had arranged to pass a day and a night before making my way to Salisbury and on to the west.

Although the village was small, there was a decent inn, and that afternoon I took tea in its public room. I was directed to a table next to one at which a man and woman sat in earnest, and even animated, conversation and I confess that my instincts as a man of the press made it impossible for me not to eavesdrop on their talk. They were speaking in low tones, but because of my highly honed listening abilities I soon understood that they were sharing their knowledge of recent scandal and murder in an Irish village. The lady was distantly related to one of the women central to the events under discussion and the gentleman was a close friend and sometime shipmate of one Captain John Massengill of the Royal Navy, who had unwittingly come into the midst of the situation and had become a key figure in its resolution.

AUTHOR'S PREFACE

In the spring of the year 1816, I felt that I must take a respite from my work as a reporter for one of London's respected daily newspapers. The tasks assigned to me had been most demanding for several months previous and I was fatigued. Accordingly, I determined to make a leisurely trip through the south-western counties. The seventh of June found me in the village of Chawton in Hampshire where I had arranged to pass a day and a night before making my way to Salisbury and on to the west.

Although the village was small, there was a decent inn, and that afternoon I took tea in its public room. I was directed to a table next to one at which a man and woman sat in earnest, and even animated, conversation and I confess that my instincts as a man of the press made it impossible for me not to eavesdrop on their talk. They were speaking in low tones, but because of my highly honed listening abilities I soon understood that they were sharing their knowledge of recent scandal and murder in an Irish village. The lady was distantly related to one of the women central to the events under discussion and the gentleman was a close friend and sometime shipmate of one Captain John Massengill of the Royal Navy, who had unwittingly come into the midst of the situation and had become a key figure in its resolution.

Immediately I sensed a compelling story, and as I listened, I realized that here was a tale I had to get to the bottom of and one that I had to bring to the public. In the society in which I found myself it was totally unacceptable to intrude on the conversation of perfect strangers, however, as a man of the press, I had not the slightest hesitation in flouting all convention and introducing myself. I used my most practiced and elegant manner and, surprisingly, my intrusion was accepted with considerable grace. I found that the lady was a local person, Miss J___ A_____, and the gentleman was himself a man of the Royal Navy, Commander [later Captain] F_____ M_____, who had come up that day from Portland where his ship was in harbor.

Commander M and Miss A had been acquainted for some years and it had been a coincidence of considerable interest that both had knowledge of the people in Ireland of whom they were in discussion. Realizing this, the Commander had taken advantage of his time in port to meet with Miss A to discuss the situation. In conversing with them I was frank to reveal my profession—not forgetting to mention my illustrious employer—and my interest in learning all I could about the story with the end of making it into a book. Miss A avowed that she was no writer and could not, even if she were, write on such a shocking subject. Commander M, for his part, made it clear that his efforts were, and for years to come would be, totally devoted to the King's service and there was no way he could think of involving himself in such a writing effort even if he were to think himself adequate to the task. Thus both were open to the idea of my producing a book about the events if the principals would allow me to do so.

As our acquaintance ripened, the two encouraged me in my plan and spent the remainder of the afternoon telling me all they could of the events and giving me letters of introduction to the principals in the story and full information about how to contact them. At the close of our meeting in the tea room I arranged to have a further conversation with Commander M, and in that conversation the Commander revealed a number of details of the affair under discussion that he had felt it inadvisable to bring to the attention of a lady of Miss A's sensibilities. These revelations served further to reinforce my plan to investigate the matter in Ireland and produce a volume.

I immediately abandoned any ideas of further leisure and booked transport to Bristol by coach and thence by sea to Dublin from which place I took coach to the village of Croome Court, the center of the events. There I met the principal characters, and with my introductions from Miss A and Commander M, was soon taken into their confidence and began to carry out the research for the most interesting story presented herewith. I have presented the story in all the graphic detail in which it happened and it is hoped that the shocking nature of some of the episodes chronicled herein will not be of a nature not too upsetting to the reader.

G. R.-S.

N.B. For the convenience of the reader, a listing of the principal characters in the narrative follows this preface. They are listed in the approximate order in which they appear.

CHARACTERS

John Massengill, son of the late village solicitor and officer in the Royal Navy

Lady Susan Seymour and her husband, Sir William Seymour, Kt, of Seymour Park

Marshall Massengill, the late father of John Massengill

John Barber, inn keeper

Lachlan Edwards, solicitor, successor to John Massengill's father, Marshall

Cynthia Edwards, wife of Lachlan Edwards

Lady Amanda Bullen Walsh, daughter of the late Sir Hugh Bullen, Bart.

Anna Watt, ladies maid to Amanda Bullen Walsh

Sir William Bullen, Baronet, brother of Lady Amanda and owner of North Hall estate

Lady Beatrice Bullen, wife of Sir William Bullen

Henry Aitken Bullen, son of Sir William and Lady Beatrice

Clara Rohan, ladies maid to Lady Beatrice Bullen

Sir Hugh Bullen, Baronet, late owner of North Hall estate, father of Sir William Bullen and Lady Amanda

Thomas Nelson Dawson Dawson, Earl de Croome, the reclusive owner of the vast Croome Forest estate, and the leading figure in the society of Croome Court and many miles around

Thomas Walsh, late major of the 40th Regiment of Foot, and until his death, husband of Amanda Bullen Walsh

William Walsh, father of Thomas and owner of a significant property centered on his ancestral home, Green Fields

James Walsh, older son and only surviving child of William Walsh

Laurence, Lady Amanda Bullen Walsh's wolfhound

Tim, Henry Aitken Bullen's spaniel

Higgins, the butler at North Hall

Quirke, the Constable of Croome Court

The Constable Supervisor, Quirke's superior officer

Thomas Allen Dawson, son of the new Earl de Croome and future inheritor of the Croome Forest estate

Captain Milton Ievers of Ievers Hall and his good wife

The Mahon family of Wildwood Manor (Alfred)

The Corry family of Corry Hall (Atwood)

Niall Bannon, son of a local farmer and sailor returned from the sea,

Padraig Bannon, Niall's father

Ailis Bannon, Niall's sister

Bowyer, Massengill's writer during naval service

Cheshire, Massengill's valet in the Navy

Otis, coxswain of Massengill's barge

Douglass, Glenn, Walters, and Womack, oarsmen of Massengill's barge

Atwood, the butler at Seymour Place

Padraic Berrigan, the head steward at Croome Forest

Laura Doss, the maid at Lady B's house in Belfast

Michael O'Day, a wealthy businessman of Belfast

Thomas Doyle, chief clerk to Michael O'Day

Terrance, one of Berrigan's lieutenants

Jonas, Berrigan's other key lieutenant.

Henry Rider, Niall O'Malley, Jarrod Whaley, and Padraig White, Clara Rohan's men

Watterson, Ievers' sergeant

Duffy, Ievers' farmer

Terrance O'Sullivan, another Berrigan lieutenant

Smith, another of Berrigan's lieutenants

Ryan, Ievers' second farmer

Lynch, farmer from Corry Hall

Nolan, Berrigan's wounded man who was interrogated.

Martin, butler at Green Fields

INTRODUCTION TO
THE PRESENT EDITION

It seems necessary to provide some introduction to the work here presented since its original publication took place over two hundred years ago and some information concerning its origin will be of interest to the reader.

In the spring of 1818 the young English journalist, Gordon Ralston-Simmons, who was a noted reporter with the respected London daily newspaper T_ T____, published a book entitled *Murder, Mayhem, and Scandal in an Irish Village.* How he came to write and publish it is outlined in his *Author's Preface.* The book proved to be a success, and during the following five years was published in no less than four editions, earning him the significant sum of five hundred pounds and adding no little to his already considerable renown. In addition to Ralston-Simmons' own gain from his work many believe that his bringing to the public a story that put the faces of real people on the life and the political situation in Ireland did considerable to pave the way for the success of the 1824 publication of Thomas Moore's satirical and gripping story of the melancholy history of Ireland under English rule, *Memoirs of Captain Rock.* Moore's work gained wide-spread success and was published in a number of editions, including a French translation.

In spite of their disavowal of any interest in or ability in writing, the years would prove to Ralston-Simmons that, although she had not admitted it, Miss Austen (for it was none other than Jane Austen whom he had met) had indeed been a writer, and a writer whose work, many years after her passing, would prove to gain great favor with the public. Further, while Captain Marryat, his other confidant, may not have had any thought of taking up the pen at the time of their meeting, his career after his retirement from a most successful career in the Royal Navy would prove that he had the stuff to become a writer of note and considerable fame in his own lifetime.

The decades have dealt differently with these writers. Miss Austen is now rightfully regarded as one of the most insightful and greatest writers in the English language during the nineteenth century, if not of all time, but Captain Marryat's work, while it undoubtedly provided the genesis for such great and widely popular current sea tales as those of Captain Horatio Hornblower and Captain 'Jack' Aubrey, currently languishes in obscurity. Both Moore and Ralston-Simmons were forgotten for decades, but an Irish house has recently republished, with impressive scholarly comment, *Memoirs of Captain Rock*. No such attention has been shown to Ralston-Simmons' seminal and engaging work, hence the current effort, which it is to be hoped will find an interested reception by the public and will help to return the work of this writer the renown it merits.

--R. D. W.

CHAPTER 1

There was a steady drizzle, it was chilly, and mud was everywhere when John Massengill approached Croome Court. The date was April 7, 1810. It had been a long road from Portsmouth, by packet around Lands End, past St David's Head, across the Irish Sea to Belfast, and by coach to Monaghan. He could have waited two days in Monaghan and ridden a coach to Croome Court, but John was not a man to wait. He was on horseback. The horse was an impressive animal, a piebald gelding fully seventeen hands high, a good fit for Massengill, who was six foot three inches tall and weighed fifteen stone of hard muscle and bone. Although the air was full of water, John Massengill traveled almost dry. A large, well worn but still serviceable, three-corner hat shielded head and face, high boots kept his feet dry, a tightly fastened set of oilskins kept water off the rest of him and sturdy gloves completed his outfit. It was said afterward—when they knew he was a seaman—that there was no wonder he knew how to keep dry.

When he reckoned he was about three miles from Croome Court, Massengill could see an equipage coming toward him through the rain. Soon he could tell that it was a handsome looking coach drawn by two fine bay horses. On the box was a coachman in excellent livery who, attentive to his passenger, brought the coach to a stop beside Massingill, who could see that a well looking and elegantly dressed blonde haired woman of some thirty years of age was seated inside. Hardly turning her head, she said, "And who might you be, sir?"

"John Massengill, madam, post captain in the Royal Navy, returning after many years for a visit in my native village of Croome Court." He tipped his hat nicely.

"Captain! How excellent! And how long has it been since you quitted Croome Court for the sea?"

"Sixteen years, madam."

"You left before my arrival at Seymour Place. I am Lady Susan Seymour. Please wait on me at Seymour Place, Captain. Our entrance is less than a quarter of a mile behind you on the right. It will be my pleasure to welcome you to Croome Court with tea and a warm fire in the grate. Turn your horse. I will not take 'no' for an answer."

She is a bold one, he thought. "My pleasure, my lady," he tipped his hat again.

The coachman trotted the rig on and Massengill turned about and continued to walk his horse. He had only a vague memory from his youth of the lady of Seymour Place, but the woman he remembered was a plainer personage who now would have been much older than the woman who introduced herself as Lady Seymour. The Lady Seymour of his youth must have died and been replaced by this fetching and forward, younger holder of the place. He sensed an interesting beginning for his visit.

Massengill reached the gate in the center of an impressive wall that fronted the property, passed the gatehouse and walked his horse down the drive to the courtyard of a fine home. He handed his horse off to a servant who met him with an umbrella that he hardly needed and walked to the door while a lad took his horse, with a canvas thrown across the saddle to keep it dry, to the stable. The door was opened before he reached it by the butler who showed him into the hall where Massengill doffed his travel gear and had his boots rubbed dry before he was led into a sumptuously decorated parlor where Lady Susan was seated. She welcomed him with a warm smile, and Massengill noted that with her wrap off, her gown was most elegant and its décolletage was eye catching in the extreme. Lady Susan was eye catching in any event. She no longer had the bloom and freshness of youth, but she was a most attractive woman. Lady Susan took a moment to examine her guest. Massengill was tall, lean, and tanned by his years at sea. His face was somewhat narrow, with an aquiline nose, a small mouth, brown eyes, and a high forehead topped by a mass of thick dark brown hair. She liked what she saw and planned to make the most of the unexpected opportunity that had come to her.

"Captain Massengill, it is so delightful to be able to welcome you to Seymour Place. Sir William is off on one of his all too frequent business trips and here I am alone." She favored him with an inviting smile. "It is a true pleasure to be able to welcome a King's officer of such distinguished rank. Please." She motioned him to a seat. "Tea, Jordan. Now, Captain, tell me about yourself."

Massengill spent ten minutes telling Lady Susan about his career in the Navy and about his early life in Croome Court. The tea arrived. "I will serve, Jordan. You may go."

"Yes, my lady."

Lady Susan busied herself with the tea and when she had completed the arrangements to her satisfaction she picked up a cup and saucer and leaned across the table to present it to her guest. During that act it happened, by purest accident, that her right breast slipped smoothly out of her gown and was delightfully exposed. She was all in shock and made charmingly ineffectual moves to shield the offending jewel from view. "Captain! Please! To the mantle and tug the bellpull—two tugs if you please to summon my maid." After a satisfying examination

Massengill had already averted his eyes and he moved to the bell pull and tugged as instructed.

"Now, Captain, into the corner, please, by the desk. How embarrassing! Please allow me privacy. Please!" Massengill did as he was told and waited. He noted, while waiting, that the mirrored cabinet over the desk gave him enough of a view of the room behind him to allow him to observe Lady Susan in all her glory. It occurred to him that this entire scenario might have been played out in exactly the same detail in the past with other guests. Lady Susan continued her attempts at shielding herself, without any effort to replace the offending globe of flesh and awaited the arrival of her maid, who did arrive quite promptly.

Lady Susan stood, and as she did so Massengill could see that she was a tall woman, several inches higher than the average. "Mary, please, quickly, unlace me and let me right this wardrobe malfunction." Mary did as she was told and when Lady Susan was unlaced she lowered her gown from her shoulders, exposing her entire bosom to Massengill's appreciative view for an instant before returning everything to its place and waiting while Mary laced her back up and departed.

"You may turn around now, Captain. I am so shocked. I am sure you have never been subjected to such an unfortunate accident, and I apologize most profusely." She smiled winningly, with no hint of a blush. "Please, please, be seated again. How can I ever apologize to you for subjecting you to this embarrassment?"

"I assure you, no apology is necessary. Such things will happen in spite of all precautions."

"You are so kind, just as I would expect from a King's officer. Please, let us resume as if nothing had happened." She bestowed yet another glowing smile.

"Of course."

They did resume their talk as if nothing had happened. Lady Susan explained that she had been married to Sir William for ten years. "I was a Dublin girl, you know. Quite enjoying myself in the midst of a glamorous life in the capital when Sir William positively swept me off my feet." After ten minutes of further conversation centered on Lady Susan's position in the social life of Croome Court and its environs, Massengill thanked her profusely for her hospitality and said that he must go to keep an appointment. Lady Susan expressed her disappointment with his departure, but after much protesting let him go with the hope that, "this brief meeting has been a satisfying example of the full hospitality that will be yours when you return to Seymour Place." She favored him with another of her glowing smiles, although Massengill thought this one had an edge of irritation that her other smiles had most definitely lacked.

Massengill assured her that he was fully appreciative of the generosity of her hospitality and that nothing could be more pleasant than contemplating a return and the experience that would reveal her fullest hospitality. He remounted his horse, on a perfectly dry saddle, and resumed his ride toward the village.

As he rode off Massengill ruminated on the tableau he had witnessed. It was too perfect to have been a genuine accident. Everything fit together much too well. The gown was perfect for the occasion; Massengill wondered if all Lady Susan's gowns had the necessary décolletage. He felt sure they did. The bureau with the mirror, the butler out of the way, the maid so readily available and so unsurprised and quick to do her work. It all fit so well. How many times had that tableau been played out before in that salon? Two, five, twenty? Massengill settled on a dozen, concluded that he knew exactly what Lady Susan wanted —and expected—from his next visit and decided to stay as far away from her as possible. The last thing he needed on a brief visit after sixteen years of being away from home was to become entangled in a scandal with Lady Susan, and it was hard to imagine how a man could be around her for long without becoming the centerpiece of a scandal. He could see that since he had left the village some things, at least, had changed in Croome Court. Was Lady Susan a harbinger of everything and everyone he was about to encounter, or was his meeting with her an aberrant event? The prospect presented by his visit home became more fascinating than any he had imagined.

As Massengill reached the edge of the village he was noticed. Faces appeared at windows almost any time there was movement on one of Croome Court's few streets, and the arrival of a coach, a wagon, or a stranger was an event to be watched by all who could get to a window or doorway. Massengill rode in on the Monaghan Road and, trailed by a gaggle of interested dogs, proceeded directly to My Lord's Wood, the only respectable inn that Croome Court could boast. He left his horse with the livery boy, gave instructions for food, water, and grooming, handed his sea bag to a lackey and went into the warm taproom. John Barber, the inn keeper, presiding behind the bar, alone among those present recognized him immediately. "You would be solicitor Massengill's boy what went off to the Navy."

"Your recall is most impressive, innkeeper. I would be the same."

"And what is it brings you back; your good father long dead and gone and no relations hereabouts?"

"I have property still in The Court, and I have long had a desire to return to the place of my birth and young life. Now, for the first time in many years, I am in possession of the time to be here and so you see me."

"Reason enough. Welcome. I presume ye will want a room to stay."

"I will."

And so he settled in to a small room that was larger than many he had lived in during sixteen years in the Royal Navy.

CHAPTER 2

Croome Court was a village that had seen its day and after its time of promise had settled in to a simple existence, neither waxing nor waning. The court of law, for many decades held there every month, had been moved to Monaghan when the Act of Union was passed, and with it moved the bustle of its comings and goings. Two of the three men at law who had served its needs moved as well. The one attorney who had stayed, solicitor Marshall Massengill, John's father, had stayed, because in addition to his work at the court, he had had the ability and the good fortune to become the man of affairs for all of Croome Court's notable families, one of whom was, in fact, a member of the nobility. Serving these families and the occasional bit of work as solicitor for villagers who had the need of his services both kept him busy and provided him with an income that made him first man in the village and part of its intelligencia, along with the vicar and the schoolmaster.

Croome Court's High Street ran in a shallow arc from north to south leading to Monaghan in the north and Cavan in the south. The Ballybay Road intersected from the east and from the southeast came the Shercock Road. The three main roads of Croome Court formed a close approximation of the Greek letter π, although there was probably no one in the village who was aware of this, to them, arcane fact. John Massengil, though, had thought of this. As a man for whom celestial navigation of ships had been an almost every day activity for sixteen years, the letter π was an important part of his lexicon, and his habit of viewing the world from above on maps and charts made an overview of his home village a natural thing and thus in his mind's eye he saw the π. He remembered it with satisfaction as he surveyed the village's few streets upon his arrival. That, at least, had not changed.

To the east of The Court, as the locals called the village, the land was gently rolling and was a patchwork of grazing fields and land under the plough bordered by rows of trees and streams and the occasional copse of woodland. Farmhouses and buildings dotted the landscape, and dirt roads, some hardly more than paths, connected the dots.

Much of Ireland was a sea of grinding poverty, and Croome Court was no pocket of riches, but it had a prosperous air that Massengill had been pleased to see on his arrival. Many of the houses were built of well laid rubble stone under slate roofs with harling on the front, and sometimes all around. A number were two stories tall and had a dignified look. Four of them, the homes of the Priest, the vicar, the doctor, and the solicitor, had handsome half circular fanlights over their front doors.

The inn, one of the most ancient buildings in the village, was of two stories with stone on the ground floor and half timbering filled with brick nogging on the first floor. With its outbuildings, livery stable and stable yard it was by far the largest structure in the village. The other main features of the village were a butcher's shop, a greengrocer's shop, an apothecary that doubled as post office, a doctor's office, a solicitor's office, a Catholic church, a protestant chapel, a shop that sold cloth, hats, gloves, ribbon, sewing supplies and other sundries of quality, and a handful of other shops. The inn was the place of dignified resort in the village, but for the lower orders there were two grog shops that, while they had no reputation for quality, nevertheless enjoyed a steady trade. In addition, there was a blacksmith, the shop of a carpenter who was also the undertaker and maker of coffins for the village, and to the south there was a mill on a steady stream that joined the River Erne a few miles to the west. Near the mill was a tan yard.

To the west of the High Street the terrain changed quite abruptly. Fields were replaced by a great forest, occasionally relieved by meadows, and frequently broken by narrow lochs, some winding along the valleys for more than a mile. The High Street had its buildings only on the east side for on its west was the wall of a great domain. It was Croome Forest, over ten thousand acres, the estate of the Earl de Croome, as he styled himself, the richest and grandest nabob of the County of Cavan, and, indeed one of the greatest in all the north of Ireland. Other than the harled stone wall, the only evidence of the grand establishment was the gate flanked by its two substantial gate lodges, either of which was as large and handsome as all but the four most prominent houses of the village. The great wall of Croome Forest extended for almost two miles along the Monaghan to Cavan road.

CHAPTER 3

A t the north end of the village, on the north side of the Ballybay Road, was a domain of some two thousand acres of
farm and woods. It was a prominent part of the everyday routine
of Massengill's youth and was a property that he remembered
well. On this estate stood a jewel box of a house, North Hall, built
in 1704, the "town home" of Sir William Bullen, Baronet. North
Hall was not a large mansion, but the elegance of its design and
the layout of its dependencies gave it a presence that completely
dominated the village that lay to the south of it. The hall was
built of carefully cut limestone, with elegant bolection molded
surrounds and modest pediments for all the windows. The
front door, in the middle of the five bays, had its own bolection
molded surround and a slightly more pretentious pediment.
The house stood two stories high over a raised basement and
under a high pitched slated roof. The main block had one-story
wings extending out to each side, and there were six chimney
stacks, four over the main block and one at the center of each
wing. The proportions of every element of the ensemble were
held in the highest esteem by all knowledgeable viewers, and the
whole impressed all viewers and awed all but the few who had
been to Dublin or Belfast or those who had seen the mansion
at Croome Forest.

The house sat back from the intersection of the High Street and the Ballybay Road and at a forty-five degree angle to each. Behind the mansion were the stables, carriage house, dairy, and other places of work. Along the street fronts were two well appointed flanker buildings, each of two stories, and each of the same fine cut limestone. The flankers sat in front of and beyond the ends of the main house forming the anchors of a handsome forecourt. Along the roads a clairvoie pierced by two gates with elegant urn-topped posts connected the two flanker houses and a circular drive leading from the gates swept up to the front door of the mansion.

The flanker facing the Ballybay Road housed a number of the servants and the flanker facing the High Street was the home of Amanda Bullen Walsh, sister of Sir William. Amanda's life had been centered on North Hall. In her childhood she had been the darling of her parents and had been educated at home by governesses and tutors, her mother not wanting to have her exposed to the rough world outside the family domain. Her mother had died when Amanda was only twelve and her father had taken on the task of raising a dutiful daughter. At the time of his death, when Amanda was seventeen, she was a model of decorum, daughterly fidelity, and the accomplishments expected of a young lady.

Upon her father's death Amanda was left in the care of her older brother, William, now the owner of the North Hall estate and the baronetcy. By the time of John Massengill's return to Croome Court Amanda was also widow of the late Major Thomas Walsh, second son of William Walsh of Green Fields, and at the time of his unfortunate death by malaria, recently promoted Major in the 40th Regiment of Foot. Green Fields, the boyhood home of Thomas Walsh, was the third of the impressive properties in the vicinity of Croome Court.

The Walsh family were of the gentry, not of the peerage, but, nevertheless, had become highly prosperous landowners in the almost one hundred years since their forebear, an English officer who had come to fight the Irish, had been rewarded for his service with a tract of land that he and his descendants had assiduously maintained and enlarged. As the second son, Thomas was not to inherit and had been gifted by his father with a commission and was sent to the army.

Seven years later, Thomas returned home a Captain, toughened by action and hard living, and much devoted to the profession of arms. He had two months in Croome Court, and during them he renewed his acquaintance with Amanda Bullen, who had been a charming child when he left and had since grown into an unusually lovely eighteen year-old. She had the lightest of blond hair, blue eyes, a fair face, a complexion not too pale, and a most pleasing figure. She had never been away from home, so she lacked the polish she might have gained at a boarding school of quality, but she had all the elegance one could have obtained through the offices of a good governess in a small Irish village. She had a keen mind nurtured by much reading, a gentle personality, a small fortune of two thousand pounds and no prospects at all.

Thomas Walsh quickly took all this in, decided she was all he could wish for in a wife, courted her assiduously almost from the moment he saw her, and within a month, her parents being dead and her brother in whose care she lived being happy to see her set up in matrimony, even if the match was not a great one, they were engaged to be married. Because time was so short, the marriage took place in one week, in the parlor of North Hall, under the offices of the local Protestant clergyman. They had three weeks together and Captain Walsh was gone, never to return.

It had been agreed that as a married woman Amanda would move from the main house at North Hall into the High Street flanker where she would have her own small, but quite elegant, establishment, well furnished with all that gives dignity and comfort to a home. She had her own ladies maid, housemaid and cook. Thomas was able to supply her with a modest income and her brother out of the love he had for his sister provided her abode. She was able to easily supply her personal needs with her own income and the income from her husband. When the word came that she had become a widow, a childless widow, her financial situation changed. Her father in law provided her with a modest stipend and her brother assured her that she could live out her widowhood where she was established. She was twenty-two years old.

CHAPTER 4

The news of John Massengill's arrival in Croome Court traveled swiftly, and before the end of the day had reached all but a tiny few of the two hundred-odd residents of the village. One who was told was Amanda Walsh, who heard the news from her ladies maid. "He rode in on a fine horse and he's staying at the inn. He is said to be a most handsome and impressive man." Amanda remembered John Massengill, not so much as a person, but as someone who had been spoken of from time to time in the past. She did remember Marshall Massengill, because he had dealt regularly with her father and her brother, and she made plans to make the acquaintance of his son. Few interesting men came into her life now, so she determined that she would make the most of this opportunity. Amanda went to the main house and found her sister-in-law, Lady Beatrice, called 'Bea', and boldly opened the matter with her, "I hear that the son of Massengill the solicitor is back in the village. He must be an officer now and is said to be a most handsome man. I think we should invite him to tea so he can meet with William."

"And with you," said Bea with a most pointed smile.

Amanda smiled back at her conspirator, "Yes, but with you, too." It was decided upon, and a footman was dispatched to the inn with a note asking John Massengill to wait on the Bullen and Walsh family at two in the afternoon two days hence.

The streets of Croome Court were either dust or mud, depending upon the weather, but the village had two carefully laid stone street crossings that could be used by the fastidious to keep their shoes and their skirts clean as they crossed the streets. One of these crossings led from the east gate of North Hall across Ballybay Road to the east side of the High Street where there was a sidewalk of stone and brick, and the second crossed the Shercock Road at its intersection with the High Street. These two crossings and the walkways in front of the buildings that lined the streets allowed the residents of North Hall, should they care to walk in the village, to go anywhere they might reasonably want to go without having to endure the grime of the streets themselves. Shopkeepers along the High Street regularly had boys clear the crossings of horse droppings and windblown debris, so they stayed neat and clean. The North Hall footman, mindful of the cleanliness of his shoes, used these crossings to walk to the inn where he was fortunate to find John Massengill at home, delivered his message, got an affirmative reply, and returned to the ladies at North Hall with his news.

On the morning after his arrival John Massengill was out early so he could walk all the streets of the village in the morning calm and cool. The weather was sunny and the mud was drying. He knew that anyone walking the streets that early would be a curiosity, but he was happy with that. He wanted to be noticed. He wanted to see old friends, if there were any left. A few early wagons were moving along the streets, bringing produce and meat into the shops and passing through from the mill. The wagons from the mill were at the beginning of the four-day trip to Belfast where there was so much demand for foodstuffs that money could be made transporting flour all the way from Croome Court. The wagons would not return empty from Belfast; they would be loaded with iron for the blacksmith, fabric and fancies for the ladies shop, and sometimes glass, brass fittings, and special ordered items. It was a good trade, both going and coming.

As John walked the village he saw that not much had changed. Some buildings had a new coat of whitewash, or even of paint, some tile and thatch had been replaced, the paved sidewalks had been extended, a house had burned and the site was left in rubble, another vacant lot had a trim new cottage. Soon enough, he met one of his school fellows and fell into the kind of pleasant conversation he had hoped to enjoy. One friend was joined by another and soon they repaired to the taproom at the inn and spent the morning sharing stories. He learned much, told stories of life at sea over and over again, and enjoyed the talk as others found the gathering and joined in.

The John Massengill who returned to Croome Court was a man far different from the boy who had left for the sea. He had lived a hard life, eaten poor food, drunk sickening water, fended for himself, learned his profession, and risen through the ranks to a position of honor in Britain's senior service. He had endured many battles, seen much blood spilled, seen his friends and shipmates cut to pieces by cannon ball, grape shot, and splinters. Massengill had endured the rigors of a French prison and had suffered the illnesses of the feted coast of South America and the islands of the Caribbean. He had become a leader, a commander who led men into the jaws of death and used the wisdom of years of service to bring back as many of them alive as he could with their job done and the King's honor upheld. No man in the village had led a life that could approach the one he had led and no one could tell the stories he could tell, so he was the center of all attention and admiration.

After a lunch shared with several of his fellows John went to the office of solicitor Lachlan Edwards. When it became clear that the life of a solicitor was not for John, his father had sought a proper young man to read the law with him and take over his practice when the time came. Lachlan Edwards was that young man. He was from Belfast and had been fortunate to attend Trinity College in Dublin, but he had no connections that offered a secure profession so he was happy to accept Marshall Massengill's offer, which came some two years after John had left for the Navy. Lachlan had proved a good pupil, had devoted himself to the law, and his appearance, ability, and manners had found acceptance in Croome Court among Massengill's clients. He was soon a valuable part of the Massengill practice and ten years later when Marshall died, Lachlan Edwards was able to continue the practice without interruption.

Even though John and Lachlan had never met, they knew each other well enough. John had heard much about Lachlan in letters from his father, and after his father's death—John's mother having died several years before he left for the Navy—Lachlan handled the Massengill estate with competence and care, and he and John had traded many letters over the four years. The exact date of John's arrival was not known, but Lachlan was expecting his visit, so his arrival was no surprise.

Lachlan had a clerk who announced John to him. Lachlan was delighted, "John Massengill! Come in! Come in! I am so glad to see you. Even though we have never laid eyes on each other I feel like a brother to you. Welcome!"

"You have been as true as a brother would have been, Lachlan, and it is my pleasure to see your person."

"Seat yourself, and let us talk." And so they talked for well more than two hours. John was brought up to date on the estate. Lachlan and his family were living in the Massengill house, with most of its furnishings still in place. He used the law office and paid rent to John for both the office and the house. The cash in the estate and the rent as it came due were invested in the five percents as had been agreed, and Lachlan brought forth from his strong box the bonds in the proper total so John could see the bonds with his name on them. They discussed future arrangements, which they concluded would remain as they had in the past.

"Will you be coming back to The Court to stay at some time?" Lachlan asked.

"That is my hope, but not in a permanent way for years to come. As the war continues I expect to be at sea for the duration, which I fear will be years yet. But someday I will come back."

Lachlan took John to see his old home. John found it moving to see so much that he remembered from his young life, and he found it good to see that it was all in use by a family. That was much better than having his furnishings in some storage or sold off to who knows whom. John met Lachlan's wife, Cynthia, and his small son, and after a proper visit he bade them all good-bye and walked back to the inn to finish the evening in reading and a dinner.

CHAPTER 5

The next morning, as was his usual practice, John awoke early without being called, had a full breakfast of eggs, sausage, bacon, toast with butter and marmalade, tomato, and coffee. He ordered the piebald saddled and set off to ride the neighborhood. He went south, passed the entrance to Croome Forest, its farm entrance farther to the south, the end of its domain wall, and rode on to the tan yard and mill. The end of the domain wall was the place from which in his earliest teen years John had led his fellows on illicit forays into the Croome Forest woods. He was not only the tallest of his fellows at the village school, he was also the most adventurous and the one who either led them into trouble or kept them out of it, depending upon which seemed to offer the most satisfying result.

Two farm wagons were at the mill and the wheel was turning. He could smell the wheat and flour; it brought back happy memories. He gave a salute to the men in the yard in front of the mill, received their waves in return, and rode on across the mill bridge. The mill stream was the only stream near the village that was large enough to merit a bridge and its crossing was a structure of poles laid across four stone piers and just wide enough for one wagon to cross at a time. The other streams had fords, and the Erne was a genuine river, far too large for the county to afford a bridge, so Croome Court was connected to the lands to the west of the Erne only by a ferry that was nine miles away. The ferry was past Cavan, so far away that for the purposes of the village the land to the west of the Erne did not exist.

Once the tan yard was well behind him the smells of the countryside became pleasant. John had reveled in the country smells, blunted though they were by the rain, on the ride from Monaghan, and in the dry wind of this morning the smells of the county side were more pleasant than before. The freshness moved him; it was far from the constant rotting smells, tar, sweat, decaying food, urine and offal that filled the air of the ships and ports he was used to. He fancied that he remembered these country smells, but he thought that in truth sixteen years at sea had probably erased all the smells, and even some of the sights of his youth. He was glad to be recapturing them.

After forty-five minutes of steady walk he came to a cross-roads, that was simply known as 'Crossroads', and turned left onto a track that he knew would take him within another two hours to the Shercock Road. The countryside was in fields, most supporting animals, and others that were under the plough. Copses of trees, streams, stone walls, and treed fence rows dotted and divided the landscape. The ride was calming. Occasionally he would see a farmer in the fields or a farm wife in the dooryard and, without stopping, would give them a salute. Near the Shercock Road he watered his horse in a rivulet, tied him to a tree and sat to eat the lunch the innkeeper had provided for him. Two hours later he was back in Croome Court. John whiled away the remainder of the afternoon sitting in the smoky tap room talking with old friends who returned to tell him what had happened in the village since he departed and to hear his tales of life in the navy. He dined, and because his father had taken pains to make him a reader from the time he had achieved good command of his letters, John read a bit by candle light before retiring.

CHAPTER 6

O n the morning of the day appointed for his visit to North Hall, Massengill arose early as usual, had breakfast and retired to his room to read. Books had been his constant companions all his life. It was reading that had put the wanderlust into his mind, it was books that had nurtured his career in the Navy, and it was books that allowed him to while away his occasional idle hours in pleasure.

After lunch he carefully dressed for his visit to North Hall. As Massengill laid out the outfit he was to wear he thanked God with enthusiasm for his valet, Cheshire. Cheshire was back in Bristol only because Massengill had refused him permission to come on the trip to Croome Court. Cheshire's devotion to Massengill was beyond dog-like, it was near fanatical, and being separated from his captain for more than a few hours was both torture and abandonment to Cheshire. Even though he had tried every method at his command, ranging from pleading to petulance, to near threats, Massengill had refused to let Cheshire accompany him. He wanted no excess baggage on the trip and Cheshire would be excess indeed.

The sea bag he had brought with him had not been large, but it held all he would need. Cheshire had selected its contents, and he had selected well. He had packed fully as well. Every item had been carefully spread, rolled, and packed so that when

Massengill took out the jacket and trousers he was to wear there was no untoward wrinkle to be seen even though the bag and its contents had been through a considerable sea voyage, coaching, horseback riding, and some judicious unpacking. That, too, had been though out by Cheshire: the things that needed to come out first had been packed last and the items in every subsequent removal had been packed in their proper order.

Massengill gave Cheshire full credit: odd duck though he appeared and though he surely was, Cheshire was a master of his trade. He knew how to pack, he knew how to launder, he knew how to remove virtually every kind of spot Massengill was able to get on his clothing—and Massengill was expert at leaving spots. Cheshire was also an expert with the needle. He could mend, cut, and sew at a level that would gain admiration from any seamstress, and in addition he was an expert at whiting with chalk, and using any number of concoctions to dye a thread to match the background of a uniform's cloth. It went without saying that Cheshire could polish brass to a perfectly gold-like shine and could polish boots to a mirror sheen.

Even though he was over two hundred miles away, Cheshire was still right there with Massengill, and he was only one of a group of men who, through hard years at sea and the stress of battle, had become so devoted to Massengill that they would follow him anywhere. Indeed they wanted to follow him anywhere and hungered for the next call to duty.

Massengill put on a cleaned and brushed jacket, newly shined boots, brushed his hair carefully, inspected himself in the tiny mirror the room afforded and, satisfied, walked the short distance to the Hall. He was admitted by the butler and escorted to the parlor where the party awaited him. The parlor was a dignified and warmly welcoming wood paneled room, with bolection moldings around the fireplace and windows that matched the moldings on the façade of the house. It was handsomely furnished and carpeted and the walls were hung with portraits and landscape paintings. Silver gleamed and mirrors glowed. All was as Massengill had expected it would be.

The group within consisted of Sir William Bullen, his wife, Lady Beatrice, Mrs. Amanda Walsh, Sir William and Lady Beatrice's five year old son, Henry, Henry's spaniel, Tim, and Amanda Walsh's wolfhound, Laurence. Laurence maintained a dignified presence next to his mistress, but Tim immediately came forward to examine Massengill. Sir William called Tim off and exhorted Henry to mind his dog. He then greeted Massengill courteously, "Massengill, it is a pleasure to see you again after all these years."

"It is my pleasure as well, Sir William, to be here and to be received by you and your family."

"Allow me to introduce my wife, Lady Beatrice, who made her appearance in Croome Court a number of years after you left us."

"Lady Beatrice, I am honored." Bea was about five and a half feet tall, with a fair complexion that had never seen the smallpox, a fine figure, and a full head of almost coal black hair. It could be said that her face lacked perfection because of a nose that was somewhat too prominent, but withal she was a most handsome woman. She held out her hand without speaking and Massengill took it and made a small bow.

"And my sister, Mrs. Walsh, whom you will remember as Miss Amanda, although to many in the village she has been known as Lady Amanda, even though she does not deserve the honor."

"I do remember her as Lady Amanda, but as a girl, not as the delightful lady I see before me. Lady Amanda," he smiled, "it is a pleasure to see you again." Amanda extended her hand with a smile, murmured, "Captain, you are most kind," and received a bow in return. Massengill immediately decided she was the most beautiful woman he had ever seen. She stood the same height as Beatrice and had the same fair, unmarked skin and the same fine figure, but her hair, like that of her brother, was blond, and her face, with high cheekbones and strong blue eyes, was the face of a Nordic princess—or a goddess. Massengill remembered such faces, few even there, from the time he had been ashore in the city of Copenhagen when it was taken by the British fleet under Nelson in 1801. Amanda left an impression that he knew would never fade.

"This is my son, Henry."

"How do you do, sir? Are you a sailor?" asked Henry.

"I am well, master Henry, and indeed I am a sailor and have been for these many years."

"Please, let us be seated," said Sir William. "Ladies, let us have tea and let us talk." Amanda poured tea, everything having been made ready on a tray that sat on the tea table.

"Massengill, you must tell us about your adventures."

"Sir William, ladies, and Master Henry, in sixteen years in the Navy I have, indeed, had some adventures. They have been set between months of featureless sailing and eventless watch after eventless watch on ship board. The Navy life includes much more routine and boredom than adventure. As Sir William will remember, I left The Court in 1794. Even though my father wanted me to follow his career and could have established me well here in the village as he did Lachlan Edwards, I wanted none of it. The village was too small for me. I wanted to see the world, and what better way than to go to sea? I had read books of the sea and was fixed upon it. When my father finally realized that there was no way to tempt me into following him into the law he was able to use his connections in Dublin to buy me a place as a midshipman, and that launched my career."

"Tell us all," begged Amanda.

"My first vessel was a ship of line, a second rate having 84 guns. I was one of what seemed to me an excessively large number of midshipmen and my job was to learn to be an officer. I worked diligently and early in 1798, after four years almost completely spent at sea, I passed the examination to be commissioned a lieutenant. Passing the examination did not insure a promotion but I was most fortunate later that year to obtain a commission. Some time after I became lieutenant, I was transferred to a much smaller ship, the brig sloop *Speedy*, and my service in *Speedy* was the basis upon which all of my future successes in the Navy were built."

Henry and Tim by this time were seated on the floor by Massengill, both apparently hanging on to his every word as were the ladies, and even Sir William. "In March of 1800 Lord Cochrane, then a commander by rank, took command of *Speedy* and my true education as a fighting man began. Lord Cochrane was the greatest naval officer I have ever encountered, a man of broad intelligence, vision, daring and courage. *Speedy's* cruise under Cochrane was a string of daring, and usually successful, raids on French shipping along the Mediterranean coast of Spain. I was able to learn from Lord Cochrane every day. I was fortunate to take part in many fights, both with ships and shore batteries, and every action taught me a new lesson of Lord Cochrane's brilliance. I cannot say enough about the man. He made me."

"Captain," asked Amanda, "did you actually feel that to be in battle was a fortunate thing for you? I would think it would be a horror?"

"Battle has its terror, no doubt, but for a naval officer to make himself he must distinguish himself in battle. Except for influence, there is no other way to gain promotion, and I had not enough influence to signify, so battle was my route to success and promotion. I was indeed fortunate to see—and to survive—many battle experiences."

"Amazing," was all Amanda could say.

"Did you ever get shot by a cannon?" asked Henry.

"Henry, I have been hit three times, once by a cannon, I believe, and the other times by riflemen."

"Is that why you walk the curiously way?"

"It is. The cannon shot grazed my leg and took away a hunk that has never come back." This brought a murmur of "How terrible," and "Awful," from the ladies, and "My word," from Sir William.

"Tell more!" Henry begged.

"I will tell you about a great turning point in my career. On the third of July in 1801, in a battle against odds we could not overcome, *Speedy* was captured by a squadron of French ships and all in the crew were taken prisoner, me among them. In just a few days Lord Cochrane was exchanged in return for a French captain, but I was not so fortunate. I remained in captivity for four months before returning to England. I used that time in France to learn the language, and although no one will mistake me for a native, I have to this day a serviceable knowledge of the French language. Upon his return, Lord Cochrane was promoted to the rank of captain, which rank he holds to this day. I, no doubting it, based on my service with him, was promoted to commander after my return to England. I served for a time in Lord Nelson's fleet and in 1802 was given command of a brig sloop of my own, *Fox*."

"Which fox?" asked Henry, to the amusement of all.

"No particular fox; just in honor of them all. Just so there is the ship *Elephant*, not named after any particular elephant, but in honor of all elephants." Henry was satisfied by this information.

"What happened to you on *Fox*?" asked Lady Amanda.

"Much of the time was spent harassing the French along their southern coast and in the sea between France and Spain. In 1804 I was made commander in a much larger ship, the very *Elephant* that I have just mentioned".

"What does the commander do?" asked Lady Amanda, who was taking a most serious interest in John Massengill and his career in the navy.

"The commander is the chief assistant of the captain and insures that every daily activity of the ship is carried out properly. I was commander in Elephant for two years and we saw action in the Mediterranean and in the Bay of Biscay. In 1806 I was given command of a ship of the fifth rate, a 32-gun frigate, *Espirit.*"

"That one is not an animal!"

"True enough, Henry. I think perhaps there are not enough animals in the world to provide names for all the King's ships, so some other words have to be used."

"And what of *Espirit*?" from Bea.

"I was most fortunate to be assigned to the West India fleet and to cruise, sometimes with the fleet and sometimes alone, amongst the islands of the Caribbean Sea and along the coast of South America. Those were good times and some of my actions were most successful. In 1808 I had the great good fortune to be promoted to the rank of post captain and I returned to England to take command of a new built forty-gun frigate, *Leader.*"

"Post captain, I am most impressed, Massengill." High praise from Sir William.

"Is post captain the same as Colonel Arbuthnot?" asked Lady Beatrice.

"It is the equivalent rank."

"But he is so old, and you are so young!" came from Lady Amanda.

"True, I am not so old, but during the last sixteen years the time I have spent on shore totals hardly more than one year, and fifteen years at sea is a lifetime."

"How wonderful," enthused Amanda, "and what do you do next? Do you go back to *Leader*?"

"No, my command of *Leader* is past. I am now between ships, but I will shortly report to the Bristol dockyard where I will assume my next command."

The family brought Massengill up to date on their lives, including Amanda's marriage and the death of Major Walsh, as well as the situation of Earl de Croome and the other notables of the area. "Captain, have you been able to reacquaint yourself with society in Croome Court since your return?" asked Bea.

"I have had the pleasure of meeting a number of old friends and I have met for the first time in person Lachlan Edwards who has managed my affairs here, and as I rode in to the village I met Lady Susan Seymour, who married Sir William after I left Croome Court."

"Oh", from Amanda, "Lady Susan. And how did you find your meeting with her?"

"Most remarkable."

"I can imagine."

"It may be that you cannot." This brought quickly stifled smiles from the ladies and a guffaw from Sir William. Massengill realized that his suppositions about Lady Susan had been on the mark. He quickly left the subject of Lady Susan and stated his intention to call on Major Walsh's family, and after a few more words Sir William rose and said, "So good of you to call on us, Massengill."

Having been thus dismissed, Massengill made his good-byes to the group and departed.

CHAPTER 7

"William, what did you think of the Captain?" asked Beatrice.

"Impressive for a village boy."

"William! He is a bit more than a village boy. His father was your man of business for years, and your father's before you."

"My point, exactly. And he is rather a bit dark and worn looking, wouldn't you say?"

"You are a hard man, said Beatrice, "and Amanda, what of you?"

"I cannot think of a more impressive man in all my acquaintance. He may have been a village boy, but he is no more. He is most respectful, but one can see that he is used to command. He has commanded many men—even sending them to the risk of death! William, I say he is no village boy. And surely one would expect him to look a bit worn from all those years at sea—and in the tropics, too. Withal, he is handsome, he has a fine bearing, and has enough graces to be made into a gentleman if properly handled."

"My dear, do you not become enamored. He has only the most modest fortune, if any at all, and you are in need of a husband who has a fortune of significance. And besides that, he will go back to the sea at any time with only a moment's notice. You must remain in the search for a proper husband, but do not look to Captain Massengill."

"It is just as well that I take your advice, William, because like him or not, it is true that he will return to the sea, and I do not wish to see another man go off to war. I shall probably never see him again."

"As much as you might wish to," was Bea's final word on the subject of Captain Massengill.

Amanda had already formed the idea of seeing John Massengill again. She would walk in the village and hope to see him. Amanda was a familiar sight in the village, because unlike her brother and sister-in-law who felt being seen in Croome Court other than passing through in a carriage was quite beneath them, she often visited the ladies shop and spoke kindly to all she met. Amanda was always accompanied by her dog, Laurence, so her safety was never in question. Although she went out the very next afternoon she did not see John Massengill. He had chosen that day to ride again, this time out the Ballybay Road both to review the countryside and to visit the home of the Walshes, the family of Amanda's late husband.

A leisurely ride of just over an hour brought him to the Walsh establishment, a handsome three story brick house over a raised basement in the style of the period of William III. It had been built in the most up-to-date style soon after the battle of the Boyne when the Walshes had made their fortune. It was seven bays wide with a string course at the base of each floor, little adorned but with fine proportions that gave it a sense of dignity and repose. It had a neat graveled drive and a number of fine trees around it. The farm was of almost a thousand acres of good soil and the Walshes were one of the leading families of the neighborhood.

William Walsh, father of the late Thomas and Thomas' older brother James, was at home and received John Massengill with pleasure. Visitors were rare enough at the old man's hearth and the visit of the long unseen son of a man who had been of much value to him for many years and who was, in addition, a boyhood friend of his late son was an event of significance. Their conversation was long and warm, lasting for well over an hour. There was much talk of Thomas, Amanda, and of the old man's late wife, but little mention of James. This was no surprise to Massengill who had heard in the village enough bad reports of James to make him pity old William, father of one son dead and another useless, and with no sign of a future generation of heirs to a handsome property that he had husbanded for near fifty years. Massengill took his leave, promising to call again when next he was in Croome Court, and made his way back to the inn. The next day he planned to meet again with Lachlan Edwards to go over his affairs in Croome Court for a last time, make a goodbye to a number of his friends, and prepare himself to depart for Belfast on the following day.

The following morning Massengill arose, breakfasted and took the short walk to the office of Lachlan Edwards. They talked for over an hour and both were satisfied with the arrangements for Edwards to continue to manage John Massengill's affairs in Croome Court. Edwards was to maintain the properties in first class order, was to invest all remaining rental funds in the five percents and was to forward a statement of accounts to Massengill two times each year.

John Massengill strolled the now dusty streets and made goodbyes to everyone he met. Most were friends, or at least acquaintances, of old, but even those who had not known him in his youth now knew well enough who he was and were anxious to speak with a native son who had left the village, made a success of himself as none had in memory, and had come back and handsomely shown his regard for those who had remained behind. They spoke to him, if for no other reason, so they could make the occasion a permanent part of their future conversation.

He lunched at the inn with some of the best remembered friends of his youth. They had begun their lunch by shooing a stray chicken out of the taproom and had found great joy, both at the expense of the chicken and in their conversation. Massengill was parting from them at the door of the inn when, by the merest chance as she later said, Lady Amanda Walsh and her dog, Laurence, happened to approach the scene. When her approach was noted, Massengill's friends, as if acting out a script, all made hasty goodbyes so he could properly greet Lady Amanda as all knew was his fate and his desire. "Lady Amanda, how delightful to be able to see you again. I leave tomorrow and anticipated no such pleasurable occasion before my departure." His pleasure was evident.

"I am so glad to see you, Captain," she smiled. "Your visit at the Hall was most pleasant and I have wished to have the pleasure of your company again. Could we talk?"

"With the greatest pleasure." He ushered her into the inn and they were quickly shown to the most private table available. Tea was offered and they accepted and settled into conversation. Their conversation was somewhat awkward. Each was greatly attracted to the other, and each felt there was no future for them. He knew that in the Bullen household, post captain or no, he was still a village boy, one who would not be seen as a suitable suitor, let alone husband, for Amanda, and she knew that he was about to leave perhaps never to return. In spite of the impediments the attraction was magnetic. They spoke of the village, of the lack of society, of his life at sea, of his rekindled acquaintances, and of his rides through the countryside and his visit to the Walsh home. Both expressed their pleasure with the old man and she spoke glowingly of his kindness to her. Massengill opined that he would have expected nothing less and spoke of his good memories of her late husband, who was a mere two years older than he. Amanda then looked at him most directly and told him that she had a great aversion to James Walsh. She did not elaborate, and John knew not what to do with this information, but he did note it well.

They continued to talk as long as, in fact longer than, propriety would allow and Amanda rose to go with a reluctance that was matched by John's reluctance to see her leave. They walked to the street. Laurence, who had been waiting patiently near the door, joined his mistress and they said their goodbyes. Amanda turned with a final smile, and walked toward the Hall with Laurence at her side. She soon rested her hand on Laurence's silken head; they were a team. John watched them go until they were about to cross the Ballybay Road. He went into the inn; she had not looked back.

The next morning John mounted his horse and rode toward Monaghan. He nodded to those he met, and as he rode past North Hall he looked at every window, hoping he might see her face, but he did not. John Massengill was much talked of in Croome Court, the subject of some knowledge and much speculation. Lachlan Edwards was able to add a number of useful facts to the sea of speculation. One thing that no one knew, or suspected, not even Lachlan Edwards, was that Captain John Massengill, through the hard-earned bounty of prize money that was available to all those who went to sea for the King and that was particularly lavished upon commanding officers of ships, had become a wealthy man. He had a fortune of some forty thousand pounds, carefully invested in the safety of government bonds, a fortune that placed him well above the wealth of the Walsh family and the other well to do landowners of the area, and perhaps on a par with the Bullen fortune.

As John departed he took with him good memories, and above all, the memory of Amanda Walsh. He remembered her as she was today and as a girl of about eight years; a beautiful child whom he had seldom seen and never spoken to except for a shy "Good morning, my lady," and for whom he had hardly existed. He suspected that she would soon forget him, but he knew he was not going to forget her.

For Amanda it was much the same. She remembered the boy John Massengill more by association with his father than in person, and as deeply as he attracted her, she did think she probably would never see him again. Thoughts of what might have been under other circumstances flooded her mind, but the flood ebbed and life for Amanda returned to the seldom varying normal in Croome Court and at North Hall.

CHAPTER 8

A quiet morning was thrown into chaos when the door to Amanda's parlor from the outside burst open without warning and Beatrice and her maid, Clara, rushed into the room, slamming the door behind them. They were disheveled and perspiring. Bea's face had a look of panic such as Amanda had never seen. "My God, Amanda, we are destroyed!"

Amanda was stunned. "What is it? My God! Be seated. Tell me. What can I do?" Beatrice slumped into a chair and Clara stood beside her. Bea gathered her senses for a few seconds and then began a rush of words, "Your brother had cast us out, utterly and forever!"

"Bea, what can you mean? How can you possibly believe that? Why? What is it, I beg you? What makes you say this?"

"Amanda, dearest, I can hardly tell you this. I know it will be outside your understanding, but you must know, because you must help us."

"Be calm, Bea, and tell me."

"Amanda, do you know that some women love each other?"

"But of course. I know that I love you, and I have since you first came to North Hall, and I always will."

"I pray to God that is so. But dear girl, I am speaking of love in the way that a woman would love a man. I mean that women give their bodies to each other. Clara and I love each other in that way. And William has found us out."

Amanda was incredulous. "Good God, Bea, what can this mean? Does this mean that you do not love William? I don't understand."

"Dearest, I do love him, but I have found that I am a woman who does not find herself attracted in the sexual way to men. It is my own sex who attract me. I do not know why, but I know it is so. For years I did not realize that I was different from other women. I thought we were all alike and that the sex act with men was something we simply did because we had to, and not because we wanted to." Bea stopped, out of energy to speak further.

"So, is it Clara you love?" asked Amanda.

"In this special way, yes. From the time Clara came into my service I was famously attracted to her, she is a beauty, as you know and as you see. For two years nothing happened, and then one day in summer last year when I was bathing I realized that Clara was looking at my body with a hunger that I had often felt for her. I asked her to rub soap onto my shoulders and neck, and instantly I felt in the touch of her fingers the fire that I had seen in her eyes. We became lovers from that time."

"My God! And now William knows!"

"Yes, in spite of all. We have always taken the greatest care to keep our love close. The last thing I wanted was for him to find out. My life seemed complete and I wanted nothing to change it. I had a husband who treated me well and gave me an elevated place in society, a home and fortune, a son whom I love most dearly, and the woman I loved. But now it is all undone. William has found us, and he flew into a rage such as I could not imagine. His blood rushed to his head so that I thought he was going to have a stroke. He told us to get out of the house instantly and to never come back. He said he would kill us both if he ever saw us again. All we have is the clothes we wear and my jewel box, which Clara scooped up as we fled. We are come to you for help, but it must be quick. We must go. I fear that he will kill us if he sees us. And I fear, too that you will be ruined if he knows that you have helped us."

"Bea, I am at my wits end. I do not know what to say. This is too much for me to take in. But, of course I will help. I do not want you to come to harm. What can I do to help?"

"We must have ready money."

"I have it. Wait." Amanda dashed up the stairs to her bedroom where she kept her supply of coins and paper money. She had almost twenty pounds, and brought it all down to Bea.

"Thank you, thank you. This will save us."

"Bea, what will you do?"

"We will go to Belfast. What will happen there I do not know. Listen, my dear, we may never see each other again, and it tears at my heart to leave you, but even more it destroys my soul to leave Henry. William will never let me see my son again. I know it. So you must become his mother. Promise me that you will care for him and raise him as if he were your own. You must, for Henry and for me." This thought hit Amanda as if she had been struck by a hammer blow. Beatrice was leaving forever, and forever she was leaving behind her child. Amanda was speechless.

"Amanda, speak to me! You will do this for me? Dearest, you must. You must."

Amanda recovered herself. "Of course. I will, of course. Do not think my hesitation is a sign of unwillingness. It is a sign of my shock only. I am most willing, and I promise you that I will love Henry as if he were indeed my own child. If what all you say is true, he will be mine."

"Oh, God, my heart is relieved. This is a tragedy beyond belief, but it is only too real. Amanda, my dearest one, we must go. We cannot wait." They embraced, and Anna, Amanda's maid, who had heard all, opened the door, saw that there was no one in sight and no face that she could see at any window of the Hall, and motioned Bea and Clara out.

When they had safely gone, Amanda collapsed into a chair. Anna was clearly so distraught that Amanda told her to be seated as well, something Anna had never done before in the presence of her mistress. "Anna, I find this incredible. I cannot believe it, but I must. When I collect myself I will go to the Hall and see what I find there. You understand that you are to speak nothing of what has happened here or in the Hall to anyone. No one at all, not in the village, not in the Hall, nowhere. Do you understand."

"I do, my lady. This is disaster beyond belief. Depend upon me."

CHAPTER 9

Amanda collected herself for some minutes. She wanted to think about Bea and Clara. What had she seen pass between them that could have warned her of what had just happened? In spite of her puzzlement she knew she had work to do, so she put such thoughts out of her mind and braced herself for a visit to the Hall. She had to determine the state of her brother and she had to take Henry in hand. There was no knowing what Henry had heard or what he knew or the agitation of his mind. Henry needed her, and perhaps William did as well. Amanda was met at the door by the butler, Higgins. Higgins was clearly shaken, his face was white and he was trembling. "What has happened, Higgins?"

"My Lady, I do not know. The master is in a state of rage. He has broken things in the parlor. He has sent Lady Beatrice and Clara away. I do not know why, but I know this is a horror."

"He is in the parlor now? Where is Henry?"

"The master is in the parlor. He has gone quiet in the last few minutes. Henry is playing in the east meadow with Tim. He knows nothing."

"Thank God that Henry is out. I will go in to my brother."

"I will be here if you need me."

"Thank you, Higgins." Amanda opened the door of the parlor in fear. The first things she saw were a tea caddy smashed onto the floor, its contents strewn around, and the remains of a large China bowl that had been hurled against the wall and shattered onto the floor. A chair lay on its side. William was seated in the corner of the room, his face so red it was almost purple. He stared at her for a few seconds and then shouted, "I have sent the bitches running. They will never be back."

"William, what is it? What has caused this? What has happened?"

"I found them out! I knocked on the door and went into her bedroom to ask a simple question and found the two of them naked, entwined like animals on the bed. They are a perverted pair! Beatrice tried to make nothing of it. Some insane story. There is no explaining such godless perversion. How long this has been going on I do not know and I do not want to know! I never want to hear the woman's name again. You are an innocent and cannot have an idea of who and what they are." He arose and glared at her, "They will never be spoken of again. Do you understand?"

"William, this is more than I can believe. Are you sure? Is it so terrible? Is there no way this can be righted?"

"I am sure. The door to that infamous room is locked and it will never be opened. There is nothing else to be said. I am ruined. The two whores have brought themselves down and me as well. They are never to be spoken of again. Hear me! Never again."

"I don't know what to do," said Amanda quietly. "Although they may have done something so terrible they cannot be rescued, how is it possible that they have brought you down as well?"

"They will not be rescued! They are banished! It will be known! The whole story will be known and I will be a laughingstock. Ruined. Go! Now! Leave me. Go to Henry. You are his mother now."

"Yes, I will go to Henry. He will need help. Does he know anything? "

"Nothing. You must think of what to tell him. I count on you to save him from this."

Amanda left, shaking and weak. Higgins was waiting, relieved that nothing untoward had happened. Amanda was barely able to tell him she had found out from her brother what had caused him to send Beatrice and Clara away. Amanda told him that it was unfortunate and sad, something that Beatrice could not help and that William could not accept. Beatrice and William would live apart for the foreseeable future, and she would take over the responsibility of raising Henry. She enquired again whether Higgins understood what had caused the break, and assured that neither he nor anyone else in the house knew, she instructed him that the staff were to carry on as usual and nothing was to be said about the situation, inside the house or outside, except what she had just told Higgins.

Higgins promised faithfully to carry out her orders and to insure that the rest of the staff did as well. This was comfort to Amanda, but it was cold comfort because she knew a situation like this would generate rumor within the house and without, and where that rumor would go she could not guess. Perhaps some would guess the truth. If they did, there could be no proof, but proof would not matter, no matter what the story. One rumor would be just as damaging as the next, and she despaired that William was right: they were all ruined.

Ruined or not, they must carry on. She would go to Henry and devise a story that would save him from the worst, but whether she could put his heart at rest she did not know. She knew that she had to be strong and that she had to be cunning enough to save what could be saved of the Bullen family reputation.

As Amanda walked through the fields looking for Henry she tried to make sense of what had happened. How could it be? It was true that Bea had moved to Croome Court from far away, but surely that was not the cause of this. Then there was Clara. Clara had been referred to Bea by an agency in Dublin that provided servants of a high grade. Clara was from Dublin and had good references and had, indeed, made an excellent impression when she had been brought to North Hall for an interview. All seemed well, and Clara was engaged for the position. When Amanda thought about the two years since Clara had been engaged she could find nothing amiss. Clara had served well and had behaved impeccably, but there must have been something wrong, some bad seed in Clara. It simply could not have been Bea who caused this; it must have been Clara who lured Bea into such a sinful relationship. That had to be the answer, but even having come to this conclusion, Amanda still couldn't understand. Why? What had made Clara who she was? Amanda could not find an answer and decided she had to live without one. Sick at heart though she might be, she simply had to move ahead.

CHAPTER 10

Amanda's mind was spinning. She had to make sense of what had happened and she had to decide upon what to do. What could have caused this? Her mind was leaping from one idea to another. The same thoughts kept coming back and then disappearing. Bea was from far away, it was true. William had met her at a house party in Hampshire, in the south of England. He had been to London and a friend he had made there had invited him to Hampshire. What a fateful invitation that had been. It was easy to see why he had been instantly taken by Bea. She was a beauty and had a lively mind. Had coming so far, and to a quiet village, been such a strain on her mind that she had developed this love for Clara as a way to repair a broken life? But how could that be? Women left home and family to move many miles to their new married homes every day without this happening. Had William treated her so monstrously that she fled to Clara's arms for succor? It was hard to believe. Why hadn't Bea come to her, her sister?

William was self centered and could be head strong, but men everywhere seemed to be much like him and their wives didn't flee with their maids. Was it Clara? Was she evil and had she cast some spell over Bea that tore her from William? That was the answer that kept coming back to her, but Amanda had never heard of such a thing. She had never even read of it in one of the novels that had come into her possession. Nothing seemed to be the answer.

Suddenly, it came to her: Clara was possessed by a demon and that demon had allowed her to corrupt Bea. This was it. The Bible said there were demons in people; she remembered a verse. Amanda was not like the dissenters who memorized verse after verse from the Bible, but the Bible was important to her and it held the answer to her conundrum. She went immediately to her copy of Mr. Cruden's concordance and turned to the page that showed where the word 'demons' was found. She looked, and what she had remembered was there. According to scripture demons had inhabited many people, and so it must be with Clara. She had found the answer, but it gave her no peace.

It was not an answer she could speak to anyone, let alone the staff of the mansion or the public, or William, or Henry. She had to create a story for all of them.

Lady Beatrice had been taken suddenly and seriously ill. It was clear that no help was to be had from the local doctor or apothecary so she, with her maid Clara, had been sent urgently to Monaghan and on to Belfast for medical care.

This was the story Amanda decided upon. She told the staff and knew that it would soon spread. In two weeks she released the second part of the story: word had come from Belfast that the illness was serious, but there was hope; Beatrice was being sent to the spas at Bath in England where the physicians and the waters hopefully would affect a cure.

Amanda's stories satisfied many, but not all. Bea's sudden departure fit the story and it was noted that she appeared agitated and flushed when she left, but she did seem physically strong so the story of illness seemed a bit weak. As William had predicted, rumors began. Bea was involved with another man. William was involved with another woman. William was mistreating Bea. Bea had found the quiet of Croome Court unsupportable and had fled to the excitement of Belfast, or Dublin, or even London. Stories abounded, but the actual reason for Bea's departure was never even speculated upon. The idea of a Lady falling in love with her maid was outside the experience of Croome Court and was never thought of, let alone put forth as an actual possibility. This suited Amanda perfectly. There was damage, but even the wildest speculations were contained within the realm of normal, even acceptable, scandal. And there was no proof of any of the speculations because none of them were true. That was the best that could be hoped for.

Immediately, Amanda moved into the mansion and took on the task of raising Henry, as well as the tasks of running the house and trying as best she could to keep William from completely falling to pieces. The dogs, Laurence and Tim, reached an amicable accommodation: Laurence was lord and Tim was willing follower. Henry was distraught at the departure of his mother, whom he did love and who had loved and cared for him, but the familiar and loving presences of his aunt and his nanny gradually calmed him and returned him to his routine. William was the most affected by Bea's betrayal of him. His pride caused him to cling to the idea that he would become a laughing stock and would never be able to be seen in public without being followed by sniggering and whispers. He simply stopped leaving the estate. It was difficult enough for him to face his own servants, although due to Amanda's instructions and her carefully maintaining and adding news to the story she had created, the estate servants and farm workers, at least in the presence of the family, accepted the situation and, at least openly, maintained their respect for William.

Bea's disastrous denouement had taken place only weeks after John Massengill's visit to Croome Court, and only weeks after Bea's departure a third momentous event occurred in the village. It was the death of Thomas Nelson Dawson Dawson, Earl de Croome. The demise of the Earl was not unexpected; he had been a recluse for almost three years and stories of his declining health, both mental and physical, had been regular news in the village. Even though it was not a surprise, the Earl's death sent a shock wave through Croome Court and the entire surrounding area.

The Earl was the largest and wealthiest landowner for many miles around and a significant amount of the commerce of the area was derived from the Earl's estate. Purchases were made in the village to serve the mansion, the estate's tenants and staff also made their purchases in the village, the forestry enterprise of the estate, a large effort, employed sawyers, draymen and boatmen on the river, all of whom added to the commerce of the area. How would the Earl's death affect all of this? It was a matter fraught with uncertainty because the Earl had no direct heir. His wife had been dead for many years, so the heirs to the estate were distant relatives who lived in England.

The Earl's funeral was a lavish one. It took place in the protestant chapel and the burial was in the family burial ground at Croome Forest. None of his family were in attendance, they all living so far away, but all of the locality were at the service, including William and Henry Bullen and Amanda Walsh. It was one of the few occasions when William left the shelter of his own home. After the funeral, life on the Croome Forest estate continued much as before. Lachlan Edwards continued handling the affairs, the butler continued to run the mansion, the farmers continued to farm the land, the forestry steward continued to operate the forestry enterprise, and the chief steward oversaw it all.

CHAPTER 11

There was an heir to the Earldom and the Croome Forest estate. He was a first cousin once removed of the late Earl. The new Earl's grandfather, a younger brother of the late Earl's father had become a clergyman and had found both a good living in Wiltshire and a wife who brought him a handsome dowry. The grandson of the clergyman was a landowner who lived on a large estate in Wiltshire that had come from his grandmother's family. He was well established, and while he was extremely pleased to receive the Earldom he had for many years expected, and the fortune that went with it, he had no plans whatever to move to what he considered the wilds of Ireland and live on his new estate.

As it turned out, the new Earl did not even visit Croome Forest. He sent his only son and heir, two servants, and a solicitor from the London firm that handled his business. They arrived about six months after the death of the last Earl to inhabit Croome Forest. The party rode into the village in a bespoke coach and, although the coach slowed as it rode through Croome Court, it did not stop. Viewing the village through the coach window proved to be all the prospective heir to Croome Forest needed in order to dismiss Croome Court from further consideration. The coach entered the gate of The Forest and was not seen again.

Thomas Allen Dawson, the son and emissary of the new Earl, found himself, to his surprise, impressed with the Croome Forest mansion. The house was of only moderate size, and the exterior was unprepossessing save for the handsome stone porch, but the interior, while not large, was as elegantly decorated as any grand house he was familiar with in his home county. He wrote home to this effect, but since the family had no intention of living at Croome Forest, the house was of no interest to them. Thomas' task was to survey the contents and arrange to bring home to Wiltshire everything worth moving. The task of the solicitor was to inform Lachlan Edwards that henceforth the affairs of the estate were to be handled by the London firm of Fortesque and Hoare, to whom Edwards was to be completely subordinate, but that Edwards was fortunate to have been selected to become the local agent of that august firm, thus he would remain closely associated with the operations of the estate.

Having determined long before he set foot in Ireland that nothing short of a disaster that reduced the family's possessions to its Irish estate alone would induce him to return, Thomas spent only cursory effort in reviewing the ten thousand acres his father had inherited. He took two carriage rides around the farms, not troubling even to visit the river front, and concentrated his efforts in the mansion.

There were items of interest: all of the family papers in the late Earl's library were boxed up, every piece of silver and silver plate in the house was carefully packed into sawdust filled barrels, a two hundred and twenty-eight piece set of Worcester porcelain tableware was similarly packed for shipment, and the eighteen family portraits in their gilded and mostly very ornate frames were carefully boxed up for shipping. Except for a set of the books of Richard Brinsley Sheridan and a handsome leather bound volume of *The History of Tom Jones, a Foundling* the hundreds of books in the library were left untouched. Anything bearing the family crest was packed to be shipped. Furniture, mirrors, and clocks, although handsome, were not needed at the home estate and were deemed to be too bulky or too fragile to bear the cost or stand the rigors of the trip to Wiltshire so all were left in place. A number of turkey and Axminster carpets were folded, wrapped and placed in wooden crates. Two Savonaire carpets that had probably been smuggled in from France via the River Erne were packed as well. Some China ware and other porcelain pieces that caught Thomas' eye were packed in sawdust filled barrels. All else was left.

It took Thomas and a crew of workmen from the estate and carpenters and laborers from the village a month to make the assessment and complete the packing. When it was finished there were fifty-one barrels and forty boxes to be shipped, yet the house to the casual eye seemed fully furnished. It took twenty-one large wagons to transport everything and, as Thomas wanted everything to move at the same time and under his eye, wagons had to be hired from freighters for miles around.

When the massive wagon train moved out Thomas Dawson left the same way he had arrived, in the coach that did not bother to slow when it exited the gate of Croome Forest and passed through the village. Only Lachlan Edwards and the workers who had been packing, crating and loading had laid eyes on him. Nevertheless, his departure was cause for sadness and unease in Croome Court because it marked the end of an era. The time of departure of the wagons was known and the village turned out to see them off. The High Street was lined with individuals and small groups who watched in silence. In the lead, the coach created its cloud of dust and each wagon added to it. As the villagers watched wagon after wagon in fear and wonder, the dust slowly settled over them, but they paid it no attention. It was clear that there would never again be an Earl at The Forest, and it was unclear what the future of the estate would be or how this would affect the future of the village.

CHAPTER 12

After Thomas Dawson took from Croome Forest what the family wanted, life there settled into a routine. The mansion was empty; many on the staff were let go, with only the butler, and under cook and two maids left. The furniture was covered and dust slowly began to settle on everything within the house. Outside, things carried on as normal. The farms were farmed, trees were felled and shipped, rents were paid, and gentle decay began.

In the village much remained the same as well. There was almost no custom from the mansion at The Forest, but farmers and workers still did their business in Croome Court and the other landowners in the area carried on as usual. Although things were not bad, they were not what they had been and there was always a sense of unease. No one, not even Lachlan Edwards, knew what would happen to the estate. A good new owner or tenant could be good news for the village, the current state of stagnation could be lived with, a miserly owner or tenant would be bad news. They could only wait to see.

At North Hall nothing returned to normal. Bea was gone and while Amanda took Bea's place with Henry she could never fill it completely. As time passed, Amanda became more and more unsure how to handle Bea's continued absence. Was it possible that, as Bea and William had said, that Bea would never return? If so, should Amanda create a story of her death and put the matter to rest? It would be cruel for Henry to hear this because he continued to believe his mother would come back when she got well, but it might be better to bring closure to the matter so he could move on with his life. But what if Bea 'died' and then returned from the dead? How would Amanda ever be able to explain that? After much thought she decided that the only thing she could do was to continue dribbling out reports of Bea's lack of progress at Bath mingled with rays of hope that there would eventually be a cure. This was the story she kept on doling out in bits and pieces every few months.

William, of course, never wanted to see Bea again. Amanda had told him how she was handling the matter for public consumption and William was satisfied. He did not believe the story would convince or quiet the rumors, but he hoped, when he could rise out of his own misery, that Henry would believe the story and would be comforted by it. William remained mired within his own despair. His conviction that Bea's departure had been the end of him as a figure in society could not be shaken, and he continued to remain secluded at North Hall, seldom even going out of doors and often remaining in his bedroom all day. Amanda tried to convince him that he was not ruined, but nothing she could say made any impression on him.

While she had no real interest in society and she had many duties to keep her at North Hall, Amanda had decided that she was not going to be a recluse. She was determined that she would both go into society and visit the village on a regular basis. Her visits to the village now were frequently in the company of Henry with both Laurence and Tim, and frequently a footman to act as hostler to the dogs when Amanda and Henry went into a shop or stopped for a protracted conversation. Amanda had always been well received in the village and, to her relief, such continued to be the case.

The society of the area was another matter. It revolved around Lady Susan Seymour. Lady Susan, still relatively young at thirty-one, still a striking beauty, second only to Amanda in the eyes of the men of the north of County Cavan, and extremely commanding and quick of wit, sought to, and did, rule social life for the upper class in the area of Croome Court. As the wife of the much older, at fifty-eight years, Sir William Seymour, owner of an estate that had been in his family for generations and a business man whose investments and activities were thought to be spread as far abroad as Belfast and even Dublin she was a figure of importance. In addition, Lady Susan was an outrageous and highly successful flirt and was eyed with distaste by almost all the women of her circle. Even so, she had created a position for herself that necessitated the forbearance of all the wives and young husband seekers of that part of the county. Amanda, although she did not find her sympathetic and found her difficult to respect, was able to tolerate Lady Susan more easily than most of the rest of her circle because she was the acknowledged superior beauty, she did not have a husband who needed to be protected from Lady Susan's wiles, and she was not looking for a husband in the local population. This did not mean that she liked or trusted Lady Susan, only that she dealt politely with her.

The other leading families of the area, now that Croome Forest was empty, were the family of Amanda's late husband, the Walshes, the family of Captain Ievers of Ievers Hall, the Mahons of Wildwood Manor, and the Corrys of Corry Hall. There were other lesser gentry who were part of larger gatherings and balls, but most social life for Amanda, as it had been previously for her and for William and Beatrice, was centered around the Seymours and the four families mentioned.

CHAPTER 13

It was Amanda's habit two times each year to make a visit of a few days to Belfast. She was able to enjoy a bit of the city's society, attend a concert of music or a play, and could visit the shops and dressmakers to obtain items not available in the village. On occasion she also made purchases for the Hall. Each trip was an outing she looked forward to for weeks, all the more so since life at North Hall had become so sad and reclusive.

Late in the month of April, almost exactly three years from the time Beatrice had been cast out of North Hall and Croome Court, Amanda was in Belfast braving the unpleasant smells, noises, smoke, and crowds of the city to reach the shops she wished to visit. She had made some purchases and was walking in Bond Street to her next destination when she saw Beatrice walking straight toward her. She was both astonished and overjoyed, and called out in her loudest voice, "Bea!"

Beatrice was no less astonished and no less overjoyed. The two clung to each other and Amanda said, "Bea, you look so wonderful. You appear to be well in every respect."

"Dearest, I am. You cannot imagine how I have missed you and how much I love you still. Seeing you is an answer to my dreams. Tell me, first, are you well, and then tell me about my darling child."

"I am well in every respect. You need have no fears for me. Henry is a wonderful child. He is the apple of my eye and you can be sure that, as I promised, I am devoted to his care above all else. I have moved into the Hall to be near to him at all times. It will delight you to know that he grows beautifully in stature and in intellect. He can read and write and is beginning to know his numbers. I teach him myself, but we will soon get a tutor. His father is devoted to him although he finds little time to spend with his son. Oh, and Tim is well also."

"Thank God. You cannot imagine how much I have longed to hear this news. We have had no way to have contact with anyone in Croome Court. I have been afraid to write to you for fear William would find out and would have wrath and take it out on you."

"I am afraid you have been right. Your departure has crushed William. He is filled with shame and anger and he seldom goes into the village or into society. He knows there are rumors of all kind flying everywhere and he does not want to address them in any way. I confess that I know not what to say to stop them, either. I have made a story of your departure due to illness and that you are now at Bath. I embellish it from time to time with news about your condition and hopes that you will be cured. It is a poor effort, but the best I have been able to do.

" William has much taken to drink and can be most unpleasant, even hurtful, when in his cups. Our life is greatly burdened and I have great difficulty explaining the situation of you and of his father to Henry, but he is accepting of what I tell him and remains hopeful for your return. I try to find other subjects with which to keep him occupied. I can say that Tim remains his constant companion. All is as well as it can be. Now, tell me. What of you?"

"I will tell you all," said Bea, "but let that wait until tomorrow if you can come to visit me in the afternoon. We can talk in comfort and in private. Can you visit me?" Amanda was overjoyed to see Bea and said she would be most happy to have a long visit the next day. Bea gave her address and they fixed the hour. With many happy words they parted, each to finish her own errands.

Amanda had some unease the next afternoon as she entered the cab that was to take her to the address Bea had given her. What would Bea's home be like? As they passed through Belfast she became more relieved as she realized they were moving from the commercial area into an area of not unhandsome residences. The cab stopped and Amanda was delighted to see that she was alighting in front of a three story brick residence of quality. The entrance door, which had two windows to its left, was surmounted by a handsome semi-circular fan light and the steps leading up to it were lined with elegantly worked iron railings painted a dark green. All was excellently maintained. Both relief and wonder flooded Amanda's mind. It was a relief to see that Bea was living in such a pleasant house, but she wondered how the woman who had left Croome Court in such panic and with almost nothing could have become mistress of this fine home in only three years. Had she married again? That seemed unlikely. How had she done it?

The door was opened by a neat young maid wearing a linen cap, a dark blue long sleeved shirtwaist with lace at the neck and wrists and a long white linen apron. She was obviously expecting Amanda and greeted her by name. "Please come into the parlor my lady. I will tell Lady B you have arrived." She backed a few steps into the hall and indicated a doorway to the left. Amanda was impressed and relieved to see the excellence of the furnishings of the hall; the pier table was heavy and glided, had a large mirror above it and was flanked by two gilded wood chairs with flame stitched seat covers. A large portrait of a fashionable woman hung on the wall opposite it and there was a turkey runner on the floor. The furnishings were old fashioned, but of excellent quality. They looked as if they had been sold from some fine home that was being refurnished in the latest fashion by a new, young wife. As she entered the parlor Amanda encountered a room whose walls were painted in a deep rose color, with an Axminster carpet in red and blue covering the floor and a suite of furniture in the French style. There were portraits and landscape paintings on the walls, silver candlesticks and candelabra and porcelain bowls on the tables. All was elegance. She was thrilled with this display.

Amanda seated herself on a settee covered in light blue silk and looked up in time to receive a shock such as she had never had before. The maid turned, grasped the door handle and left, closing the door behind her. Unbelievably, Amanda saw that from the back the maid, who had seemed so demurely dressed from the front, wore absolutely nothing below the waist but her well polished slippers. The shirtwaist ended at the ribbons and bow that cinched the apron and below that was only a pair of beautifully rounded buttocks and two elegant legs. Amanda's heart stopped, her breathing stopped, and she instantly flushed and grew faint. Had she not been seated she was sure she would have collapsed to the floor. Had she come to the wrong place? No, the maid had known her. What could this be? Where was she? What was Bea doing in this house? She sat with her heart now beating almost out of control and was unable to move or put together coherent thoughts.

The door opened and Bea came in, looking elegant and almost radiant. Amanda could only look at her and stammer, "The maid?"

Bea panicked. She realized what had happened. She had to make amends; she could not lose Amanda now that she had found her. "Oh, God, Amanda," she said, "What have I done to you, dearest? You are safe. It is my fault. I was so foolish. I told Laura a lady was coming and she assumed you were a client and dressed the part. You should not have seen that."

"But what is this? What kind of client? Why is she dressed so incredibly?"

"Dear girl, you are ever the country mouse, and you have found yourself in the heart of the evil city without the slightest idea what is happening to you. I am so, so sorry. I will explain."

"Yes, yes," she looked at Bea with pleading eyes, "what is this?"

"Do not worry yourself. You are safe with me. Nothing is going to happen to you except that you are about to find out more about me than you wish to know." Bea was almost crying and she was all reassurance. Amanda remained collapsed in her seat. She was beginning to regain her color and her heart was slowing down, but she knew she was still too unsteady to stand. "Bea, I have no idea what has happened to you. I do want to know. You must tell me."

Bea sat next to her and took Amanda's hand in hers, "I so much regret the trouble caused at North Hall, and wish with all my heart it had never come to pass. I am afraid my story will be a great shock to you, but you must know it so I will give it to you as briefly as possible. As you remember, when Clara and I left Croome Court we had nothing but the clothes on our backs, the few items we were able to purchase in the village, my jewel box, and the money you gave us, dear heart. We arrived here in Belfast and had to make our way. Your money kept us going at first and we were able to find a goldsmith who would buy my jewels. We doled them out slowly to keep ourselves going and to keep the smith from realizing all that we had. We had to decide how to make our way. Another marriage, which would, of course, have been bigamous and therefore illegal in any event, seemed impossible. Any man of substance who might have been enticed into marriage would almost surely have had the means to find out my story and would never have married me, and only a man of substance would have been suitable. In any event, I had to keep Clara. I could not do without her, husband or not. I could have sought to become mistress to a man of substance—I could do that, you know—but I would have always been at the whim of a man, and that I did not want."

"But you have done well. You live elegantly."

"Yes, dearest. Just as Clara and I found our love between our legs, we found our fortunes there as well. When all our opportunities were considered with care, I determined that my only way forward was to set myself up as a courtesan of the highest class."

Amanda was shocked, almost speechless. "My God, Bea, I cannot believe this! But I thought you did not wish do such things with men. How can it be? How can you do it?"

"Believe you must. You are right, of course, I do not wish to lie with men, but I can, and so can Clara. That is the means by which we have made our way. We rented a decent premises and Clara was able to ingratiate herself into certain society where word of the favors I had to grant could be spread. She found a suitable client—we had determined that we would serve clients of only the most respectable type—and I pleased him in the most lavish way. The word of our services spread from that encounter and we soon had a growing clientele. Clara served some and I served the most discerning. We were most careful in every way, and because of the propriety of our premises and the great satisfaction we rendered we were able to prosper. It came slowly, but the growth of our prosperity was steady."

"I am astonished. I am unable to imagine you living such a life." Amanda's heart rate was going up again and she felt herself flushing.

"Of course you cannot, there is no way you can imagine what the life of a woman such as me must be like, and although you have suffered, you have not been thrown onto the street in an instant as I have, and had your entire life snatched away from you in that same instant. One does what one must do—and what one can do."

Parnassus Books

3900 Hillsboro Pike, Suite 14
Nashville, Tennessee 37215
(615) 953-2243
Join us every Saturday @ 10:30
for children's storytime!

	Date:	11-06-2014
Sale: 171473	Time:	06:04 PM

An Irish Mystery
1634439899   Item Price: $12.95 $12.95

1 Items   Subtotal: $12.95
                   Sales Tax (9.250 %): $1.20
                              Total: $14.15

                   Credit (Visa) Payment: $14.15

                      Amount Tendered: $14.15
                          Change Due: $0.00

Printed by: admin   Register: Drawer #2 (Apollo)

November 6, 2014 06:04 PM

Thank you for shopping with us today! Follow us on Twitter at
ParnassusBooks1.

"Beatrice, believe me, I do not condemn. You have been the best of sisters to me and the affection and love I have ever had for you still remains. It is that I am unable to imagine that your life has made such a turn, and I confess I am unable to imagine how you can do what you do."

"You can appreciate that society and men, in the form of your brother, have cast me out, and perhaps you will be able to understand that I retain little regard for the ways of conventional society and am happy to use it, including the desires of both its male sex and its female sex, to my advantage."

Amanda was silent for near a half minute and then said, "I do see." She thought for a few seconds longer and then asked, "But you said the maid thought I might be a client. How can that be?"

"It is this way: our business in servicing the needs of men prospered so well that both Clara and I were worked to our limits so we took in another suitable girl. We continued to prosper and added more girls and then we rented a much larger premises and furnished it, not in the best manner, but in a manner most suitable to what it was—a brothel of the highest class." This caused Amanda to shudder visibly. Bea went on, "We continued to prosper and less than a year ago we were able to purchase this house, much smaller than our establishment of business, but much finer and in a more elegant part of the city. We planned it as our home, and as you can see, we have furnished it in the finest way and it is an oasis for us."

"But you have clients here?"

"Yes, but only a select few. It happened by chance. I seldom venture out; meeting you was a dazzlingly fortunate event. Most of my outings are a ride in a hired carriage out into the countryside for a picnic with Clara. We enjoy getting out of the city, away from our clients, and we crave the opportunity to be alone with each other where there is no chance of prying eyes.

"On one occasion, however, I was making necessary purchases at a shop of quality when I recognized that a woman was watching me closely. She approached and I was afraid she might be the wife of a client who had somehow realized who I was and that there would be an unfortunate scene. It was not the case. She was indeed the wife of a client, and with his description she did discern who I was. But there was no scene. Instead, she most quietly let me know that she knew my profession and that she knew her husband availed himself of my services on a regular basis. I was quite astonished at her calm demeanor, but she soon astonished me even more by suggesting that if I were willing she would like to become my client as well. She told me who she was and I realized that her husband was a peer who was, indeed, a regular and most satisfied client. Almost every client will complain of the coldness of his wife when making his explanation of why he would need my services or when complimenting me on his extreme satisfaction with my labors, but in this case the wife made it clear that she had no use for her husband and he had no use for her. She had been seeking a female to love for years and when her husband described me to her in most fulsome terms, as was his habit when he had been given great satisfaction by a woman, she felt there was no chance that I would ever be in a position to betray her to anyone in her circle and had decided to take the chance of revealing herself to me. It had taken her several months, but she had found me.

"I was intrigued by her request, and after thought, told her I would consider it. I immediately revealed the conversation to Clara and we considered what to do. We knew it would be an opportunity to greatly increase our income because such women, of fortune of course, would pay very well. We would enjoy such a liaison, but the concern was that such liaisons might separate us from each other. We solved that problem by agreeing that we would both together service and enjoy any such clients."

"Your story grows more incredible by each word!"

"True enough, I am sure." She looked pleadingly to Amanda, "I sent a note to this woman telling her to come for a visit. She arrived by carriage the next afternoon and we made the arrangement. Our first meeting turned out to be as much as we could have hoped for in terms of both gratification and monetary gain. She is now our regular client and we have developed a very small, and very select, and very loyal clientele in the same line. They never meet each other and they come only in the afternoon, which leaves us available at night to oversee the business at our other place and in the mornings to rest and refresh ourselves. It also leaves our clients available to meet their husbands' needs in the evening, which they do with more—at least apparent—ardor after they have had a satisfying session with us. We do not work on the Sabbath. I think this is more than you have ever wanted to hear, but here it is." Bea was silent for a moment. "But now you must excuse me for a moment, my dear."

Bea left and Amanda tried to digest all she had heard. She knew, in the vaguest way, that there were women who served men sexually, but it had never occurred to her that there were women who served women sexually, and in spite of almost unceasing wonder over the years about Bea's fate, it had never occurred to her that whatever happened to Beatrice, it would be this. Bea shortly came back with a small purse which she pressed into Amanda's hands with the words, "Here is the return of your loan my dear one. Your unconditional kindness will be in my heart forever."

"Thank you, dear. You know you need never have paid me back, but I accept this with pleasure. You are kind as always you have been. Tell me, I do wonder, is not what you are doing outside the law?"

"It is, but there is no worry. As I have intimated, our clientele is from the highest circles of the city and this includes members of the constabulary, the military, and the municipal and even national government. They have no desire to expose us because in doing so they would become exposed as well—and they would lose our services which they value most highly. We make regular payments in specie or services to the lower ranks of the constabulary and so keep them firmly attached to us. Believe me, we are safe from the law and we take every precaution to be safe in our persons as well."

"Bea, I can hardly take this in." Amanda paused, "We must stay in communication so you can know Henry's progress and so I can be assured you are well."

"From the minute I saw you in Bond Street I began to think of that as well. I do not want to lose you again, my dear one. Here is what I have devised: You will write to a fine shop here, one from which you might be expected to make purchases, and inside the envelope you will enclose a smaller envelope addressed to 'Lady B'. I will ensure that they know this may happen and that the letter you enclose will be brought to me. I will have my letters to you taken to the shop and will instruct them to enclose them in an envelope on which is shown their name and address; you will therefore never get a letter from me nor will you write one to me that can be seen by William or anyone else."

Amanda was delighted. "That is a fine plan. It will work well. You are so wise to be able to devise such an arrangement and to have the means to carry it out."

"Yes, my dear." Bea gazed at Amanda and thought for a moment. "After all this shocking revelation I think you need to leave—you must have time to recover yourself. I have not even offered you tea! But I think it is best that you go. Take care of my boy. Devise every way you can to let him know his mother loves him." There was little more to be said, so after hugs and kisses Amanda took her leave. It was agreed that on every visit Amanda made to Belfast they would meet in person. Amanda returned to her lodging and early the next morning she took post for Monaghan where she would stay the night and be met by the North Hall carriage. By late that second day she was home, still filled with both shock and relief.

CHAPTER 14

There was no doubt among the connoisseurs of the sex trade in Belfast that Lady B's house of pleasure was the most elegant of the city's brothels, but it was only the gilded tip of an iceberg of commercial sex. Jimmie Kelley was one of the other titans of the trade. He owned three brothels in the city, all located near the waterfront in the most densely built up and most unpleasant parts of the city. His houses catered to the seaman and the working man and they were well located for their trade.

Jimmie had grown up poor and rough in a Catholic section of Belfast, but in spite of the poverty of his upbringing he had achieved an education that was impressive for a boy of his class—eight full years in school, and he had applied himself well during those years. Somehow, Jimmie had gotten the idea that an education would stand him in good stead, and in spite of a lack of parental support, except for the important support of letting him stay in school, and in spite of jeers and bullying from his peers who were less inclined to pursue an education and more inclined to start a fight, he had persevered. Although he studied, he did not eschew fighting and took part in at least his full share of neighborhood scrapes and in the Catholic boys' fights against Protestants. By the time he was fourteen years old he was a good reader, knew arithmetic like the back of his hand, and could brawl with the best of them.

Jimmie's talents did not go unnoticed and he was offered a position with his neighborhood drug dealer. He had already run errands and done other small work for his mentor and when he finished his schooling he was offered full time work with an impressive—to him—salary. He would keep the books, collect some of the easier to bring in debts and do some sales. The trade was in opium and laudanum. Opium had been coming into the port of Belfast courtesy of the East India Company for over fifty years and more recently the British Levant Company was bringing in very adequate quantities from Smyrna in the Ottoman Empire. Business was good. Jimmie's mentor was not one of the major importers but he was a major distributor and Jimmie spent the years of the 1780s and early 1790s learning the business and growing into it. In 1794 his mentor retired to a cottage in County Down and Jimmie Kelley became the proprietor of a good business. He had only to make a fair payment to his mentor each quarter of the year for the next five years to secure the business, and he did this with true religious devotion.

Along the way Jimmie had realized that a person who was in thrall to opium was in thrall to his—or her—opium supplier. He put this knowledge to work by putting to work on the streets a girl who needed her opium and would do whatever it took to get it. He kept her in necessities, a place to live, and opium, and she made a profit for him. Within a year he had three girls working for him and in 1796 he was able to take the lease on a house where they could live and work. It was much better for the girls than working the streets and it proved much better for Jimmie as well. By 1810 his drug business was continuing profitable and he had three brothels that were all bringing in good money. He had a large staff, including a stock of rough men who kept order, collected debts, sold drugs, and did any work he set out for them.

His houses of prostitution catered only to the lower classes, but they were religiously neutral, filling the needs of both

Protestant and Catholic. The drug trade was the same, and Jimmie had often pondered the fact that sex and drugs had the wonderful facility to be able to erase religious distinctions and animosities. He felt good about his part in that bringing together of humankind. He did, however, recognize, and often indulged in, the fact that both of his trades did tend to generate animosity and even violence for reasons other than religion. Jimmie's drug trade had one virtue that his sex trade did not: his drugs found a good market, indeed a very good market, within the upper class. The upper class wanted drugs just as much as the lower classes and they had the money to pay for them.

Jimmie had connections with the upper class of Belfast through his drug trade, but he had never been able to translate that upper class drug business into his sex trade. That was a source of disappointment, not because he wanted to mingle with the upper class—that wasn't going to happen under any circumstances—but because he wanted more of their money. A high class, wealthy man would pay good money for a high class woman. One upper class customer could be worth as much to him as ten of his present customers. He wanted that trade, but didn't know how to break into it, and when 'Lady B' opened her establishment he was both envious and jealous of her success. All he could do was watch, and he did watch. He learned about Lady B, how she ran her business and how she lived. He learned everything there was to learn and kept watching and hoping for a way to cash in on that knowledge.

CHAPTER 15

B eatrice Bullen to Amanda Walsh:

"My Dearest Amanda,

Your letter has filled me with shock upon shock. It is difficult enough to believe that William is dead, and that he has taken his own life is hard to bear, even after all that has passed between us. I count myself to blame in part, because the shock of my denouement was, I know, beyond anything he could have imagined might happen to him. But what could I do? I tried my best to keep the secret from him, but I am what I am and can no more change it than I can fly through the air. And he was what he was and brought himself to his own end.

My second shock is the realization of what has happened to Henry. My dear child has lost his mother and now his father. The only beam of light in this picture is you, my dearest sister. You have been every bit a mother to Henry, and you will now be both mother and father, for I have given careful thought to your suggestion that Henry might now spend some time with me. I do not feel it can be so. You are acquainted, at least in a general way, with my situation, and I could never allow Henry to enter my world, even for a short time. At some point in time and in some manner he would learn the truth, and I could not bear that, for his sake or for mine. So there is the end to that idea.

I do have a plan, and I blush to say that I have put it into motion without first gaining your consent. I know you, my dear, and have every confidence that you will see the merit of my plan and join enthusiastically in allowing it to be carried out. I have engaged the limner Adam Buck to paint you and Henry in little for me. Mr. Buck is highly regarded in Dublin where he bases himself and I have seen his work here in Belfast. It is of the finest quality.

Here is the plan: he will come to North Hall where you will allow him to establish himself while he does his work. Henry will be told that you have engaged him to paint a portrait of Henry for you and one of you for him. And that will be done, but at the same time he will paint one of each of you for me. Thus I shall always have a portrait of each of you who are so dear to me. Henry will be none the wiser. All of the arrangements have been made. Mr. Buck will bring with him the gold cases to complete the work. All is paid. I am told he is a gentlemanly sort of man. I expect he will be with you within two or three weeks of the time you receive this letter.

Keep me always in your heart, and continue to love my child as your own. Write often.

Your loving sister,
B. Bullen"

The limner Adam Buck arrived at North Hall twenty days after Amanda received Bea's letter. Amanda was pleased with Bea's plan and Henry was fascinated with the entire process. Buck did all the work he was engaged to accomplish and one thing more. Amanda had him paint a third portrait of her. She did not know what she would do with it, but she had a hope that she would need to give it to someone, and she wanted to have it ready against that day. After almost four weeks Buck departed for Belfast to take the two portraits she had commissioned directly to Bea. Henry was pleased and Amanda was pleased; the images Buck had produced were most perfect and were highly satisfying. When she received her portraits, Bea, too, was greatly gratified by the results of her plan.

CHAPTER 16

The end of the Napoleonic War had greatly reduced the Royal Navy's need for officers and seamen and Captain Massengill was one of the many who had been released from active duty and placed on half pay. Although being relegated to half pay caused financial distress to many officers it was no burden to Massengill, in fact it was a welcome change. He had been twenty years in the Navy, more than enough for any but a man who could not adjust to life ashore, and during those years he had been one of the rare few who was fortunate enough to amass a large fortune through prize money. His fortune amounted to almost one hundred thousand pounds, enough to supply him with a lifetime income that ranked him with many of the nobility and the most prosperous of the merchants and manufacturers. When he left the service he took with him part of his boat crew and his two most trusted servants. What each of them would do in the new life was not clear, but all had been with Massengill for almost ten years and their fondest wish was to stay with him. He valued their service and their loyalty and had determined to insure they would be honorably employed and taken care of for the rest of their years.

Upon his release from the service, Massengill had closeted himself with his London bankers, who had also served him loyally and well. When they learned that he was to retire from the Navy they had assured him that he was an extraordinarily wealthy man who had the money to do anything he pleased. He had indicated that his pleasure was to return to the place of his birth and buy a property upon which to live the life of a gentleman. Baring Brothers & Co. began the search for suitable properties and they very quickly found that the firm of Fortesque and Hoare, solicitors, were, in behalf of the Earl de Croome, at that very time offering for sale a large property in Ireland that was adjacent to the village of Croome Court. "Perhaps it would be the perfect property for Captain Massengill," they suggested. The estate was comprised of 10,000 acres, a fine mansion house in the early Palladian style with much of its furnishings, and a full complement of farm and forestry buildings and facilities. The price of twenty thousand pounds, while substantial, was well within the Captain's means. The property could be expected to return a full two thousand pounds net income each year and the Captain's remaining funds would return approximately three thousand five hundred pounds a year, thus giving him an almost princely income of five thousand five hundred pounds a year and a fine property upon which to enjoy his income.

It was hard for Massengill to believe that the solicitor's son, a village boy, was in position to buy the most magnificent property he had ever known as a young man—a property he had never even dreamed of owning. He asked for the use of a small office where he could sit in quiet to consider the matter. In one-half hour he emerged and instructed Messrs Baring to have their solicitors close the sale.

Upon completion of the sale, Messrs Fortesque and Hoare notified Padraig Berrigan, the chief steward of the Croome Forest property, of the sale. He was advised that the new owner was one John Massengill, late of the Royal Navy, and that Massengill could be expected to arrive at Croome Forest within the next month. This was bad news for Berrigan. He had known that the property had been put up for sale and that the completion of the sale would mean that the conditions that had allowed his enterprise to prosper at Croome Forest would come to an end. Now it had suddenly turned out that he had only a fortnight or two to arrange for removal of all evidence and to reorganize the activities in such a way as to allow them to continue unnoticed by the new owner. The fact that the new owner was a former naval person was additional bad news, for such a person could be expected to pry into every aspect of the estate, always looking to have everything ship shape and Bristol fashion as Berrigan had heard it said.

Berrigan started a search for new premises and he told his confederate John Barber what to expect. Upon hearing the name Massengill, Barber realized exactly who the new owner was, although he could not conceive of how John Massengill, the solicitor's boy, could have come into enough money to buy the Croome Forest estate. Perhaps a magnificently advantageous marriage? Or perhaps the prize money fortunate naval officers were said to be able to come by? Barber told Berrigan what he knew.

CHAPTER 17

Before leaving London to take up his new property Massengill had made arrangements to purchase a coach and a wagon in Belfast. Both were to be of good quality, but not of extravagance; they were to be part of the permanent equipage at Croome Forest since it had been suggested to him that there might be no suitable coach remaining in the estate's inventory, and he needed the wagon in any event. The carriage maker had them ready for his review when he arrived and both passed his inspection so the purchases were completed. With this important task taken care of, Massengill, with no little help from his men, had spent the better part of a week purchasing horses and equipment that he needed for the journey to Croome Court, and when all was ready he and his men started on their way.

The party had left Belfast behind and was hours into the countryside on their first day of travel. Massengill had one seat in the coach to himself, allowing him to face forward and to look out either of the side windows as he chose. Most gentlemen being driven in their coaches would not bother to look out the windows, finding the countryside and its people both trivial and uninteresting, but Massengill was cut from a different cloth. He was a man who observed, and he spent much of his time on the road looking out one window or the other, interested in what he saw and cataloging the information for future use or enjoyment.

After a considerable time of passing through open countryside they entered a copse of trees that stretched for some distance along both sides of the road and suddenly there was an incident that seared itself on John Massengill's memory. They rolled toward a large tree that stood on the south side of the road and suddenly from behind it stepped a wisp of a girl. To Massengill's eye she looked to be not more than four years old—if that. She was the chief of a party, and her party consisted of two still smaller children, one perhaps near three years of age and the other less than two, barely able to toddle.

The three waifs were dressed alike, in neat, clean, white frocks of a cloth that appeared to be a most ordinary cotton. The oldest girl had honey colored hair in tight curls and the mass of her hair was long enough to be tied behind her by a ribbon of the lightest—no doubt faded—pink. The two younger ones had the same hair, but theirs was short and formed curly helmets on their little heads. But it was not their appearance that transfixed Massengill; it was what the leader of the party did. As they stepped along their path, came to the road crossing and left the shelter of the large tree, the chief of party saw the oncoming coach and team, heard the thundering hooves and the grinding wheels and instantly flung out her tiny arms so her two charges would not patter into the danger that was charging toward them. The look on her little face was one that Massengill knew he would never forget; it was a mixture of fear, courage, and determination. The child's gaze was fixed on the coach and wagon, and as the coach and wagon passed the little party Massengill turned to watch. When the danger was past the little leader wasted not a moment; she lowered her arms and led her charges across the road and onto the path beyond.

During twenty years at sea Massengill had seen looks of fear, courage, and determination on the faces of many battle hardened men and he knew well that all of those emotions had appeared on his own face. But to see all this on the face of a four year old child and to see her instant move to safeguard her tiny charges was moving beyond anything he could remember. He marked the tree in his mind so he could find this spot again, and as he turned the incident over in his mind he came to see the little girl not just as a courageous and determined child; he was much moved when he realized that he saw her as the embodiment of Ireland, itself.

What but poverty could have sent out such a waif with such a charge? What important, even desperate, errand took them away from their home and to the dangers of the road? But what other than pride could have dressed the party in the clean, white frocks that were either new or carefully mended? And where but in Ireland would a child of such tender years have already been inured to duty, become aware that the world was full of things to fear, and become armed with resolve to do her duty to protect her charges at any cost? She was the living soul of Ireland, a country of poverty, pride, duty, resolution…and fear. This was the Ireland to which he was returning, the country of his birth with which he was casting his lot. He saw Ireland as he had never seen it before. What was this Ireland going to bring to him, and what was he going to bring to Ireland? He was filled with wonder. The coach lumbered on without pause.

CHAPTER 18

It was an August day in the year 1814 when John Massengill returned again to Croome Court. His arrival was much different from what it had been in 1810. The weather was sunny and still warm. He arrived in a coach. It was seen to be a new, dignified vehicle of good quality, painted a dark blue with gold striping. The coach was drawn by four bay horses and on the seat was a well but plainly dressed coachman, who handled the team with skill. The driver of the coach was named Walters, and beside him on the box sat another man, Glenn. Inside the coach were three men, John Massengill, a man named Bowyer, and a man named Cheshire. The coach was followed by a sturdy wagon, also obviously new. A carter and two men were on board along with a cargo of boxes and luggage. The driver of the cart was named Otis, and the two men with him were named Douglass and Womack. Bowyer had been Massengill's writer in the Naval service, Cheshire was his steward, Otis was the coxswain of his barge and Douglass, Glenn, Walters, and Womack were four of the barge's oarsmen.

Upon finding that Massengill was to purchase a coach in Belfast and travel in it to his home, three of his men, Otis, Glenn, and Walters, announced their early lives as farm boys and proclaimed their ability to drive. It would not be necessary to hire a coachman and driver; they would do the work. In fact, they were so anxious to drive that a strident argument broke out between them as to who would have the honor of driving the coach. The argument became so contentious that Massengill finally said he would thrash them all if they did not shut their mouths. He would decide by toss of the coin who would do what. The drivers and helper set out to do their duties as the coin had decreed.

Although he was the owner of Croome Forest, when Massengill and his party arrived in the village they stopped at the inn where the number of rooms they required had been reserved by message two days before their arrival. Massengill had given considerable thought to his arrival in Croome Court and he had decided that placing the mansion in good order would take some time so it would be both appropriate and convenient to stay at the inn until his home was in good order. He had also considered whether he should announce immediately that he was the new owner of the Croome Forest estate and he had decided that it would be much of a shock to the populace to get such information with no preparation. Accordingly he had instructed his men that they were to say nothing about his ownership of the estate, only that he was coming back to Croome Court to retire from the sea. He would establish himself with his friends and acquaintances and only then would he reveal the outline of his fortune and his ownership of the estate. He felt that thus he would lessen, and possibly remove, the shock that might be caused by the revelation of his almost staggering turn of fortune.

The arrival of the party was noticed by everyone who could get onto the street or to a window. The populace had been alerted by barking dogs and the sound of the equipage and had come out en mass. They were most impressed with what they saw and were excited to find that the occupant of the coach was none other than their own Captain John Massengill. As had happened on his visit in 1810, Massengill immediately became the talk of the village.

After settling himself in his room, Massengill repaired to the office of Lachlan Edwards where he spent well over an hour informing Edwards of his purchase of Croome Forest and the good news that Edwards was to become, once again, the man of affairs for the property. Massengill made it clear that he did not want the news spread until he had had time to feel the pulse of the village. It was a meeting filled with satisfaction for both parties.

John Barber sent a message to Berrigan informing him of Massengill's arrival and of his visit to Lachlan Edwards.

CHAPTER 19

Berrigan had to decide quickly what to do. Massengill had arrived almost ten days before he was expected. Arrangements had not been made. Things were not in place. The first order of business was to keep Massengill from starting a thorough examination of the property—one that could alert him to what was happening. There were two problems in addition to that. Barber had told him that Massengill had arrived with seven men, mostly a rough looking lot. Did this mean that he had somehow already found out what was happening and was planning to take Croome Forest by force? And the visit to Edwards. Edwards knew enough about the financial situation of Croome Forest to realize the flow of cash from the property was not what it had been before the late Earl's death. He might ascribe this to general laxity in the absence of an on-site owner, or he might be suspicious or cunning enough to think something untoward was going on. If Massengill did not know, could Edwards have alerted him to a problem? If he did know could he have compared information with Edwards, confirmed his knowledge, and told Edwards what he thought was happening at Croome Forest?

There were too many "ifs", and almost any of them could lead to exposure of Berrigan's work. Something drastic had to be done. Massengill might or might not know or suspect. In any event, he had to be kept out of Croome Forest at least long enough for proper arrangements to be made. He could simply be killed, but the final solution of killing him was too much, at least for now. The death of the new owner would focus too much attention on Croome Forest and that could unravel everything. Massengill had to be contained but not killed.

Edwards was another matter. His records were dangerous and Edwards himself was potentially dangerous. If Massengill did not know what was going on he could find out from Edwards' records even if Edwards himself were unaware, and if Edwards did know, or had found out, it was too dangerous to allow him to stay alive. Edwards had to die and his records concerning Croome Forest—and Massengill for good measure—had to be stolen and destroyed.

CHAPTER 20

It was the earliest riser of the village, the baker Terrence O'Doul, who found Lachlan Edwards' body. O'Doul rushed into the inn's bar room, banged on the counter to raise the inn keeper and shouted at the top of his lungs, "Hit's the attorney, and he's dead enough! Come out, Barber! Come out!"

In no time a small crowd surrounded Edwards' body, which had been easy enough to find since it was lying in the dust in the middle of the High Street. He lay on his face, an obvious bloody gash in the back of his head, and a trickle of blood in the dirt near his head. "Foot pads!" "Done him in, right here in the street." "Bloody murder." Dastards!" "By God, he were a good sort." "Who done it?" There was a flood of comments and ideas.

The Constable was called and he took charge in a most official manner. Constable Quirke was a man of medium height, but of sturdy build. He was sandy haired, light of complexion, square of face, and slow to talk, but he had been the constable of Croome Court for over a decade and he had the respect, if not the friendship, of the people of the village. "You idlers there, move the body to the undertaker. I'll tell his wife and family. All the rest of you, to the pub and wait for me there."

Edwards' wife was told, and she collapsed immediately. A neighbor woman was called in to tend to her, the rector was called to comfort the widow and begin the preparations for the funeral and burial, and Constable Quirke returned to the pub to begin his interrogation of the witnesses. It turned out that there were no witnesses, only the man who found the body and the curious.

Massengill and most of his men had joined the crowd by this time, and after it had been established that there were no actual witnesses, Massengill suggested that he and Constable Quirke return to the scene of the crime to see if there was any evidence there. They did, and nothing could be found. There were footprints everywhere, but it was clear that there had been so much coming and going since the body had been found that it would never be possible to determine which footprints, if any of those that were visible, were those of the murderer, or murderers. Massengill took the constable aside and said, "Constable, I have a thought."

"Very well, and tell me, who are you, my man?"

"Captain John Massengill, born in this village and back after twenty years service in His Majesty's Navy. Lachlan Edwards was my counselor at law and the successor of my own father, Marshall Massengill, long the solicitor here. I saw Edwards only yesterday afternoon."

"Ahhh, I do remember you, Captain." The Constable was satisfied.

"During my years in the Navy I have seen more blood spilled than I can ever recount to you and the curious thing about this scene is that there is precious little blood in the street. I've seen many a similar wound and they bleed prodigiously. I believe he would have been killed elsewhere and his body brought here."

"It is possible. And where would you think he had been attacked?"

"His chambers are just there. Perhaps we should start there since you have apparently established by your visit that it did not happen at his home." They went to Edwards' chambers, found the door unlocked and walked in. The front office, the domain of Edwards' only clerk, appeared normal in all respects.

"Nothing out of the ordinary here," noted the constable after a look. "No sign of a break-in, so if it happened here my experiences tells me the perpetrator would be someone Edwards knew."

"True enough." They went in to Edwards' office and there the scene was different. Although the office did not appear to be the scene of a fight there was a large pool of blood on the floor near Edwards' chair.

"Here is where it happened. So it was not a footpad on the street bent on thievery. You have most recently been in this office, Massengill. Do you see aught that is different from what you remember?"

Massengill perused the room thoroughly and saw two things that were amiss: "Look there, behind the desk, at his books of files. They are in alphabetical order and some are missing."

"Which?"

"The large gap would appear to be the papers for Croome Forest, no doubt his most important client, and the smaller gap to the right is his file on my own affairs."

Quirke was instantly alert, "Yours, sir? Why would they be missing? "

"I have no idea. Nor do I have an idea why the Croome Forest papers are missing."

"Most curious. So he was murdered because of some papers? Why not just steal the papers?"

"Constable, I would think it was because Edwards knew what was in the papers and even if the papers were gone he would be able to tell the story—whatever it might be. He had to be silenced. I cannot imagine what would be in the papers concerning the very ordinary matters he handled for me that would be of the most vague interest to anyone, let alone a cause for theft and murder. But the Croome Forest papers could have been much more interesting, and perhaps more dangerous."

"Possible indeed. And, pray, Captain, what time did you leave Mr. Edwards yesterday?"

"At half past five. I hardly need say that he was in perfect health when I left him."

"Of course. Was his clerk present when you left?"

"No. He had gone."

"Oh, I see."

The constable made a second visit to Mrs. Edwards, now in the care of two of her neighbors, and found that after an evening spent together she and Edwards had retired to bed at about ten PM after which a loud knocking at the door came at about eleven PM. Her husband got up to answer this most unexpected summons and shortly came back saying that it was an urgent business matter that required him to go to his chambers immediately for a time. He dressed and left, telling her to go back to sleep, and she did sleep. Her first realization that anything was amiss was in the morning when the constable had knocked at her door with the tragic news. How many people had been at the door the night before? She could not say, "perhaps more than one."

"Were they Male or female?"

She was shaky, but managed, "I could only hear muffled voices. But probably male. What woman would be out at that time of night wanting my husband's presence?"

There wasn't much to go on. It was clear that Edwards had survived his afternoon visit with Massengill, but there was no telling who had come back in the night. Could it have been Massengill himself with one or more of his men? Or was it someone else? Who could have wanted Edwards dead? The constable began to mull it over.

Word of this most astonishing crime in living memory in Croome Court spread everywhere in the village within an hour of Edwards' body being found. It got to North Hall where Lady Amanda was astonished, fearful, and determined to learn whether this could be the beginning of a concerted series of attacks on the gentry or whether it was likely to be aimed only at Edwards. She understood that John Massengill had come back to Croome Court and had seen Edwards only hours before he was murdered. She wanted to know what he knew. A footman was sent and shortly after noon John Massengill presented himself before her.

Amanda greeted him warmly, "Captain, I am so glad to see you after all these years, but I regret that the circumstances are so shocking."

"Indeed they are, my Lady. I would say that I am glad to be back in The Court, but under the circumstances I can hardly say that. I can say, however, that I am most pleased to be able to see you. How can I be of service?

"You are most kind. Captain, you must help me. What has happened? Is this a crime against Edwards only, or is this the first part of a terror spree aimed at the gentry and nobility? I am sure Edwards must have made enemies among the tenants, though I think the tenants in the area of Croome Court are treated well. All the main families have been settled here for many years and we have a good relationship with our people. But violence against the gentry and nobility seems always to be bubbling at the surface of our life. Do you know if there is general unrest? Is it the local ruffians? Could it be the Whiteboys…? "

"I do not know," Massengill admitted, "although it does appear that the area is quiet in general. Having left Ireland when I was but a lad and having been away these twenty years I have no first-hand knowledge of the situation. However, during my ride from Belfast I saw nothing that indicated a general level of unrest, so my best estimate is that the crime had to do with something Edwards knew that would be destructive to someone if it became public knowledge. What he knew or who it might have damaged, I do not know. I do not believe you have anything to fear. I do not think the Whiteboys or other rebels are involved."

"I am glad of it. I have been most worried. I am sure that if anyone in the village would understand the situation of the country, it would be you. Thank you for answering my request for a visit. Please, let us be relaxed. I will call for tea. Could we now talk of what has happened since we last saw each other?" They spent near an hour talking over tea and biscuits and were still talking at a lively pace when Higgins knocked, entered, and announced, "Madame, the constable is here and wishes to see Captain Massengill."

"Send him in, please."

The first words out of the constable's mouth were, "John Massengill, I arrest you for the murder of Lachlan Edwards."

Amanda and Massengill were astounded. "You must be out of your mind, man! What possible reason could I have for murdering my long time friend and man of business? He is—was—a man I felt to be as much a brother to me as any man on earth."

"Constable," cried Lady Amanda, "this is outrageous. It simply cannot be true. Captain Massengill is no murderer."

"So you think, My Lady. But the evidence says otherwise. Captain Massengill was the last person other than Edwards wife who is known to have been with Edwards before he died. Massengill had arrived in the village only hours before with a group of hard men and the first thing he did was to meet with Edwards. Something happened in that meeting. Something Massengill was expecting, otherwise why would he have arrived with his men—his murder squad? I will get to the bottom of this and Massengill will be in my custody until I do and until he is tried and convicted."

Massengill was enraged, "Sir, you are wrong in the wildest sort of way. You have no right to take me and I will not go with you. Leave us!"

"Perhaps you will not go with me, Captain, but you will go with us." He turned, "Come, now!" At this barked order three men entered the room, one of whom menaced with a pistol, and Massengill realized he had no option but to go with them.

As he was being propelled out of the room he turned, "Lady Amanda, I am mortified that this outrage has taken place in your home. Forgive me. This will be cleared. I assure you. I had nothing to do with Lachlan Edwards death. Please, send to tell my men of this."

Massengill was taken away. Amanda was outraged, first that Massengill, a man she was sure was a gentleman and no murderer, had been arrested, and second that the constable had had the effrontery to barge into her home to make the arrest. She was seething, but she could still think and she realized that Massengill's men likely would be the constable's next targets for arrest, so she immediately sent a footman to the inn to find who he could of Massengill's men and warn them to escape. She also sought immediately to help get Massengill out of the constable's custody. In ordinary circumstances her first thought would have been to call on her man of business, Lachlan Edwards, but clearly that would not be possible. Who to call? The vicar was not a forceful man, so he wouldn't serve. She finally settled on a man who had some family standing in the community and who had long shown himself—to her displeasure—to be very devoted to her: James Walsh, her late husband's brother.

Amanda sent for James and in mid afternoon he arrived. He was his usual fawning self in Amanda's presence. Amanda was repulsed by James' interest in her, but knowing he was her best hope, she told him everything she knew about Edwards' death and Massengill's visit and his apprehension by the constable and his men. She declared her certainty that Massengill could not be guilty and begged James to help get Massengill released, at the very least, and cleared of suspicion if possible. James swore he would do everything in his power for her. She was relieved. She thanked him and ended the interview as gracefully as she could. Amanda could think of nothing else she could do except to visit Massengill, wherever he was being held. She set about finding out where he was.

CHAPTER 21

Michael O'Day was gently stroking her thigh and B was thinking that of all her clients he had to be her favorite. He had time for her. When he was satisfied he didn't just up and leave like most, he stayed for her, and she knew it was for her, a little gift. Michael was wealthy and important. Not just wealthy, but super wealthy. His father had left him a good mercantile business and he had made it into a giant. He sold lumber, hardware, other building materials, fabrics from simple cotton to luxurious silk, wine and foodstuffs. He had warehouses, warerooms and shops. He had ships, a number of them. He had his own docks and his ships traded in Baltic timber, timber and foodstuffs from Irish ports, goods from England, and from France. And in spite of all this he was not accepted by the nobility and other upper society. They might do business with him and buy from his shops, but he was Irish and the English thought he was not good enough to be invited into their homes. That was probably lucky for B, because she knew that if he could get into the homes of the men he did business with, he could get into their wives' bedrooms as well and then he might have no use for her.

Michael was in his forties, but still slim, strong, with dark wavy hair. His good looks and surprisingly good manners could have gotten him into the beds of half the women in Belfast society, but he never had that chance, and how good that was for B. She was his pleasure and he paid well for that pleasure. Michael was not interested in having another girl along with B as some clients were, he was interested in none of the rougher forms of love, and he certainly was not interested in having another man in the ménage as were a few of her clients. She had men working for her as security, as handymen and drivers and she could supply a man if he were needed. But Michael was interested only in her.

Michael continued his exploration of her thigh, moved up to her belly and placed one fingertip in her naval while he caressed her with the rest of his hand. B was enjoying it. It could be Clara's hand there; he was just as delicate as Clara. He moved up to her breast and gave a gentle pull to her erect nipple. "I think you are most interested in me," Bea smiled at him.

"And I think you may be interested in me, as well as in my purse," he murmured.

"You are mean to me," she purred as she spread her legs. He was in her and she wrapped her legs around him as they both liked. This time it took longer than before and when he was finished B let out a well practiced moan of pleasure and both were well satisfied. This time Michael did get up to leave.

" I must go. I have business."

"Business? Truly? At near midnight?"

"Truly." He got up and got dressed and as he was finishing B swung out of bed, put on a dressing gown that she did not fasten in front, leaving all her charms in view. She snuggled against him, one hand on the bulge in his trousers and the other around his neck.

"Come back soon." He gave her kitty a stroke and told her there was no fear. He would be back.

CHAPTER 22

James Walsh had no intention of helping get John Massengill out of custody or out of suspicion. He wanted Amanda and he would do anything he could to get her, but getting a rival for her affection out of trouble was not an action that seemed to be helpful to his cause. And he could tell that Massengill was a rival. He would, of course, do what he could to make it look like he was working for Massengill, but he would also do what he could to make sure those efforts bore no fruit. He decided to seek the advice of a trusted confederate, Lady Susan Seymour. Lady Susan was James' confederate in every way. In fact, she was his mistress and she was often available to him since her husband was very frequently away on business trips to Dublin, Belfast, Galway, Sligo, or Derry. His many businesses were said to be involved with shipping and all were in sea ports. These trips were a godsend for Lady Susan and James. At fifty-eight, and probably with romantic interests of his own in his various cities of business and being so often absent to boot, even when he was at home Sir William hardly satisfied his wife's sexual needs, which were many and varied. James, a good twenty years younger, was eager to make up any deficiencies.

The loving couple made an effort to shield their trysts from interested eyes outside the Seymour estate, but at home Lady Susan worried not. The servants all knew that Sir William knew and cared not at all what his wife was doing so no one had to keep secrets from anyone else. Lady Susan also knew all there was to know about James' infatuation with Amanda, but she did not care because she knew that Amanda was not her sexual rival and she also felt sure, in spite of what James hoped, that Amanda would never take him away from her by marrying him, or any man like him.

They talked about Amanda and Massengill and, while Lady Susan would have been happy for Massengill to sweep Amanda off her feet and out of James' life, intrigue was stock in her trade so she supported James in his plan to do all he could to hurt Massengill. She did remember most clearly that, years before, Massengill had not availed himself of the charms that she had so clearly offered him, and she could neither forget nor forgive that snub. How nice it was to be able to have a measure of revenge.

Having dealt in great detail with Massengill, they spent time puzzling over why Edwards had been murdered and whether Massengill might actually have done it. What could have happened between them? What did one of them know that either enraged or terrorized the other? James had no clue so Lady Susan was free to evaluate all the possibilities she could imagine. After they had thoroughly discussed the matter and she was through with James and had sent him on his way, Lady Susan lay abed and continued to think on the matter and her thoughts began to coalesce around one possibility.

CHAPTER 23

The bark *Champion* arrived in the port of Dublin on August 14, 1814, after having been away from Dublin for six months and two days. The voyage had not been an easy one; punishing North Atlantic storms had all but sunk the ship on not one, but three, occasions during the passage to Nova Scotia and back. An early spring departure had been a mistake to begin with, and having survived the crossing *Champion* had spent time in Nova Scotia for repairs and loading cargo. The voyage had not been easy for anyone on board, and for the crew before the mast the general rigors of the voyage were increased by poor pay and even worse food. After consideration that had not had to be very lengthly, young Niall Bannon, ordinary seaman, had decided he had had enough of the sea. He was going to return to the family small holding in County Cavan and use his meager savings to help his father improve the place that he knew would be his someday.

First, though, he headed for a brothel in Fenton Lane whose name and location were well known to the crew members who hailed from Dublin. He was greeted outside the door by a large man of tough mien who asked who he might be. "A sailor home from the sea."

"You have come to the right place. And what kind of money do you have?" Niall showed a silver coin and the door was opened and he was ushered inside without another word.

The room was dimly lit, smoky from candles and tobacco and smelled of candle, tobacco, sweat, stale food, and sex. He moved into the room and a woman, clad but scantily, left a group of idlers and came to greet him. It was his sister Ailis. His knees almost buckled but he was able to scream, "God Damn! What are you doing in this shit hole?"

She said in a low, even voice, "The same thing you are, fool, getting screwed."

"God Damn! You are my sister!"

The outburst had drawn the door keeper into the room. "Is this bounder your brother for true?"

"He is. And he's not welcome here." Her voice carried a mixture of anger and despair.

"God Damn!" It seemed to be the only thing Niall could think of to say.

"Outside, you two, and sort out whatever is between you. No quarrels in this place!" The door keeper herded them outside, pointed them down the street and said, "Sort it, and be quick about it. You have work to do, miss."

"What is this? What is this? You are a whore in Dublin? How? What happened to you, girl?"

"I was tricked. It's true. I never set out to be whoring, but I was fooled into it.

"Who did it?"

"It was John Barber, that bastard of an inn keeper in Croome Court," she said with venom. "He told me he could get me a good job in service with a fine family here in Dublin and I believed it and let him put me on a coach to get here. But it wasn't that way. When I got here they took me to this rotten place and a whole gang of those toughs who guard the house and bounce out the bad ones took me in a back room and raped me one after the other. I came here as a virgin girl and they ruined me. I was raped! They locked me up and made sure I knew that I was a ruined girl and that there was no way I could return home."

"Damn their souls. You can come home. I'll take you."

She shook her head and stared at him, "No, I can't. The toughs would be sent after me and when they found me they would kill me. They would have to, because I know too much. They have made it clear to me."

He was incredulous. "What do you know? What could be worth killing you, for God's sake?"

"I know that the owner of this place, who makes all the money, is none other than Sir William Seymour, our own fine knight from County Cavan. They could never let me loose to go home and tell that. I would be a dead woman, and besides, our own pa would murder me if he found out I had been whoring. There's no home for me but here. And no work but on my back. I am ruined."

"Jesus, Mary, and Joseph! Is it really true that Seymour owns the place?"

"Yes. And he owns others, too, in other cities. And that high toned bitch of a wife of his knows all about it. She never comes here, but she knows. She does the money, and they talk about her. The rotten bitch," she said bitterly.

"I'll take you home. Now. I can make it all right."

"No. No, you can't. Get it through your head: I really will be dead if I show my face in County Cavan. They will have me killed. They are evil, and they have too much to lose if the secret gets out. I have to stay here. Now you go. Get away from here and leave me alone. Go home. Don't ever mention me or this place or the Seymours. It's best for us both." She turned, ran up the street and back into the only home she had. Niall Bannon watched Ailis go and vowed that he would bring her home, and home safe. He turned that minute and started for home. It took him eight days of walking, sleeping rough, riding in the back of empty carts, and one ride in a coach to get to the farm, and when he got there he had a plan.

CHAPTER 24

John Barber was ushered into Lady Susan Seymour's parlor and as he stopped before her he made a small bow, accompanied by what looked to Lady Susan like a totally unacceptable smirk. She determined to deal with that. "To what do I owe the honor of this must unusual summons, my lady?"

"Please be assured that it is an honor that is unlikely to be repeated. You are here because I have information for you and I seek information from you. You are paid well by my husband to be of service and I expect service." She was terse.

Barber gave her a hard look, "You know full well, my lady, that I and my associates have for these many years provided most important service to you and your husband and we do so not because we need you but because you need us."

She glared at him, "You need our money. There are others who could provide us the service you supply, but I know of no one else who could provide you with money in the amounts we make available. Do not be impertinent with me. We could reveal your secret without involving ourselves."

"My lady," Barber said very slowly, "it would be of great value to you to recognize the folly of what you suggest. We can provide such proofs concerning your enterprise as would be impossible for you to deny. And we would do so without hesitation if we thought you had any idea of revealing us. You might make accusations about us, but you can be assured that if we thought you were going to be foolish enough to do so we would murder you in addition to ruining your reputation. You and your husband would be far too dead to do anything to rescue your standing. I doubt you could be buried in consecrated ground." He stared at her. "I do not believe you are up to murder, but I would gladly kill you with my own hands if you were to convince me you were going to cross us. Do we understand each other?"

Lady Susan was stunned. Up to this minute she had thought Barber was her man to be used as she pleased, but she now saw all too clearly that she was his woman to be used as he pleased. "Barber," she said, carefully and quietly, "you know I would not reveal any of your secrets for any reason. You simply jarred me with your attitude. I am sure it will never happen again. Neither of us will be so rash in the future. Don't you agree?"

He gave her a hard smile, "I agree. I think we understand each other full well. Now, if I may ask, what is the subject of our visit?"

"I have some information that I think will be of use to you. It appears that Captain Massengill has found out some information about goings on at Croome Forest and has came to Croome Court with his band of men to stop you. He is a King's man, you know. I believe that in his conversation with Lachlan Edwards he determined that Edwards knew what you are doing and was a part of your group. He became so enraged that he killed Edwards, took all the pertinent records and he plans to out you. You must do something to stop him. And I know that he has told Lady Amanda Walsh all he knows. She believes him and will do anything she can to remove him from the custody of the constabulary so he can expose you. You do know that the constables have taken Massengill? You must do something to stop him and to stop her, too."

Barber was impressed. "My lady, this is indeed useful news and I thank you for it. I can see that in spite of your somewhat impertinent remarks in the past you are truly on our side."

"Of course, I am one of you. Remember that always—always."

"You can be assured that we will remember you—always. As long as Massengill is in the custody of the constable—who is a man of limited intelligence—he will not be able to expose us because he does not have the documents at hand and will only seem to be making wild statements to gain his own freedom. I do not think he will waste the information on such a useless attempt. He will wait until he has everything in hand and can show proof. We will do all we can to insure that he stays in custody and we will silence him if he should gain his freedom. You might be interested to know that we had already surmised what you have told me about Captain Massengill, but the information you have given me about Lady Amanda is news indeed, and news that we will act on. You can be sure that Lady Amanda will not expose us. You do have our thanks."

"I am glad, Barber, to have been of service."

"How good that our service to each other can be mutual. I will take my leave, my lady. I have arrangements to make."

CHAPTER 25

John Barber made his arrangements.

On the night of August 23, 1814, the household at North Hall retired to bed as usual. By ten o'clock Lady Amanda and Henry were in their beds. By midnight the last of the servants had finished their work and were in bed. At some time around two in the morning Lady Amanda awoke. Laurence was barking. She was confused. She could hear noises and she could smell an unusual odor. Everything was a blur of confusion, but gradually things began to sort themselves out. The rumbling sound did not reveal itself, but the other sounds were people shouting, shouting to each other and shouting her name. The odor was resin; the smell of fat pine wood. She was beginning to identify the pieces, but the pieces failed to come together until she suddenly realized: fire!

Amanda leaped out of bed, and without bothering to put on her dressing gown, rushed to the door to the landing and opened it. Heat and smoke hit her like a wall; flames seemed to be dancing everywhere. Smoke was pouring into her room. It was clear that the center of the house was an inferno so she slammed the door shut. Even after the door was shut she realized smoke was seeping into her room through the crack under the door.

She couldn't think what to do, but then she knew: Henry—she must get Henry. She thanked God they had adjoining rooms with a connecting door and she flew into Henry's room with Laurence behind her. Smoke was seeping under his door, too, but he remained asleep, totally unaware, although Tim, on the bed with him, had his head up and eyes wide open. Amanda wakened Henry and said, "Quickly, Henry, we must go into my room. There is a fire." Why her room instead of his she had no idea, but her room was hers; she knew it. They got into her room, dogs and all, and closed the connecting door. "Henry, stay calm. We will be all right; we will get out the window and the servants will help us."

They went to one of the front windows and opened it. The fresh air was an instant relief; already the room was filling with smoke and breathing was not easy. Now Amanda could hear even more clearly the rumbling of the fire and the cracking sounds and thuds as timbers weakened by the fire broke loose and crashed to the floors below. The smell of burning pine wood was heavy in the air. They thrust their heads out the window and the sound of voices became clear. There were servants and some village people milling in the entrance court, their faces glowing in the reflected flames. Constable Quirke was in the crowd, already moving about to keep those who were doing nothing out of the way of those who were trying to help. One of the men below shouted, "Be calm, my lady, we are getting a ladder. Come to the side window. We can get you off the roof of the wing. The ladder is tall enough to get to you there. You will soon be safe."

"Bless you," she shouted. "Please hurry. The smoke is thick and we feel the heat already." Henry was remaining calm, almost amazingly so, and Amanda thanked God she did not have a panicked child to deal with as a part of the disaster that was unfolding. Amanda opened the side window and she and Henry looked down the slates to the edge of the roof. Wonderfully soon the top of the long ladder that was used to get onto the roof for repairs poked above the roof edge and the face of O'Reilly, the farmer of the home farm, appeared.

"My Lady, put the lad out the window and let him slide down to me. I can catch him; he will be safe; but quickly." Amanda did as she was told, holding on to Henry's hand as long as she could, then she let him go. He slid down the slates and O'Reilly scooped him in. Henry looked back and yelled, "Tim!"

"He is coming. When you are down. Go!" O'Reilly went down a few steps and handed Henry to one of the group waiting below. He came back and Amanda hoisted Tim over the window sill, handed him down as far as possible and let him go. It was all dog paws, frightened eyes and yowling puppy, but O'Reilly caught him without trouble and handed him down as he had Henry.

"Now it's you, my lady!"

"No. Laurence next."

"He's too big. He is a dog!"

"He will come. I can do it and so can you." She had to struggle to get Laurence onto the sill; he weighed full three –quarters as much as she did. Finally he was on the sill, but Laurence was not about to get out onto the roof.

"Hurry, my lady! Slide him over. I will catch him." She did and the result was a huge flail of howling wolfhound sliding down the roof. When he hit the top of the ladder, O'Reilly grabbed him but the force of his arrival pushed O'Reilly and the top of the ladder back from the roof edge. Two men were already steadying to bottom of the ladder but when it tipped out others rushed to help. They stopped the ladder when it was perfectly vertical and managed to push it back to the roof edge. O'Reilly struggled with Laurence and finally took hold of his collar, swung the dog down, lowered him as much as he could and let him drop. Laurence landed on two of the men below who tried to catch him, knocked them down, broke his own fall, and they all survived.

"Now, Lady Amanda, it is you!" Amanda hoisted her feet over the sill, sat on the sill, slid off, still grasping it with both hands and let herself start sliding down the roof. The top of the ladder was just too far down for O'Reilly to catch hold of her feet so she had to let go of the sill and try to let herself down slowly by holding on to the mortar joints between the stones of the wall. Her fingernails ripped and her finger tips bled, but she slowed her slide down the slick slates enough so that O'Reilly was able to get an arm around her legs and control her descent. In addition to the damage to her fingers, Amanda suffered an indignity that she was not aware of but that the crowd below fully appreciated. As she slid down her flimsy nightgown slid up revealing "the best leg seen in this county." The sight was dazzling: perfect ankles, perfectly turned calves, charming knees and delicious thighs. As she began to slide down the crowd had grown quite and when the delightful spectacle came into view there was an audible gasp of appreciation.

As quickly as it had happened it was over and O'Reilly was bringing her down and getting her feet on a rung of the ladder. She did think for a second that no man had touched her so intimately since her husband had gone off to war, but there was no time to dwell on that; she had to concentrate on getting down the ladder rung by rung with O'Reilly going down below her step by step. In her bare feet the ladder rungs hurt, but it was nothing compared to the relief of being out of the burning house and on the way to the ground. When Amanda's feet touched the ground a cheer rose up from the crowd. "O'Reilly, God bless you. You have saved us all," she gave him a kiss on the cheek.

"God bless you, Milady; it was only my duty."

"Thank you. Thank you. You are a good and true man, O'Reilly."

Anna, who was already holding Henry's hand moved forward and took charge of Amanda. "This way, my lady, we will go to the lodge. They have it ready for you." The lodge that had been Amanda's home before Bea left was kept in readiness to receive visitors, so Anna knew it would be available to receive Amanda and Henry. Quirke cleared the way and they moved to the lodge.

The fire was blazing out of control. The roof was aflame and it was clear that the entire roof of the main block would burn and collapse onto the floors below it, with the remains of each floor collapsing on to the one below it until the entire main block was burned out. Nothing could be done to stop it, but the task that was possible was to keep the fire from spreading into the wings and into the basement whose ceiling was masonry arches.

By morning the main block was gone. The walls still stood and, amazingly, on them much of the woodwork, some doors, and some mantles and window frames still clung to the walls, virtually undamaged. The floors, though, were gone and the roof was gone. The wings had survived and they and the basement had escaped with only damage from the smoke and some water that was put on the fire. Every piece of furniture in the main block burned because the open front door was a sea of flame when the first rescuers arrived and nothing could be removed, but to the amazement of everyone, two portraits that hung on the walls of the parlor remained where they hung, a bit smoke blackened, but otherwise intact.

After a good dose of hot tea, treatment of their cuts and scrapes, and time to calm, Anna had firmly placed Amanda and Henry in beds and ordered them to sleep. Their dogs were close by them.

CHAPTER 26

When morning came the smell of smoke was everywhere in the village and the scene at North Hall was a tragic one. The ruins were still smoldering and the walls of the Hall were stained with smoke. Debris and ash were scattered all about the mansion. As the servants and villagers began to survey the damage a greater tragedy was realized: Higgins was nowhere to be found. His first duty, indeed his first instinct, would have been to save the family—his family, the family he had served for near forty years and the family who not only employed him but loved and respected him. Soon there was no doubt in any minds; Higgins' body was somewhere in the ruins. Debris was high within the house and the scene was still so hot it was not possible to search. It was late into the next day before the debris could be sifted and Higgins body was found there in the collapsed remains of the main stair.

John Barber sent word that Lady Amanda, Henry, and any of the servants who needed a place to stay would be welcome at My Lord's Wood. Guests would be turned out to make space if necessary. At the same time he dispatched a hostler to the Seymour mansion with a note to Lady Susan,

"Lady Amanda has survived the unfortunate fire at North Hall. You should insure that she makes use of your hospitality. It is necessary. Waste no time. B."

Lady Susan wasted no time. As soon as a carriage could be readied she was on the way to North Hall.

Amanda had awakened early to full knowledge of the disaster. Anna had been busy and had collected from the best clothes of the staff and farm families an outfit that was presentable enough for Lady Amanda and clothes for Henry. The dogs had been fed. Amanda washed and was dressed by Anna. She and Henry were fed and Amanda went out to survey the ruins of her home. It was shocking. The walls stood, smoke begrimed but solid, the roof was gone, the windows were empty holes with a few fragments of frame remaining but all the glass had been blown out by the heat. The forecourt was scattered with ashes and pieces of burnt wood. She saw that everything in the main block of the house was gone, and then the news about Higgins was given her. Amanda burst into tears and sagged against Anna. "Oh, God. I can't believe it. Higgins has been here all my life. He was our rock. Oh, God, how can it be? This disaster is beyond my strength."

"My lady, he was trying to save you and Henry. He was doing his duty and, in truth, if his time had come he died as he would have wished."

"I know it, and that makes it all the more horrible. We have lived and he has died. It is not right for God to let such a thing happen. I cannot imagine life without Higgins. And poor Henry—he has lost his mother, his father, his home, and his beloved friend. I don't know how he can survive. I must go to Henry. I have to tell him."

While Amanda went to Henry villagers were swarming the scene and those who felt they were expert of one sort or another began to speculate on the cause of the fire. Very soon there was agreement: the fire was a case of arson. It had clearly started in the entrance hall where there was no reason for a fire to start. Those early on the scene were able to testify that the hallway was an inferno by the time the first to respond had arrived. There had been, and indeed still was, the smell of fat pine in the air and there was no such wood in the structure or furnishing of the house. It was clear that someone, no doubt more than just one person, had broken open the front door, had loaded the hall with pine kindling and logs and had set it ablaze. Someone wanted to destroy North Hall. But why? No one could think of any reason. There was simply no reason at all, but arson was clearly the cause. It didn't take the constable to figure out that a crime had been committed, every simple farmer understood.

Not long after Amanda had gone in to Henry the gentry began to arrive. Carriages came from the Seymour Estate, Ievers Court, Corry Hall, Wildwood Manor, and the Walsh place. The parlor of the Lodge was soon crowded and everyone was offering help of every kind. William and James Walsh, her closest kin, insistently offered their home as the appropriate place to stay. Lady Susan announced that, with her present there to be of every assistance, Seymour Park was much more suited to Lady Amanda's need, that everything she had to offer was available to Amanda. She made it clear that she would not take no for an answer.

Amanda was overwhelmed. She knew she did have to make some arrangements; the Lodge was too small for her, Henry, and the dogs, and even if that had not been the case, she could not face getting up every morning to see the ruin of her home. She turned over the possibilities. Green Fields was an obvious choice, but James would be there and his attention was something else she did not relish having to face every day. Ievers Court, Corry Hall and Wildwood Manor would all be crowded with their own families and that left only Lady Susan and Seymour Place as an alternative. The prospect of having to deal with Lady Susan on a daily basis was not a pleasant one, but upon reflection it appeared to be easier to live with than facing James Walsh. She did not want to disappoint William Walsh, however, so she made the choice Solomon would have made. Henry, who would not be fully welcome at Seymour Place, and the dogs, who would be even less welcome, would go to Green Fields. Henry loved his godfather, William Walsh, and knew him well. Both he and the dogs would be welcome, and James would pay no attention to Henry while William would dote on him every hour of the day. His nanny would go with Henry. Amanda and Anna would go to Seymour Place. Lady Susan would be placated and Amanda would be spared James. And so it was done. William Walsh was well pleased, James was disappointed, Lady Susan was relieved, and the others understood.

Lady Susan hoped her relief was not too obvious. When she had received Barber's note she had immediately realized everything: Barber had caused North Hall to be set ablaze so Lady Amanda would die and would no longer be a threat. It hadn't worked and Amanda had to be controlled—or destroyed some other way. Her job was to get Amanda and keep her away from everyone else. Thank God she had succeeded. She realized, to her excitement and to her horror, that she was engaged in a matter in which lives were cheap. Barber and his men were to be feared—and obeyed. She was scared, but she was determined to meet the challenges that were ahead of her.

All the necessary arrangements were made and Lady Susan handed Amanda, Henry, his nanny, and Anna into her carriage and hurried them off, first to Green Fields to get Henry properly settled, and then to Seymour Place.

CHAPTER 27

As soon as Amanda was settled in at Seymour Place Lady Susan was beside herself wanting to talk, "Well, my dear, you are the talk of everyone for miles around. What a coup!"

"I can imagine. The fire was horrible. Our dear Higgins is dead. Henry and I are homeless. How could we not be talked about?"

"My dear, that is all true, but it is the show you provided last night that is on the mind and lips of every man in the district—and every woman."

Amanda thought about what had happened. "Yes, I am sure that climbing down the ladder in my night clothes was most undignified and would be the subject of talk, even ridicule."

"Come, my dear, your gown was the least of it. It was the magnificent display of your beautiful legs as you climbed onto the top of the ladder that is the center of excitement among the men and envy among the women. You will never be forgotten. I only wish I could hit on some device that would give me the opportunity to make such a dazzling spectacle of myself. I suppose a fire would be too much, but I would be delighted to find some engine that would allow me to be imprinted on every mind in such a dazzling way."

Amanda couldn't believe what she was hearing. She had no idea exactly what she had done, but it must have been scandalous if Lady Susan were so anxious to be able to become the center of a similar display. She thought again of what had happened: the house was gone, Higgins was dead, she and Henry were homeless and farmed out in the neighborhood, and all the scandalous Lady Susan could think about was an unwonted and unaware display of her limbs. "Good God, I had no idea," was all she could manage. She wondered if she would not have been better off going to Green Fields and undergoing the attentions of James Walsh.

The Seymour Place housekeeper and maids were immediately set to work to alter some of Lady Susan's clothes for Amanda, to make new under garments and to find shoes to fit her. Anna, too, was to be provided for as needed. Work went on that day and the next day and by the end of the 25th Amanda was adequately fitted up and rested. Lady Susan could not do enough for her, hovering all the time and making Amanda constantly uncomfortable.

On the morning of August 26, another sunny day, Lachlan Edwards was laid to rest in the graveyard of the protestant chapel in Croome Court. Between his death and the fire at North Hall the village and the entire surrounding area were all in shock. Edwards' service was well attended. He had been an important man in the village, and more than that, he had been liked as well as respected. That same afternoon at St Michael's Catholic Church the service of burial was held for Higgins. Lady Amanda, Henry, the Walshes, Lady Susan, many of the gentry, and all the servants and farmers of the North Hall estate were there at both of the services. Higgins had no family—only the Bullen and Walsh families—and Lady Amanda arranged with the Priest to have Higgins buried in the family plot at North Hall.

On the evening of the 26th Sir William Seymour returned home and, after a hurried briefing by Lady Susan, welcomed Amanda to their hospitality. That night they dined in the state that Lady Susan always demanded and afterward were in the parlor having conversation. It was not an easy time for Amanda. Lady Susan's cloying attention was wearing on Amanda and, in spite of his almost relentless bonhomie there was a menace about Sir William that kept Amanda on edge.

At shortly after nine in the PM there was a loud knock at the front door. This was most unusual, since the gate keeper should have barred the arrival of anyone at that time of the night. Both Lady Susan and Sir William were instantly alert. The butler unlocked the door and before he had swung it back six inches it was flung open by the visitors, knocking the butler to the floor. Six men, masked and armed with pistols, pushed their way into the hall. One knelt beside the butler, placed a pistol against his head and said, "Don't move or I'll blow your brains out." The butler, stunned in any event, wisely obeyed. Four of the men barged into the parlor and another waited at the parlor door so he could see both the hall and the parlor.

Sir William was almost apoplectic. "What is this outrage?" he shouted.

"Quiet, you fool! Quiet all of you if you value your lives. We aim to kill if we need to. Sir William, Lady Susan, on the floor."

"What?!" Sir William got a blow from the barrel of a pistol and was knocked to the floor, bleeding.

"Down, woman." Lady Susan, almost petrified by fear, almost hurled herself onto the carpet. The thought of being hit in the face in a way that marred her beauty frightened her almost more than the thought that this encounter might be fatal. Both she and Sir William knew what was happening; all this was meant for Amanda, but they were still frightened for their own safety. Violent men might get out of control or they might take the opportunity to settle real or imagined scores from the past, and these were violent men.

One of the men unrolled onto the floor a large piece of canvas he had been carrying over his shoulder. Another moved to

Amanda, jerked her around and quickly tied her hands behind her back. He then placed a gag over her mouth and pushed her down onto the canvas. She hit hard and let out a muffled cry. Two of the men then rolled Amanda into the canvas, picked up the roll by its ends and carried it out of the room. The man who was clearly the leader of the group stood over Sir William and Lady Susan and barked, "You two, not a word until morning, or we will come for you. Keep the servants in check." He walked out to the hall where the man with the gun and the watcher were now presiding over two footmen stretched on the floor next to the butler. "Out. Now."

They went outside where two wagons were waiting. Amanda had been placed into the back of one of them. The crew got aboard and headed down the drive. When they got to the gate a seventh man who had been holding the gatekeeper at the point of a pistol knocked him down just as the other had knocked down Sir William and they rumbled off into the night at a steady pace; not fast enough to attract attention but fast enough to cover the distance they needed to cover before dawn. Amanda was in a near panic, finding it hard to breathe and stunned by what was happening. She had no idea why these men could want her, and the violence of the whole episode was unexplainable and terrifying.

CHAPTER 28

The next morning a footman was sent from Seymour Place to summon the constable. When Constable Quirke and his men arrived, Sir William and Lady Susan were seated in the parlor with as much dignity as they could muster in spite of Lady Susan's lingering panic and Sir William's rage. Sir William's head sported a bandage. He could understand that all appearances had to be that they were victims, but he knew full well that he had been treated much more roughly than need be and he was determined that he would have revenge. They both knew why the abduction had happened, and were not about to tell the constable what they knew, but their anger at the treatment they had been subjected to was so real that the constable was quickly convinced they were innocent victims of an outrageous and completely unexplainable crime. The constable interviewed them at length and interviewed all the servants who had had a direct part in the situation, including the gate keeper who had shown his bloody gash and poured out his story the minute the constable and his two helpers had arrived at the gate.

Constable Quirke was totally out of his depth and he knew it all too well. During eleven years at Croome Court he had had to deal with many a scuffle, frequent enough theft and two drunken murders. But they were all explainable as the normal violence of village life. There had been nothing like this: a murder, a fatal arson, and an abduction, all involving members of the gentry and all within one week. He needed help and he immediately sent a messenger to Monaghan to bring the Monaghan constable, the area constable supervisor and as many useful men as they could bring with them.

Late that day the party of lawmen from Monaghan arrived and went into conference with constable Quirke. Quirke told them all he knew and they were as baffled as he was, but the constable supervisor came to one conclusion: "This is a large matter. All of these things are related one to another, and there is much behind this that we do not know. The gentry have been the target and this suggests that it may be the Whiteboys or their ilk. This being the case, constable Quirke, it must be that your Captain Massengill is not a guilty party since he has been in custody during both the arson and the abduction."

"He has been in custody, but what about the gang of men who came to town with him? They melted away before we could get to them or we would have taken them into custody as well. It would appear that someone at North Hall warned them."

"True. Interesting. Think of this: if they were warned by someone at North Hall why would they have been party to burning the Hall and abducting the Lady?" pointed out the Chief Constable.

"Right enough, Sir. But recall that there were seven men at Seymour Place during the abduction and Massengill had seven men with him! We must find them and determine where they have been during the times of the crimes. That will tell us the story."

The Chief Constable thought about the matter and pronounced his decision, "Considering all things, let us release Massengill, get the word out that he is free so it gets to his men and brings them in. We will then find where they were during the crimes and that will tell the story. We will watch Massengill all the while. This can be done easily by telling him it is for his protection." His plan was carried out, and by the next day Massengill's men had come back in to the village. After their stories were heard and checks were made, there was enough evidence of their whereabouts to show that they could not have done the crimes, and in addition, it was realized that they had no way to get the pinewood necessary to start the fire at North Hall, and that they had no access to the two wagons used for the abduction. The evidence was convincing that Massengill was not the perpetrator of the deeds so he immediately went from suspect to confederate.

The lawmen wanted to know everything Massengill knew and, unfortunately, he could think of nothing that might help. He and Edwards had had a friendly reunion. Little had been spoken of business and Edwards had told him nothing that gave Massengill any reason to believe anyone would want Edwards dead. There was nothing in Massengill's records that would be of interest to anyone, let alone reason for murder. It was, however, suspicious that the Croome Forest records had been stolen. As to Lady Amanda, nothing had passed between them that would indicate her having knowledge of or being involved in anything that could make her the subject of the disasters she had suffered. He was filled with disbelief that she could be involved in anything that would make her the subject of arson or abduction. The constables considered Massengill's information and were collectively little further toward a solution than they had been before talking to Massengill. It could be the Whiteboys; it could be local ruffians; it could be someone else.

CHAPTER 29

In the early morning of August 26 Michael O'Day knocked at the door of Lady B's establishment. It took a while for the door to be opened, but the door man recognized him immediately. "Sir, we are not open for business at this hour. If you could return at eight in the PM?"

"I do not come on business. I must see Lady B. It is a personal matter of importance to her."

"Sir, she does not live here. You cannot see her. Could we take a message to her?"

"No. I must see her. Take me to her. This is most important to her. There will be trouble for you if I do not see her. Now, man." He talked the door man into sending a messenger to B to ask her to come to the establishment, but under no circumstances would they take him to her home. O'Day went inside to wait. It was forty-five minutes before B appeared.

She was worried, "Michael, what can this be?"

"B, I have news for you that will be both bad and good. First, I must tell you that I read all your letters and that is how I know of your interest in what I have to tell you."

"Letters? What letters are you talking about?"

"Your letters to your dear Amanda and her letters back to you," he explained.

"What? This is an outrage! How can you even know about those letters, and how dare you read them? They are sealed. They are always sealed! How can you do it?"

"I know about your letters because the manager at my gold-smith's shop has told me about them."

"You own Fortnum's?"

"Yes. My manager values you as a customer and as one who has referred other valuable customers to him, but he values my approval more. He has been true to you in that no one else knows, but he will always tell me of anything out of the ordinary, and your arrangement for mail was most unusual and therefore interesting. Although I did not want to intrude on your privacy I felt I had to know the nature of your correspondence. It could have had to do with business. I have had the letters delivered to me and I once I read the first one I confess that I was not able to stop. I have read them all. I understand your story and I find myself much in sympathy with you. You are fortunate to have such a loving helper as Amanda and your son is in the best of hands."

"But how can you get into the letters without breaking the seal?"

"We are careful, and you must realize that goldsmiths make seals. We have recreated both your seal and Lady Amanda's. We replace the wax most carefully—and skillfully—to match the original imprint, reseal them and send them on."

"This is monstrous." She was angry.

"That may be so, but there it is. If you consider, I think you may feel that you are fortunate that I have read the letters even though it be monstrous, for it is because I read your letters that the intelligence I have about events in Croome Court can be passed on to you."

"Croome Court? Tell me." Her demeanor changed instantly; she was eager.

"Two nights ago there was a fire at North Hall."

"Oh, God!"

"Henry and Lady Amanda survived with only minor injuries. And I might say that if the word of my informant can be trusted, and I think it can, your sister-in-law has a body fully as beautiful as yours."

"How on earth can you know that?"

"It seems that her gown was somewhat disarrayed during her escape from the fire and her beauty, particularly that of her dazzling legs, was available for all to see and to appreciate. In spite of all, she is well. Lady Amanda has been removed to Seymour Place, a mansion in the neighborhood, and Master Henry is at the home of his godfather, William Walsh. North Hall is destroyed. The butler, Higgins, has apparently died in the fire. This is not certain since the ruins were still smoldering when my informant left Croome Court, but Higgins was nowhere to be found so it is presumed that he is dead."

"Good God. How awful. Higgins was a most valued man. A dear man. How did the fire happen?"

"I am not sure, but there is suspicion that the fire was set deliberately. It seems that, although she survived the fire, Lady Amanda remains in danger. A man who grew up in the village, one John Massengill—"

"I know him!"

"...Massengill has returned to the village and appears to be in possession of information that he has passed on to Lady Amanda. This information is potentially dangerous to certain persons and they have determined that it shall not be revealed. One man, Edwards, the solicitor, who also talked with Massengill, has been killed to keep him from revealing it."

"This is unbelievable." Her face was ashen, "what could that man have told Amanda that is so important?"

"Amanda is an innocent victim. She has become involved, through mere chance it appears, in matters so large that she is in mortal danger."

"Mortal danger? Incredible! Who are these men who mean to take her life?"

"I cannot tell you that. I can only say that they are Irishmen. I should not have revealed any of this to you, but I confess that never having seen her and never having heard her voice, I am absolutely besotted with her; Lady Amanda is a woman I could love. Indeed, I have fallen in love with her through reading her letters to you and yours to her. She is an angel to whom life has not been kind. And now I find out that she is a famous beauty. I am doing this for her. She is in danger. She must keep quiet. She must keep close what she knows, and she must be gotten out of danger as soon as possible. I cannot do it. I cannot be involved in any way with this matter, but you can. You must go to her or send someone you trust completely and bring her here. Once she is here I can take care of her. I can keep her safe and I will do anything for her. I know that to your jaded eyes and knowing me as you know me my devotion to her must seem incredible, and it is. Nevertheless it is what it is. You must do this, now. There is no time to be wasted. Apply at the coach office. I know there is a seat available on the coach this afternoon to Monaghan and you can make your way on from there."

"Michael, this is unbelievable, but I do believe you. I have always thought you a man of uncommon honor. I will do what you say. I must disguise myself for the sake of my son—and for Amanda, but I will be on the coach today. I will bring her here."

CHAPTER 30

The men of the law in Croome Court remained at a loss. Crime was piling on top of crime. They were confident that the crimes were connected, but what was the connection? Their confusion was only growing deeper. They decided to have a public meeting to tell the people all they knew and see if any of the public knew anything that could help. The meeting was set to be at eight PM on the night of August 27 in the ballroom at My Lord's Wood. They spread the word as widely as possible during the day, taking care to insure that the Seymours, John Massengill—whom they now thought of as one of them—and the rest of the gentry as well as the servants at North Hall were all informed of the meeting.

When the announced time for the meeting arrived the ballroom was crowded. The gentry were there, seated, while the others stood around the room. The Seymours, fresh from their outrage and the abduction of Lady Amanda, were seated in the front with the rest of the leading families. The North Hall servants were there, the Croome Forest Chief Steward, Padraic Berrigan, was there and many villagers were there. The crowd was largely male and not a few were obviously armed. The room was warm and getting warmer by the minute, and the air was filling with the smoke of pipes and cigars and the smell of hot bodies. It was a noisy crowd, not a little panicked, but silence fell quickly when John Barber mounted the small musicians' stage and welcomed all. He turned the meeting over to the Constable Supervisor and stood back against the wall. John Barber was worried. The Chief Steward of Croome Forest was worried, and even though they were in the role of aggrieved victims, Sir William and Lady Susan Seymour were fearful. This thing had to be carefully controlled to keep it from getting dangerous for them.

The Constable Supervisor echoed John Barber's welcome and added his thanks to everyone for coming out. He began to go over the events of the past week and the crowd remained silent, clinging to every word and hoping for an explanation of what had happened. The Constable Supervisor told them of the theory that everything was connected but admitted that he did not know what the connection might be. He ended his presentation and asked for help. Immediately a hubbub arose, people turning to their neighbors giving their theories and asking what their neighbors knew. No one seemed to have any useful solution to the Constable Supervisor's problem but he allowed the discussions to go on, hoping that someone would say something that triggered a valuable thought in someone else's mind.

As people continued to talk and squirm two men began working their way from the back of the standing crowd toward the front where the gentry were seated. They were the former seaman Niall Bannon and his father, Padriac. They were purposeful, but not rough or conspicuous as they moved forward. The Constable Supervisor and the rest of the law men on the stage saw them and hoped they were seeing the answer to their conundrum approaching. The two Bannons reached the row of chairs where the gentry sat and stopped behind it. The Constable Supervisor looked at them expectantly and to his horror saw each draw a pistol from inside his jacket. The law men all thought they were seeing the malefactors and that they, the law, were to be the next victims. Other hands reached for pistols and swords but before anything could be done the Bannons fired and Sir William and Lady Susan Seymour's brains were blown out of their heads.

"Whoremongers!" shouted Padraic Bannon, "they ruined my daughter and now the bastards are dead! They have paid for what they done." The crowd was stunned into silence and inactivity, and they watched with shock as Padraic Bannon turned and walked toward John Barber. Barber knew instantly what was about to happen and, in terror, threw up his hands and pled, "No!" But his plea was in vain and the quiet was broken by another explosion as Padriac Bannon drew a second pistol and shot John Barber dead. Both Bannons threw their empty pistols onto the floor. "Do what you must, constable, we've done your work for you," Padraic shouted.

The meeting exploded in frenzy. Most of the crowd struggled to the doors and fled the room. The law men and several other armed men drew pistols and leveled them on the Bannons. The noise was almost deafening, but Constable Quirke shouted over it all, "Quiet in this room!" Those left in the room quieted, the Bannons were taken into custody without any resistance, and the three bodies were checked to see if they were indeed dead, and they were.

The Constable Supervisor was stunned. He now had four murders, an arson that had caused another death and an abduction, all within one week and all involving the most elevated gentry in the area and one of the most prominent tradesmen. The bodies were collected by the undertaker and his helpers and inn servants were set to work scrubbing the room clean of the remains of the three victims. The Bannons were taken to the constable's office and placed in the only cell. The constables and Massengill sat in the office.

"Could all of this be connected?" asked the Constable Supervisor. "Is it possible that the Seymors and Barber are indeed involved in prostitution and that Edwards found them out and was murdered to keep him quiet and that Lady Amanda, too, knew about it and was burned out and abducted to silence her? She was taken from the Seymour house. This suggests it may all be at the hand of local ruffians and that some outside force is not at play here."

There was silence as each thought about the possibilities. Massengill broke the silence. "I begin to think that is not the case that Edwards and Lady Amanda have been singled out because of something they knew about the Seymours. If Edwards had had such knowledge and was so in danger that he was murdered within hours of when I saw him, I feel he would have said something of it to me, or at least I would have detected a degree of unease in his demeanor. In fact, during near two hours we spent together he was perfectly at ease. We talked of old times, of his handling of my affairs, of his family. There was nothing of tension. If Edwards knew anything of importance, he had no feeling that he was in danger because of what he knew. I am sure of it. And Lady Amanda—how could she have been privy to information about prostitution and the stealing of girls into the trade? I cannot imagine it."

Quirke was eager to contribute, "But how can all of this have happened one after another, in a village that is almost always quiet, and they not be connected? This is too much for coincidence."

"Quirke, you may be right," said the Constable Supervisor. "Let us examine. First we must question the Bannons to see what they know. There must be something to their accusation or it cannot be conceived that they would have resorted to bloody murder, and have been so wrought up they would do the crime in public. Let them be examined carefully." The Bannons were examined, with the Constable Supervisor and Massengill asking the questions. Niall's story was so straightforward and so detailed that it was believable, and he never wavered from the tale.

The Bannons were put back in the cell and an urgent message was sent to the constabulary at Dublin outlining the situation in Croome Court and asking if there was a prostitute named Ailis Bannon in a Dublin brothel on Fenton Lane, and if so, who controlled the brothel. This having been done all retired for the night and agreed to gather the next morning at ten AM to continue discussing the situation.

CHAPTER 31

Late that night there was a knock on Massengill's door. It was Cheshire, "Cap'm, a servant is here which says a lady must speak to you. The lady is waiting in her coach. She says it is most urgent that she speaks to you, immediate like." At sea, a summons at this hour would have been nothing out of the ordinary. In Croome Court it was extraordinary, but John Massengill had come to realize that nothing that was happening in Croome Court was in the ordinary. He was not surprised; a summons at near midnight was only to be expected. "I will be there directly, Cheshire. Have her wait."

"Aye, Cap'm."

Massengill dressed quickly and went out to the pitch black street where a coach was waiting. He walked to the door and was asked by a female voice to enter. He did so and sat on the seat facing her. "Captain, I am greatly in need of help and know no one else to whom to turn. You do not know me, but I know who you are and I hope you can help me."

"Madame, your voice sounds familiar to me."

"Sir, I am sure it is not. But that is of no importance. I am a friend of Lady Amanda Walsh and a mutual friend recently informed me that she was in great danger. He told me that her home had been burned and that the fire was an attempt to murder her to keep her from telling authorities something she knows. He understood that she had survived the fire but told me she remained in great danger from those who wanted to silence her. He begged me to come to Croome Court, find her, and bring her away from this place. I came here and found she had been abducted. Those who wanted her have taken her and I fear the worst. Her life is in danger! There is no doubt! This is unbelievable! Captain, she must be saved! Who has her? Why do they have these evil designs on her? What does she know that puts her life in danger? You must help," she begged.

"I want nothing more than to find Lady Amanda. Her safety is my very first concern, but I am most sorry to say that I know little more than you do. You must help me. Who told you this information, and how does he—or is it she?—know?"

"I am unable to tell you who my informant is. He swore me to secrecy. How he knows what he knows I do not know. If I did know I would surely tell you. I promise it."

"Lady Beatrice, I do know who you are. I remember you well. I know of your illness and that you have been living elsewhere for a number of years. Now, you must tell me all you know. Amanda's life depends upon it. Where have you come from?"

"All right, Captain. You have found me out. My story is too long and complicated for me to tell you all, but I will tell you where I have been living. You must promise me that you will tell no one that you have seen me or that I have spoken with you about anything. It is for the sake of my son and our family. Do you agree?" she beseeched him.

"I will not mention your name or our meeting. Now, tell me."

"I have been living in Belfast," she said. "The person who told me this information is a man of consequence in that city. I truly do not know how he found out the information he gave me. He must have been told by someone from Croome Court, because I know he has never—at least not in recent years—been to Croome Court himself. But he does know. The information he gave me was all true."

"Did he tell you anything, anything at all, about how he obtained his information, anything about those who wanted Amanda, or why? Please, anything at all. Anything, no matter how trivial it may seem. Remember, Amanda's life is in the balance."

"As I have told you, he said Amanda knows something that could destroy them—wreck their plans—but he did not say what. He said of the men only that they were Irishmen."

"Irishmen? That would seem to be all of us. How can it help? So that is all you know."

"That is all he told me. He said she was in great danger."

Massengill fixed his stare on Beatrice's eyes, "But you do know one other thing, his name. What is it? We must try to talk to him. He knows more than he has told you. His name, Lady Beatrice."

"Please! I cannot tell you. He made me promise that his name would not be associated in any way with what has happened."

"We have no designs against him. You must tell me. For Amanda."

"I cannot. I beg you, I cannot. He might be put into the same danger Amanda is in. I could not do that to him."

"We know nothing here. I am close with the constables, so I know all they know. We don't know who has her, where she is, why they have her, or what we can do to help her. The man who sent you here is our only hope. He knows something, even if it is only the name of someone else who knows what we need to know. Remember, we have no designs against him. It is our only hope. You must tell me so we can contact him and find out what he knows."

She faltered, "I could go back to Belfast and ask him."

"Time. Time means everything. We cannot wait for you to go to Belfast and report back. You must tell me now—for

Amanda. If we know who he is we have means to find out what he knows, and quickly."

"Oh, God!" Bea shuddered and wrung her hands. "All right. You are right. Amanda is my child's true mother and I cannot let anything else happen to her. She must be saved. Henry might be in danger, too! The man is Michael O'Day. He is well known. But he must not, he must not, know I said his name."

"It shall be so. We will do everything to save Amanda. You should return home. Go. Now." Massengill got out and the coach immediately began to head north along the High Street. He went back to his room and spent some time turning over what he had just heard before he fell asleep.

CHAPTER 32

On the morning of the 27th the constabulary, Massengill, his coxswain Otis, and the men of the gentry met at the constable's office to try and find a way ahead. The constable's office consisted of one outer room that was the office itself, a smaller room with a secure door that was the cell, and one more small room that was for storage. They smell of dust and a growing aura of human sweat saturated the room. It was crowded. Quirke, the Constable Supervisor, and Massengill sat; all the others had to stand. No one had any new ideas and no one had any new information—except Massengill. He told them of his meeting the night before with an unknown woman who had come from Belfast to warn Amanda that she was in danger and to take her away. The interesting fact was that she had come all the way from Belfast, and very soon after the fire, and that a man there had known of the fire and had come to this woman to warn her of Amanda's danger and to say that she must be removed. Why had a man in Belfast known about the fire so soon after it happened, and why had he been concerned for Amanda?

The unknown man had a connection in Croome Court; that was clear. The fact that he knew the fire was not just an accident and that he was so sure that Amanda was the target and remained in danger fell in line with—and foretold—Amanda's abduction. It was clear that the fire and the abduction were part of the same plot. It seemed, more and more, as if Edwards' murder was also related, but there was as yet no hard proof of that. The deaths of Barber and the Seymours might be related, but they could be completely separate incidents.

Captain Ievers raised the possibility that Amanda had been taken as a part of the prostitution ring, to be forced to work in one of their brothels. She was, after all, a most beautiful young woman and her beauty had been underscored to dazzling effect, remembered by all who were there, when her beautiful legs were exposed to view during her escape from the fire. Perhaps whoever was luring the girls into prostitution had been there and was so excited by what he saw that he was sure she would be a dazzling addition to his stable of girls and had had her abducted.

Constable Quirke was quick to support this theory, "It's most true. I was there at the fire and I can confirm most heartily that any man there would have been dazzled by her display— meaning no offense to the Lady, of course. Of course, sirs, no offense! It was all most inadvert, of course. I dare say she had no control…"

"Yes, Constable. Thank you. We will discuss it," the Chief Constable quickly broke in to keep Quirke from becoming completely muddled by his enthusiasm and confusion.

Quirke was not the only one for whom this theory of the abduction seemed likely to be true. There was a general discussion, but in the end the theory was dismissed because it was agreed that even men low enough to be in the trade of white slavery would realize that a person of Amanda's breeding could never be kept as a prostitute. If she had not escaped on her own, virtually the first client who came in contact with her would have heard her story, recognized her quality, realized her must be true, and helped her to escape. There could be a connection between her abduction and the murders of the Seymours and Barber, but it could not be an attempt to force her into prostitution. They would await news from Dublin on the connection, if any, between the Seymours and Barber and the brothel there, and they would question the Seymours' servants to see what they might know, but they would have to come up with a different solution to answer the question of why Amanda had been abducted. The story the woman had told Massengill pointed to some other reason for the abduction.

The Chief Constable took charge, "Captain Massengill, we must know: who is the man from Belfast?"

"I have said I would not reveal his name."

"If you value the life of Lady Amanda, you must. This man not only knows what happened he must know why it has happened and that is the key. His name, Captain. We must have it."

Massengill was torn, but he knew what he had to do for Amanda's sake. He would be breaking his promise to Lady Beatrice, but surely her first wish was the same as theirs: to save Amanda. And how could the man in Belfast be hurt by having his name known? "You are right. Yes. I have no idea how this man knows what he knows nor do I know what his connection to Croome Court may be, but his name is Michael O'Day."

"Good God," came from the Constable Supervisor, "I know the name of the man. He is a most prominent person, owner of many businesses in Belfast. We must send to the constabulary in Belfast and have the man taken for questioning. He knows what we need to know."

"Is there some way we can have him questioned without letting him know that he, alone in Belfast, is a subject of interest? Both he and my informant need to be protected," pleaded Massengill.

The constables and Massengill considered this, but after a thorough discussion, no way could be determined to keep O'Day from realizing that his name had been leaked. It was decided that the only course was to bring him in for questioning, taking care to let him know that he was not the subject of any accusation. A message was written out and sent immediately by horseman to Monaghan where it could be put onto the day's coach to Belfast. Instructions were included for the Belfast constabulary to send the return information by horsemen with no delay.

It was decided that they would enlist the help of the chief steward at Croome Forest. Berrigan had been at the meeting the night before but had melted away with the rest of the crowd when the shooting took place and he had not been seen since. He was a man of consequence in the area, being the overseer of many workers, and he might have heard something or might be able to find out something that would be of value. Massengill volunteered the services of himself and Otis to contact Berrigan, and when the meeting broke up he and Otis had horses saddled and rode to the Croome Forest gate lodge.

When they arrived at the gate lodge Massengill told Otis to rouse the gate keeper. No sooner said than Otis roared, "Ahoy the gate!" Massengill loved it; this was probably the first time the gate had been thus addressed and it was possible that the gate keeper had no idea what an 'Ahoy' even meant. But whether the word signified or not, the tone of the roar did and the gate keeper soon came out. Massengill explained that they were there at the request of the constable and wished to speak to Berrigan concerning the recent troubles in the village and expected to be promptly admitted. But it was not to be so. The gate keeper, whose tone was just short of insolent, told them that Berrigan was not receiving visitors and that in any event he knew nothing about the goings on in the village. In spite of Massengill's pleas and orders, the keeper refused to open the gate. He suggested that there was no reason for them to come back since he was sure Berrigan knew nothing.

Massengill found everything the gate keeper said either unbelievable or insolent, but he felt there was nothing to be gained by continued argument so he motioned to Otis to leave and they rode away. He and Otis returned to the constable's office and found all the constabulary still there. Massengill briefly reported that they had been refused entry to Croome Forest and said he did not like the feel of the situation there. Following a few questions by the Constable Supervisor and Quirke, Massengill and Otis took their leave.

After Massengill departed the group settled down to discuss the situation. About five minutes later the door was opened and James Walsh walked in. This was both unexpected and interesting because Walsh had not been at the general meeting and had not made any previous contact with the constabulary. Walsh was welcomed and said he would like to talk with them about the incidents in the village. "Please, Mr. Walsh, tell us what you know."

"Thank you, Quirke. Gentlemen, I have information that I think may be important. I find that I am in a situation of some delicacy and I ask that, while you are free, indeed I beg you, to use this information in the fullest way possible, I ask that how you found this and my involvement be kept silent."

"We will reveal nothing of your doings unless it be absolutely necessary to further the investigation."

"I am sure that you will find no reason to reveal my confidence. I can tell you this: Lady Amanda Walsh, widow of my late brother, has long been the subject of my affection. I am deeply devoted to her and will do anything to be of assistance to her. I visit her often and I visited her only a short time after she was visited by Captain Massengill on the day after Lachlan Edwards was murdered. In the course of our conversation she told me of Captain Massengill's visit. Shortly after my visit to Lady Amanda I paid a call on Lady Susan Seymour, a long time friend."

Quirke said, "We are aware of your friendship with Lady Susan, Mr. Walsh. We have had no reason to reveal it up to this time and I trust we will not have reason to reveal it in the future."

James was surprised. "Very good, Constable. I thank you. It happened that during my conversation with Lady Susan we discussed the matter of Lachlan Edwards' death and the visit of Captain Massengill to Lady Amanda. Lady Susan questioned me in detail about that visit and I told her all I knew about what had been said, which, I must say, was little of substance. Lady Susan had what now appears to me an inordinate interest in Captain Massengill's visit to Lady Amanda. I do not know why she was so interested, but it has occurred to me that it was only shortly after I left Lady Susan that the fire occurred and Lady Amanda was abducted, and, indeed, was abducted from the home of Lady Susan. Then the Seymours came to grief.

"It all seems to be of a part and I fear that my visit may have been the spark that—so to speak—lit the fire. I do not know what the connection is between Massengill's visit to Lady Amanda and the things that took place after my visit to Lady Susan, but there must be a connection. That is what I feel is of importance. My deepest fear is that I have somehow done a thing that has lead to disaster for Lady Amanda. I will do anything possible to help you recover her."

The Constable Supervisor thanked him, "Most interesting, Mr. Walsh. As you may know, we have considered Captain Massengill's role in this matter and we will take your information much to heart as we continue our investigation. You may be sure that we will avail ourselves of your service at any time you can be of use to us."

"Thank you, Constable Supervisor, I am at your service." Walsh departed, leaving the constabulary with a new puzzle and, perhaps, useful information. What was the connection between Lady Susan Seymour and the North Hall fire and Amanda's abduction?

CHAPTER 33

In mid afternoon of the 27th a farmer from Croome Forest rode out of the gate in a wagon with a riding chair on it. He drove directly to the office of the Constable, went inside and said, "I have a message for the Constable Supervisor. I am to wait for a reply." He handed over a folded paper and the Constable Supervisor read it.

"Tell him it shall be so." The messenger touched his forelock and left. "Gentlemen, it seems that in spite of all, Mr. Berrigan is leaving his lair. He has information and wants to visit privately with the constabulary at five PM today."

Promptly at five PM Padraic Berrigan rode through the Croome Forest gate and presented himself at the constable's office. "Good evening, Mr. Berrigan. We are glad you have chosen to come out to us. As you may know, Captain Massengill and his man were turned away at your gate when they tried to meet with you. We wonder why that happened and would like to hear your explanation. What have you to tell us?"

"Constable Supervisor, I can tell you that you that you have had the man who is responsible for all of this and you have let him go."

"Most interesting, sir. And who would this man be?"

"The very man you sent to talk with me, and he's a man who strikes fear into my heart, Captain John Massengill."

"Ahhh, this is news, indeed," said the Constable Supervisor, "and how would it be Captain Massengill since we know he was in our very own custody when some of these crimes took place and his men also were not in position to have carried out some of them?"

"What has he told you about Croome Forest?" asked Berrigan.

"Nothing. He knows nothing."

"Nothing, indeed," snorted Berrigan, "I suspected as much. Has he not told you he is the owner of the place?"

"He has not. Ridiculous! How could a village boy who is only a captain in His Majesty's Navy afford to be the owner of an estate such as Croome Forest? It is not possible, man."

"Possible it is, Constable Supervisor. Massengill has made a fortune as one of the King's pirates during the wars. It is said he has one hundred thousand pounds to his name. And he is the owner. Read this." Berrigan handed the constable supervisor an envelope. The constable supervisor read the letter inside and handed it to Constable Quirke, who read it while the constable supervisor was saying, "Well, Berrigan, if this letter can be credited it appears that Captain Massengill is indeed the owner of Croome Forest."

"I can tell you for certain that it can be credited," replied Berrigan. "It is written under the letter head of the Earl's solicitors in London. In my capacity as chief steward I have received many letters from them. I know it is genuine. Massengill is now the owner and he has some murderous plot afoot."

"Very well, we shall accept that Massengill is the owner of Croome Forest, but how does that prove that he has some plot afoot and how does it prove that he is behind the crimes that have been committed?"

"Here is what I know. I am the chief steward at Croome Forest. Under me are the farmers, the staff of the mansion, the linen weavers, and the steward of the forestry. I control closely all of these except for the forestry. That is a large operation at Croome Forest and the steward of the forestry runs it as if he were independent of my control. He gives me reports, but I have not been given the ability to monitor every aspect of that operation. What I do know is that there is something rotten in the forestry. Barges are regular at the wharf. They meet with ships at the mouth of the Erne. Massengill is a man of the sea. I have suspected for some time that something is wrong because the money that should flow from the forestry operation is not what it has been in the past and so is not what it should be. Who else would know this? Edwards. And he is dead. Who did Massengill talk with after Edwards died? Lady Amanda Walsh. And her home is burnt and she is taken. From where was she taken? Seymour Place. And the Seymours, too, are killed. Massengill is silencing them all."

"But how could he have done all this when he and his men are accounted for during some of the crimes?"

"It is simple! He has the men of the forestry at his command. The ruffians he brought to town with him did not have to do the deeds and Massengill himself did not have to be present." There was stunned silence. This could explain everything. Berrigan's narrative seemed to have no holes in it; everything could be just as he said.

Constable Quirke broke the silence, "And so it could be. But what is this plot of which you speak? What would be so great that it would lead Massengill to do these crimes?"

"Constable, that l cannot tell you. I do not know what is afoot. You are the men of the law. You must find that out for yourself. You must watch Massengill. Follow him. If he is at liberty, he will lead you to the truth. You must not let him know that you know. The information I have given you must not leave this room. If he finds out you know, he will bolt and he will close down the operation and you will never know. Watch him and learn. Then you can catch him and end his entire plot and all who are in it with him. I have told you what I know. This is all I can do here. Now I must return to my work. I will do what I can at Croome Forest. I will watch for Massengill and will try to learn what is afoot on the estate. You may be sure that I will inform you of any more useful information that I am able to obtain."

"Very well, Mr. Berrigan. We thank you." Berigan took his leave and the room plunged again into silence.

"Does it make sense," asked Quirke, "that a man who has the money to buy Croome Forest would risk losing it all by engaging in some monstrous unlawful plot?"

"A well taken point, Quirke. We must consider it." responded the constable supervisor. "What, indeed, could make him do such a thing? Berrigan's story does, however, seem to fit with the information James Walsh has given us. Quirke, what do you know of the man Berrigan?"

"Sir, he is a respected man. He has been chief steward at Croome Forest for over a decade. It is a position of great responsibility on the estate of a nobleman—the leading man for miles around—and Berrigan had the complete trust of the late earl. He has neither wife nor family. He keeps to himself. He is not a man to mingle with the people, but there is nothing to be said against him."

"We must consider carefully what he has told us. His story is credible, but there is no proof. We must not leap to a conclusion. It seems we have done that before and have had to draw back, but we must now begin to treat Massengill as the suspect. We will allow him to roam free but you will have him and his men watched at all times, Quirke. Let him work with us where it is possible, but let him know nothing. That will make him easy to keep watch upon."

"Yes, sir."

CHAPTER 34

After a rough ride that seemed to last forever Amanda had been taken off the wagon, carried a short distance and put into a room. The canvas was taken off, her gag was removed and she was untied and was dumped onto a bed. "We will come for you," was all that was said. The door was slammed and she could hear the sounds of it being locked. The room was dark. She was exhausted and so stiff and weak that an attempt to get up and explore the room produced almost no movement. She lay there stunned and incredulous, but exhaustion soon put her to sleep.

She awoke the next morning to silence, but there was light, coming through a small window high on the wall near the door. She could see that her room contained a bed, two chairs, a small table holding a candle stick with no candle, a bucket, and nothing else. She could smell the mold and the layer of human sweat that clung to the walls. There was dust everywhere and where a bright shaft of light touched the floor she could see in the dust footprints of some small animal. The room was the most repulsive place she had ever been in and it sent a stab of fear through her. Why was she in this horrible place, and what was going to happen to her?

After a time that she was not able to measure, footsteps approached and the key turned in the lock. When the door opened a man she had never seen entered. "Who are you?" she asked. "Are you here to save me, or are you my jailer?"

"I'm afraid I am your jailer, milady. I am here in the role of a inquisitor. You have some information, and I must have it."

"You are one of the ruffians who took me from Seymour Place?"

"We were men which were doing their duty."

"This is infamous! Where am I? And why am I here? What is this that you are doing?"

"You are at Croome Forest, Lady Amanda. You cannot escape from us; you are being watched day and night. You have become engaged in a matter which has placed you in great danger. I want to know certain things. You met with John Massengill four years ago when he came to Croome Court and you met with him again after Edwards was murdered. What did John Massengill tell you? What did he say the first time you met?"

Amanda was nonplussed. "Captain Massengill told me nothing that would put me in danger or that would be of interest to you. We spoke of his years in the Navy. We spoke of his visits with old friends. Nothing that could put anyone in danger."

"What old friends?"

"His solicitor, Lachlan Edwards, with whom he had only corresponded before. Chums from his school years—I don't know their names, he never said. He visited Lady Susan Seymour. I can think of no other. How could this help you?"

"What of his visit with Lady Susan?"

"Only that it was—interesting, remarkable."

"And how was it interesting? What made it remarkable?"

"He did not say. Do you know Lady Susan? Do you know her reputation? He is a handsome man. We could only speculate."

"I do know of Lady Susan, and I know well her interest in handsome men, but I know more than that about her. What did she say to him?"

"I have no idea."

Her inquisitor grabbed her wrist roughly, glared at her and shouted, "Tell me, woman!"

"There is nothing to tell. He said nothing. Let go of me! This is outrageous!" The man did not let go of her arm. "Listen, lady, you may think a man like me could never dare to deal roughly with you, but I tell you now that I will break you if need be. Mark my words." The menace in his voice and look was unmistakable. "Now, tell me what happened during your meeting after Edwards' murder."

Amanda was stunned, but she managed to mumble out, "There was nothing—nothing that could make any difference to your plan, whatever it is. I promise."

He gave her arm a jerk and said, "You know we have a plan, eh. We will talk. We will leave you to think about what you know and what will happen to you if you do not tell me what I need to know." Her inquisitor went out, locked the door, and Amanda was left in silence to think about what was happening. She went over every word both she and Massengill had said and she could make no sense of it. There was nothing that could make a difference to anyone. Or was there? Had he said something Amanda did not understand but that was important? What could Massengill know? Was there some plan? Had she made a terrible error in using the word 'plan'? Had that put her in much trouble? What did she know?

CHAPTER 35

In the afternoon of August 29, his office door opened and Michael O'Day's chief clerk hurriedly entered to say, "There is a constable, Rafferty, who wishes to see you. He says it is urgent."

"Send him in."

Constable Rafferty, who had long been a friend of O'Day, had a stricken look. "Michael O'Day, sir, you are found out. A squad is coming for you. Lucky for you they think you are a dangerous man and they are assembling a group of hard men with weapons who they think will be enough to take you. You have about one half hour before they are here. If you are to escape you must leave now."

"Do they know the worst?"

"I do not know. All I know is that they want you for questioning. You will hang if they know all. You must flee now or run great risk."

"Damn all! Damn! I trust you, Rafferty, you have behaved very well in all of my dealings with you. I thank you for this warning. You have served the cause long and well and it will not be forgotten. I am leaving. Now it is time to save yourself. Get yourself away from here, you can have no connection with me." Rafferty left immediately and O'Day walked into the outer office, taking nothing with him, told his chief clerk, Thomas Doyle, that he was leaving, and gave orders to his clerks: "Call up my carriage; send the two trunks in my office this instant to the stables. Four clerks were quickly enlisted to carry the two heavy trunks to the stables and another ran to the stable to give orders to make ready the carriage.

O'Day did not wait for the carriage to be brought to the door. He went immediately to the stable and he instructed a hostler to load the trunks onto a cart and take it immediately to his brig *Ann Elizabeth*. "Tell the captain to stop all work and make ready to get under way immediately I arrive. I should be there within fifteen minutes of the arrival of the trunks. Go now, quickly." He was waiting in the carriage when the two horses were in harness and the driver was aboard. He gave an address and they left immediately, even before the cart with the trunks had gone.

O'Day's carriage stopped before the door of Lady B's residence and O'Day leaped out and mounted the steps. He was seen, and the door opened by the maid before he could raise the knocker. "I must see her."

"Sir, Lady B is not to be disturbed at this hour of the day."

"I know that, but I will see her. Take me to her, now."

"Sir, I cannot."

O'Day pulled a small pistol from his coat pocket, pointed it at the maid, and said, "Now." She instantly stood aside and pointed up the stair. O'Day went up on the double, opened the first door he came to and found the room empty, jerked open the second door and found himself facing three nude women entangled on the large and handsome four-poster bed. Lady Conconnon was in the middle, flanked by Clara on the left and Bea on the right. All three froze in place and stared at O'Day without a word. "B, you God-dammed bitch, you have ruined me. You two, get!" Clara and Lady Conconnon, staring at the gun O'Day still had in his hand, tumbled off the left side of the bed. When Lady Conconnon hit the floor she lost her footing, hit Clara, and they both crumpled to the floor. "Listen, you two, out of this room, now!" shouted O'Day. Clara and Lady Conconnon got off the floor and stumbled into the hall, closing the door behind them. While they were untangling themselves O'Day stalked over to B, grabbed her by the hair. He held her until the two were out of the room and said, "You fool, I told you that I must not be mentioned in any connection with the events in Croome Court, but you have done it. The constabulary is coming for me now—I am informed—and I must flee. I am losing everything and it is because of you. I ought to kill you. You have upset matters so large that you cannot imagine what you have done. There is no time. Here is your choice: I am leaving for France. You will come with me and spend your days serving me as I wish in penance for what you have done, or with this pistol I will kill you now and that will be penance enough. What will it be?"

"Good, God, Michael, is it really so bad? Is all lost? Is it worth my life?"

"It is worth your life and more. Choose."

"You leave me no choice. I am with you."

"Get dressed. Hurry. Hurry!" Bea threw on her clothes. "Speed, woman, speed!" She snatched her jewelry box out of the drawer of the dressing table, and said, "I am ready." O'Day took her by the arm, opened the door and headed for the stair. Clara and Lady Conconnon, both still naked and both scared near to death, cowered in the hall.

Bea looked over her shoulder, tears in her eyes, and said, "Clara, all is yours. I am gone. Take care of Henry and my darling Amanda."

Clara screamed, "Oh, God, no! What is it?"

O'Day never slowed his pace, almost tumbling Bea down the stairs. The maid, who had not moved, opened the door, her eyes full of disaster and tears, and as O'Day and Bea went out the door, Bea turned and called up the stairs, "Clara, I love you forever, I promise."

As they were getting into the carriage O'Day growled, "She can damn well hope your promise to her is worth more than your promise to me."

"Oh Michael, I am sorry. I am so sorry."

"Sorry is not enough. You cannot imagine what you have done. Damn Fool!"

"Michael, please! Please! I have never said you had anything to do with what happened. I never talked with any constabulary. I promise you."

"Then who did you tell? I know you told."

"I spoke only to one man about Amanda's danger and he agreed to help. He made me tell him your name, he said he must have it in order to save her. He made me! He promised not to use your name. Please! I promise! You know I would never hurt you."

"You promised that my name would not be used and you told me on Monday that you had not said my name. You lied, damn you. You have ruined me."

"Oh, God, Michael, I did what I did to save Amanda. You know what an angel she is. I had to."

"The hell of this," he answered, "is that you have used my attempt to help a woman I revered to destroy me. I should have kept my affections centered on a whore like you. What a damn fool I am to have thought I was falling in love. Damn, damn, damn. Lady Amanda will never come under my care and will never fall in love with me as I hoped. It could never have happened in any event. I was a fool to think it might. A lady like her could never have had love and respect for a common-bred man like me. You, on the other hand, are low enough to look up to me, and you know well how to fulfill my needs for sex. That's something."

They rode in silence for ten minutes, the coachman shouting pedestrians, horsemen and dogs aside in a rush and dodging around equipages in a bullying way. When they reached O'Day's wharf he could see that *Ann Elizabeth* had her lines singled up, men were aloft to release sails and the captain, himself, was at the wheel. He could see his two trunks on deck near the hatchway to the cabin. The second they were on board he shouted, "Bring in the brow and cast off." The first sails dropped, the brow and the lines were brought in, and the breeze was moving them away from the wharf almost immediately. "Thank God we have made it. Get below. We must not be seen. I am coming behind you. Hurry."

CHAPTER 36

Twenty minutes after Michael O'Day quitted his office in great haste the constables arrived. The Chief Constable was there and he had six other men with him. Constables, even the Chief Constable, often came to the office for one errand or another so the presence of the constabulary was not a surprise, but the presence of seven men was a surprise. The Chief Constable asked to see Mr. O'Day and when told that O'Day had left he brushed past the clerk and walked into the office of chief clerk Doyle. "I am here to see Mr. O'Day on an important matter and I am told that he is not here. Where is he? Immediately, man, where is he?"

"Chief Constable, I do not know. Mr. O'Day frequently leaves without telling me where he is going. What is it that you need? Perhaps I can help."

"You cannot help. I am here for the man himself."

Doyle eyed the crew the chief constable had brought with him, "You are taking him into custody?"

"We need to question him about an incident in County Cavan. How did he leave? How long ago?"

"He left about twenty minutes ago by carriage. The stablemen may know where he went. What has happened in County Cavan? I know of no business Mr. O'Day has there."

"Never you mind. Follow me, men." The chief constable and his posse rushed around to the stable and asked where O'Day had gone. No one knew. He had left in his carriage and had given the driver instructions, but no one in the stable had heard what he said. "Surely, men, you must know where he went?"

"No sir, we know nothing." All the stablemen nodded in agreement. One of the men ventured to say, "He sent a cart."

"A cart? Where did he send it and what was in it?"

"He sent it down to the *Ann Elizabeth* at his wharf. It had two trunks in."

"Trunks! The man is fleeing! He has been warned. To the wharf!" They ran to the street in front of the building, climbed into their wagon and were gone. Doyle had followed them to the stable and had heard the exchange. Doyle did not know what was in the two trunks in O'Day's office, which was always locked when he was not in it, but he knew their contents were important. Sending the trunks to the *Ann Elizabeth* could only mean one thing, O'Day was fleeing from something. But what? Doyle was privy to all of O'Day's businesses, and in fact handled the day to day operation of everything, but he knew that O'Day had other activities, activities that he was careful to keep Doyle ignorant of. Doyle suspected that, while O'Day's businesses were within the law, there might be something in O'Day's life that was outside the law. But if that were so, he did not know what it might be that was outside the law. He knew that O'Day ships called at ports in County Donegal for timber and at Sligo. Perhaps there was a connection to Cavan through that shipping.

Doyle ordered a phaeton harnessed up and when it was ready got aboard and drove himself to the wharf. He got there minutes after the constables had arrived and joined them on the pier where they were watching *Ann Elizabeth* disappear down the bay. The ship was at least a mile down the harbor, almost abreast of Helen's Bay by the time the constables arrived, and there was no catching it. "Well, Doyle, what have you to say about your boss? Where is the ship bound?"

"Chief Constable, I can tell you nothing. He said to me only that he was going out. I confess that his sending his trunks of valuables to the ship and the departure of the ship do make it clear that he has fled, but I do not know why. Have you asked the dock workers what they know?"

"We have not. Constables, ask you among the workers what they know of the ship's destination." The constables were back within a few minutes and reported that no one on the pier knew where the ship was bound.

"Doyle, I ask you again, where is he going?"

"Chief Constable, I tell you I have no idea. Was he fleeing you? What is this matter?"

"Never you mind, Doyle. But if he should contact you in any way, in any way at all, you are to tell us all. Do you understand?"

"I do."

"We will maintain contact with you; you can be sure of it."

CHAPTER 37

The constables in Croome Court were at their wits end. They realized that they knew nothing and had little idea of how to proceed. Massengill had once again become their only suspect, and there seemed to be ample ties between him and the victims. In addition, based on Berrigan's information, he might well have had the means to have committed—or to have had others commit—every one of the crimes that had shocked Croome Court. But why had he done these things? That piece of the puzzle eluded them and it was the piece that would tie everything together and close the case against Massengill. But did that piece exist? It appeared to be true that Massengill was now the owner of Croome Forest, the greatest estate in the locale, but was that really a factor in the situation and why would a man with such means risk it by crime? On the other hand, how had he come by his fortune? Had it been honorably obtained as a King's Officer as Massengill had intimated? No one could actually remember him saying that he had become rich in the naval service, in fact no one could remember him ever saying that he was rich. Could it be that his fortune was illegally obtained, perhaps in connection with the Seymours, and that he was eliminating all who had knowledge of how he had obtained the money so he could live quietly in the enjoyment of his fortune? Edwards could have known or could have found out. Massengill himself might have, perhaps unwittingly, revealed it to Lady Amanda, and the Seymours could have been part of it from the beginning. They all would have had to die. Perhaps Massengill and the Seymours were, in fact, partners in a massive prostitution ring that was making them rich.

They had to continue to keep watch on Massengill. It was decided to ask the Belfast Constabulary to contact the Port Captain there to learn what could be found out about Massengill's Navy career and whether or not it might have resulted in a great fortune for him. Such a fortune was, of course, possible. Captains and Admirals did gain fortunes, sometimes huge fortunes, at sea. They knew that soon they should get a message from Dublin about the Bannons' charges, so they sent a message to the Belfast Constabulary and waited for news from there and from Dublin.

The 28th was Sunday and the day of worship and rest was observed by all in Croome Court.

The 29th was another day of funerals. In the forenoon Sir William Seymour and Lady Susan Seymour were buried in the grounds of Seymour Place. There was no service and no one was there except for the staff of the estate. That same afternoon John Barber was buried in a plot just outside the hallowed ground of St. Michael's Catholic Church. There was no service and there were few at the graveside.

In the late afternoon of the 29th a coach arrived from Cavan and with it a message from the Dublin Constabulary. Upon receipt of the request from Croome Court they had moved immediately to learn all they could about the brothel on Fenton Lane. They were well aware of the place, of course, but had tolerated its existence because there was little trouble there, and perhaps because its owners had made it worthwhile for the constabulary to ignore it (although there was nothing of this in the report).

The brothel was owned by a man known as "William Henry", which was not thought to be his true name although it was the only name they could associate with him. The operators of the brothel knew only that name. They had seen him many times, but they knew little about him except that he was obviously a gentleman, he came from County Cavan, and he owned similar establishments in Sligo and Derry, and perhaps elsewhere. There was a girl named Ailis Bannon working in the house, and she was from County Cavan. The description that was provided of William Henry did fit the late Sir William Seymour. This did fit with the story that Niall Bannon had told, but it did not mean that Massengill was not involved in the prostitution enterprise with the Seymours and it did not mean that Massengill had not used—or allowed—the Bannons to eliminate the Seymours and Barber for him, although that possibility appeared to be a stretch.

The Constable Supervisor directed that letters be sent to the constabularies in Sligo and Derry outlining what they knew about the Dublin brothel and its owner and the events in Croome Court and Dublin with a request that the brothels in those cities be scoured to determine if any of them were part of the same ring of ownership, and if so, what could be found out about the owner. The letters were sent and it seemed there was little to do but keep watch on Massengill and wait. They must wait for replies from Sligo and Derry, they must wait to find out about Michael O'Day, and they must wait to hear from the Port Captain in Belfast. The replies they got could turn the investigation in any number of directions and the very number of possibilities locked the constabulary in place.

CHAPTER 38

When the door closed behind Bea and Michael O'Day, the maid rushed up the stairs and found Lady Conconnon and Clara still standing in the hall, frozen by shock. "She's gone. O'Day has took her. Where have they gone? What has happened? He had a pistol!"

Clara recovered herself enough to say, "I do not know where they are gone. Lady B has said all is mine. I don't know what to do. I can't think."

"Both of you, get dressed. You cannot think standing there naked as the day you were born." They took her advice and then came down to the parlor.

Clara sat on the settee and Lady Conconnon sat next to her. She rested her hand on Clara's arm, "Clara, you must carry on. B will be back, I am sure of it, and you must keep all against her return. We need you—I need you. Every night I go to bed thinking about you and B. You have made my life worth living. I think of you when I wake up. I think of you all day long. I must have you. You must be here for me. Promise me. You can count on me to help if you need me." Clara still could hardly think, but she nodded in agreement. Whatever happened, she owed it to Bea to carry on. They had built a small empire and it could not be allowed to die. The door knocker sounded. "That will be my driver," said Lady Concannon. "I will be back on Friday. Be here for me, my dearest."

"I will."

Lady Conconnon was shown out and Clara began to ponder over what to do next. Tonight Lady B's House would open for business as usual, that was sure. Bea was not always present, so her absence would not cause any alarm. Things must continue. People must see that all is normal, even though it eventually would be found that Lady B, herself, had left. Clara now had to concoct her own story of what had happened to Bea. She realized that she was in exactly the same quandary that Lady Amanda had been in when she and Bea had departed Croome Court in the same haste with which Bea had now departed Belfast. What could have happened between O'Day and Bea? Clearly, it was a disaster beyond imagining. Would it remain a disaster forever or would the problem be resolved allowing Bea and O'Day to return? There were only questions and no answers.

Clara thought, turning ideas over in her mind, and suddenly she had it: Bea and O'Day had eloped to get married. O'Day wanted her to the point of distraction—it was widely known that they were partial to each other—and he could not bear the thought of not having her for himself, but nor could he bear the thought of marrying a whore for all to see. The only answer had been to leave. That was a story that could work, and unless a better one came to her, that would be the story that would be told—but it needed to wait for a few days before it came out. O'Day needed a story, too. She would talk with his chief clerk; they could make their stories fit. They had to fit.

In addition to keeping the business going—both businesses—she had another pressing task: she had to help Lady Amanda. Bea had told her all that had happened and all that was known, which was that Amanda was in great trouble but no one in Croome Court knew why. Clara knew that Bea had talked with Captain Massengill, who had returned to Croome

Court just before the tragedies began to take place. She remembered Massengill with respect from his visit to North Hall and knew that Bea trusted him, and that she trusted him to rescue Lady Amanda.

In addition to the girls, the cook, the driver, and the servants, she, and now it was she alone, Clara Rohan, had six men in her employ as doorkeepers. They had to be rough men for that job and they were men who did not shy from a fight, who in fact looked for a fight. Clara decided to send four of them to help Massengill. She did not know what help Massengill needed, but given the murders, the abduction, and mayhem that had taken place in Croome Court she felt violent men were needed there on Amanda's side.

That night all seemed normal at Lady B's. Clients came in, and were wined, fed, and serviced. There was no disturbance and there were no embarrassing questions. A short time after midnight Clara had the four men she had chosen directed to the office. She sat behind the desk as she had done at times in the past, and they stood before her without question and waited on her instructions. Clara told them that Lady B was deeply troubled by what had happened to a dear friend of hers in the village of Croome Court in County Cavan and that Lady B had ordered her to provide aid to those who were helping Bea's friend in her distress. She told them of the abduction and that Lady B was so upset that she was in seclusion and might not be back until the matter was resolved. She said that Lady B had told her to send them to Croome Court to help Captain John Massengill, late of the Royal Navy, in the quest to rescue Lady Amanda. Clara made it a point to tell them of the killings and the fire as well as the abduction and then asked each if he was ready to join in an effort that might put his life at risk. As she had suspected, every one said he was ready to go. Clara knew that among them there were some weapons and she told them to take any weapons and ammunition they had or could get. She told them she did not know how long they would be gone—she did not think it would be too many days—but she advised them to take what they would need for a week, perhaps a fortnight.

Arrangements were made for the four to take the coach the next morning for Monaghan. If there was no immediate coach for Croome Court they were to hire a carriage or whatever conveyance was available and get to Croome Court as quickly as possible, hopefully before the sun set tomorrow if there was a way. She gave them money and told them to begin their inquiries at the inn when they sought to find Massengill.

They were off the next morning and Clara prepared to face a day that she expected to be difficult. She was going to have to visit O'Day's office and see if she could come to agreement with his chief clerk on a story. It might be simple; her visit might be welcomed, but she might be stepping into a hornet's nest of anger. Because she had no idea what had happened between Bea and O'Day, she had no idea what to expect.

CHAPTER 39

In the afternoon of her first day of captivity the door to Amanda's cell—as she now thought of it—opened and a man came in with a package that he unfolded to reveal some food and a jug of water. "This will keep you going. Do you have slop?" Amanda was embarrassed to tell him that the bucket needed emptying. She was conscious of the fact that the room smelled—because of her. It made her sick to think of it. The man took the bucket to the door and simply threw the contents into the yard. He brought the bucket back and without another word walked out and locked the door. Amanda was beginning to despair. She had no idea what these men wanted from her and had no idea how to convince them she knew nothing that would be of use to them—at least she thought she knew nothing that could be of use to them.

It was the next morning before anything else happened. Amanda slept some during the night but spent most of her time in confusion, hearing the occasional sound from outside, trying to understand what was going on. She had lost all track of what time it might be, but she knew it was a few hours after sunrise that the door opened again and her inquisitor walked in. "Well, missy, I hope you have something to say to me today."

"I will not be addressed in such a manner. You know who I am and I will have the respect that is due me!" He grabbed her wrist with one hand and with the other gave her a hard slap. If he hadn't been holding on to her wrist, Amanda would have fallen down. As it was she spun around and staggered before she regained her balance.

"Here, you are whoever I want you to be and you are whoever I say you are. Don't be insolent with me. I have no patience for it. I want to know what Massengill told you." The man was angry and his anger filled Amanda with fear.

"Please, I promise you, I have already told you all I know. Everything. I cannot imagine anything else to tell you."

"I don't believe it." He kept asking her, threatening her, and jerking her roughly when he was unhappy with her answers—which was almost all the time. After ten minutes of frustration for him and fear for Amanda he pushed her onto the bed and said, "I am going to leave you to think about this. I want answers, and we are going to keep you here as long as it takes to convince you to talk." He left and Amanda sank deeper into despair.

Her inquisitor walked across the courtyard and went into an office where two men were waiting for him. "Well?"

"Nothing. I have treated her quite roughly and I have told her that I am not through with her. She thinks we will keep her until she tells us what we want to hear, but I think she actually does not know anything. I believe Massengill told her nothing. I doubt she can be of danger to us."

"Perhaps you are right, but perhaps you are wrong. In any event we cannot let her go. The risk that she does know something is too great and you have made the damn fool mistake of telling her she is at Croome Forest, so if she is released she will tell that and all will know that something is afoot here. She must stay. Feed her and give her water and leave her where she is. If you want to question her more, do as you please, but make sure she stays where she is."

"We could kill her and have it done with. She wouldn't be the first to die for the cause."

"We will not. I have not yet stooped so low as to kill an innocent woman. It will do us no good. Keep her."

"As you wish."

CHAPTER 40

John Massengill was frustrated. It was two days after the constables had released him and he thought he was in their good graces, but the constables were telling him nothing about the progress—or lack of it—that they were making and they were not asking him for any assistance. He knew they were awaiting replies from constabularies in other cities that might have a bearing on the situation, but he didn't know what information the letters that had been sent out had asked for and had no idea what the answers could be or toward which direction those answers might point the investigation.

He decided he needed to take counsel and he considered who he might counsel with. Berrigan at Croome Forest seemed out of the question. James Walsh had hardly shown his face and seemed to be of little use in any event. William Walsh was a good man, but old and not in touch with life in the area. Alfred Mahon and Atwood Corry were both good and honorable men, but they were not young and Massengill thought of neither of them as a fighter. He wanted a fighter, and the one man left who fit that description was Captain Ievers. The Captain had earned his rank in the King's Army and was a man who had seen battle many times and had suffered hardship and disease in the service. He was hardened, and though not young, he was young enough to join in a fight if need be and he was active and knowledgeable about the people and the goings on of the neighborhood.

"Otis, have two good horses saddled for us. We are going to the country." With Barber gone and the village in a state of almost constant upheaval, Massengill's word was near law at the inn so the horses were ready in short order. They left the village quietly and rode for forty-five minutes, first south and then east and arrived at the gate that opened on to the lane that led to Ievers Court. It was more than a quarter of a mile through a thick forest before the house came into sight. The forest went on beyond the house; there was a garden at the rear and there were outbuildings, but all was surrounded by trees. The scene might have looked gloomy in other circumstances, but in this case it seemed warm and inviting. The house was one of the oldest in the county, three stories tall and built of brick, although with a front of well cut stone. The house was old fashioned in style, little adorned, but with a solid presence and a doll-house look that was most welcoming.

They knocked at the door and it was soon opened by the maid who showed them into a book-lined library where Captain Milton Ievers made them welcome. "Captain Massengill, I'm glad to see that the constabulary, in their great wisdom, have set you free. The idea that you would be the perpetrator of these events is quite absurd to anyone who has known your father and has known you, if only during your youth. The whole thing is absurd! Be seated and tell me what brings you to my door."

"Captain, I am much relieved to hear of your confidence and thank you much for it. We need your counsel. Allow me to present my coxswain, Otis. Otis has been with me for all of ten years, through many dangerous times—times that an army man such as yourself will understand—and he is to be trusted." Otis gave Captain Ievers a bow and Ievers nodded to him with an approving smile. "I do not have to parade before you the story of recent events," continued Massengill, "you know all too well what has happened. The problem is this: I have no confidence in the constabulary. I hardly need to say that I was enraged to be arrested and detained by them. It is true that once the Constable Supervisor arrived they did see fit to release me, but even so I believe they have no ideas about what to do. They are simply waiting for information from one place and another. What the information will be and where it will lead they know not, nor do I. Lady Amanda, if she still lives, and I hate to mention the possibility that she does not—but it is there—must be found and rescued. She is dear to this community and she is dear to me. I have some ideas about the matter and I want to gain your opinion on them and to learn if you have any thoughts to present to me."

"By all means, Captain. Lady Amanda is the dearest young woman I know and has suffered so many tragic blows that only a person of the highest type could have carried on as she has. Indeed, she is the darling of the whole area. I am at your service. I will do anything, including take up arms to help, and I feel it will be necessary to take up arms before this thing is over with."

"I am glad to hear your sentiments. I have been weighing the possibilities. It appears to me that the deaths of the Seymours and John Barber have without doubt resulted from the charge of prostitution that the Bannons made. My own brief experience with Lady Susan, some years ago, leads me to believe that even though she was a person of high station, she was a person of low character. I can believe she might easily have been involved in some way in a business that involved sexual adventure. Her husband, I have never met so I can have no opinion."

"Your assessment of Lady Susan's character is in line with my own and with that of most of local society. If the wife of a knight can be called a bawd, then I will say that of Lady Susan. Of her husband I know not much. He is of an old family. He has much business and he clearly is prosperous. He is also most close-mouthed. No one is admitted to his confidence and I know of no one who has intimate knowledge of his business arrangements. There is the suggestion of some kind of impropriety that needs to be hidden, but I can make no judgment."

"Very good," said Massengill, relieved once more to hear Captain Ievers' sentiments. "We are in agreement that they may be involved in such a low venture but, still, I find it difficult to believe that Lady Amanda's abduction and the fire at North Hall have anything to do with such a business. How could she be involved?"

"I agree. There is no way she could be involved in such a thing. So where are we left?"

"I think the fire at North Hall and Lady Amanda's abduction are without a doubt related. How any of this is connected with Lachlan Edwards' death I do not understand, however I do believe Lachlan's death has to do with the Croome Forest estate. You will remember that he was murdered shortly after I visited him. Now, here is some information that no one here knows, save Otis of course: I am the owner of the Croome Forest estate. I bought it not a month ago using a part of my prize money."

"Remarkable. Truly remarkable! My warmest congratulations. I wish you joy of your great success."

"I thank you most kindly. It is of great interest that the things taken from Edwards' office during the murder were all his records concerning Croome Forest and his records concerning my business with Edwards. I believe someone has made the connection between me and Croome Forest and the likely person to have been able to make such a connection is Padraic Berrigan, the head steward at The Forest. He would have been informed of my purchase of the property by the executors of the late Earl's estate. When I arrived in the village he would have doubtless found out about it. He may have known I met with Edwards and it may be that he thought some information dangerous to him passed between us. I think it is possible that Edwards was murdered and robbed to keep that information, which must have been in Edwards' records, from becoming public. I wonder that they may have wanted me dead as well, but when I was arrested that kept me away from them—and them away from me. You may be sure that I have been careful and have had my men guarding me since I was released." Ievers pondered. "All this seems possible."

"Indeed, and there is another important fact: Berrigan is keeping everyone out of Croome Forest. I am told that people from the village never go in except for a few tradesmen, and few enough of them. Since my arrival it seems that no one has entered. You may know that when Otis and I tried to enter we were turned away, even though we were emissaries of the constabulary. Something is going on there that Berrigan does not want to see the light of day. I wonder if Edwards was murdered because of something Berrigan thought I told Edwards, or was murdered because of something Berrigan thought Edwards told me? I do not know which, but I think one or the other is true. I can tell you there was nothing that passed between us that was worth murder, whatever Berrigan may think."

"So—Berrigan and Croome Forest. I can believe it. And how does Lady Amanda fit into the puzzle?"

"I do not know how Lady Amanda's troubles fit into this picture. I can only speculate that my visit to her caused those with evil designs to assume that I had told her something that I knew or that Edwards knew, and that they felt she must be silenced. Her friend came from Belfast to tell me she was in danger. She said she had been told of the danger by a man named Michael O'Day, but all else she could say was that the culprits were Irishmen. That could mean anyone, so it tells me nothing."

"True, we are all Irishmen. It is curious that that news should have come from Belfast. Who in this neighborhood could be doing anything that would be of interest in Belfast?"

"It is possible that this ring of brothels that the Seymours are alleged to have been involved with could be active in Belfast and that would be a connection. But how would I be connected with that? And although Lady Amanda was abducted from Seymour Hall, North Hall had been burned before she became involved with the Seymours. The only other possibility in Croome Court seems to me to be the goings on at Croome Forest. We have no idea what is happening there, but there must be something going on or Berrigan would not be so careful to keep everyone out of the place.

Ievers considered all that Massengill had told him and found himself in agreement. "That may be the answer to Lady Amanda's abduction. It appears to me, Captain, that the answer to all of the questions is behind the gates of Croome Forest."

"I think so. We must get into the place and find out what is going on."

"Agreed." Even though he was the older man, Captain Ievers was ready to defer to Massengill. It was clear to him that Massengill was used to command and that he had long experience in planning actions and was ready to meet any challenge that might be faced.

"Otis and I will make another attempt. I believe we should do it without involving the constabulary. They do not seem keen on action, and we need action. We will go now. If they let us in we may be able to find out what is afoot, and if they do not we will press the matter and see how far they are willing to go to stay secret. We will report back to you in the morning, Captain—and if we do not come back, pray do alert the constabulary."

Massengill and Otis mounted their horses and headed for the village. Although the afternoon was more than half over, Massengill decided they would make the attempt at the gate as soon as they reached the village. "Cap'm, we've no arms."

"We are not going to join a fight, Otis. We don't need to get in today if they don't want us in. We are just testing the water, so we will simply ask for an appointment to see Mr. Berrigan. If we are turned away, we will go—and we will know for sure that there is something not right in Croome Forest. If the gatekeeper offers to check with Berrigan, it may be that all is well. We will see." They rode in silence the three-quarters of an hour that brought them to the village gate of Croome Forest. This time there was no need for Otis to hail the gate; they could see the gatekeeper peering out the window of the lodge as they arrived and he was out to challenge them as soon as they had stopped their horses.

"Ye two! Ye been told there is no coming to see Mr. Berrigan. There's no entering of this gate. Move it on, or I'll move ye." A pistol was in his right hand and he waved it at them. "Git! Now. And don't come back or I'll shoot as soon as I see you coming. Git!"

Without a word, Massengill turned his horse and Otis followed him. He headed south and when they were a few yards away he said, "Otis, the fat is in the fire. There is mischief afoot in there. We are going back to Ievers Court straightaway. We will get off the road and go by trails so we can put off any one who may be following us."

The maid ushered them once again into Captain Ievers' library and, without greeting or ceremony, Massengill said, "Captain, we were turned away at gunpoint without a word being said by either of us. There is a mystery in Croome Forest and we must get to the bottom of it. I think Lady Amanda is there and I think Berrigan is behind this all. We must go in numbers, armed and ready for a fight. I have no idea how many men are in there, but I think we must go with the largest force we can assemble. Are you ready to help?"

"I am ready."

"I will be back first thing tomorrow and we can plan. Let us think on it tonight and be ready to begin making all ready in the morning."

"I will consider who we can count on to help. Come early."

CHAPTER 41

As soon as Massengill and Otis were out of sight, one of the gatekeepers had immediately left with a message to alert Berrigan of Massengill's visit to the gate, and Berrigan had decided the time for action had come. The next morning, even before Massengill and Otis were back at Ievers Court, Berrigan and his two lieutenants were meeting. "Massengill knows something is afoot. He may not know what, but he knows there is something. I have tried the best I could to keep him quiet. I think I have succeeded in turning the constables against him, but they have not been convinced to take him back into custody where we should be safe. He has tried twice to get through the gates and we have kept him out, but we cannot keep him out forever. There's only one solution left to us. We must kill him."

The men were concerned. "With Barber gone we have no one in the village. That means we must go out and do the work ourselves."

"You are correct, Terrance. I give it to you to choose two men and send them out to find him and kill him if they can. If they cannot kill him, they can at least come back and tell us how to get to him and we will determine how to do the job. Meanwhile, we must plan what to do if he cannot be stopped. If he can enlist the constabulary, and even the militia, they will be too much for us to hold off. Our only option if we are not to be ruined completely in that event is to move the arms. Jonas, I charge you with making a plan for the removal. I will try what I can to get the constables back on his case."

Berrigan and his lieutenants had hardly finished their meeting when Massengill and Otis, after a furtive departure from Croome Court, arrived at Ievers Court. They found that Captain Ievers had not been idle. "Captain Massengill, I have important news. Last evening I went into the village and had a session with Constable Quirke. I have known Quirke since he arrived on the post and we have a good relationship. We talked of the situation in vague terms. I tried to hit on many points to see what his reactions would be and within ten minutes I struck the right note. Berrigan has been with the constables and has poisoned them against you most completely. They are sure, based on what Berrigan told them—and I know not what that might have been—that it is you who is up to no good at Croome Forest. Berrigan has told them you are the new owner and they are convinced that you have a plot afoot. Somehow you have outsmarted Berrigan, according to him, and have some nefarious operation under way. The constables have determined to tell you nothing and to watch you to see if you will unwittingly lead them to your operation. Berrigan is cooperating with them—or at least he says so!" Ievers smiled and shook his head dismissively. " Whatever you do, the constables will think you are up to no good, so we must keep the constables away from our project. If we tip them to what we are doing I have no doubt they will warn Berrigan so he will be alert against us. I think you must disappear from their view. You must stay here at Ievers Court while we make our plans. Have they followed you here?"

"My God, Captain, what a hoard of information. It is by the grace of God you were led to seek out Quirke. If you had not found this out I doubt not we would have been undone. I think you are right that I must stay here while we plan. I think, too, that my men should disappear to here also. Otis, it is possible we may have been seen leaving the village, but I do not think anyone followed us into the country. Do you think we were followed?"

"I do not, Cap'm, said Otis."

"I agree that it would be wise for your men to come here out of sight of the constabulary. We can accommodate them in the cottages around the place."

"Thank you, Captain Ievers. Let it be so. Otis, you must go and round them up. Bring everything with you that could be of use in a fight. You know what to do. Keep it close."

"Aye, Cap'm, I'm off."

"Now, Captain Ievers, let us plan. Let us take stock of where we stand. We have myself, yourself, and my seven men, all men who have faced battle and can be counted on in any circumstance we may face."

"And we have Watterson, my sergeant. He has stayed with me all these years. That is ten men who are hard fighters. We will also have my farmers Duffy and Ryan. They are both tough lads and will follow where I lead. If my adding is right that means we have twelve men."

Massengill thought about it. "A good crew, but I would like to have more."

"I will get out and do some quiet recruiting."

"Good. We also need weapons and ammunition. I and my men have weapons and some ammunition, but not enough for a real battle, and I fear we may be facing a real battle."

"I have some of both weapons and ammunition and will be looking for more," said Ievers. "You will stay here. I fear for you on the roads. Berrigan knows you are a potential enemy and may have men looking for you and the constables may be looking for you as well. It is hard to know who we can feel safe with."

"Agreed. You should be able to move without fear. There is enough for me to do here." Captain Ievers alerted his wife to make a place in the mansion house for Massengill and to find what accommodations could be had on the place for their soldiers, for that was what he now thought their men were, soldiers about to go into battle against a shadowy enemy. Massengill set himself to thinking about equipment they would need and strategy for the fight that he was sure was coming. Late in the morning Otis arrived back at Ievers Court with the wagon crammed with well hidden men and cargo. He reported to Massengill, "Cap'm, we've snuck out without leaving nary a trace."

"Nothing more fair than that. Well done."

CHAPTER 42

Berrigan's first task after leaving his lieutenants was to visit the constables, both to see what they might know and to try to poison them further against Massengill. He turned the matter over in his mind as he rode. He decided he should approach the matter gently with the constables because being too bold might raise suspicion. Berrigan found only the Constable Supervisor and Quirke in the office when he arrived. He greeted them warmly and was politely received. Berrigan told them he had trusted men riding through the Croome Forest property on supposed errands who were looking for anything suspicious. He expected all of them to have reported back to him by late in the afternoon and he would notify the constables of anything they found. If there was anything suspicious he would either look into it himself or enlist the constables to help him. He, himself, was examining the financial records to see if he could track down the problems he had felt were beginning to appear. He remained in fear of Massengill and hoped the constables were keeping close watch on him. The man was dangerous.

The constables assured him that Massengill was being watched and that the village entrance to Croome Forest was being watched as well. There was no other news for him. They were still waiting on replies from several messages they had sent, and felt the replies would point them in a direction that would allow the solution of the crimes and an unraveling of Massengill's goings-on at Croome Forest. He would be informed if there was any news that would be of use to him in his searches inside the Croome Forest estate. Berrigan thanked them and left. During the ride back to his office he made a decision.

At two o"clock that afternoon Berrigan met again with his two lieutenants as planned. "O'Sullivan, what do you have to report? I presume he is still alive or you already would have told me of his death."

"He is still alive. I have had two men searching the village since we met this morning. He was seen early in the day riding out with his man Otis and has not been seen since. They rode south, but no one who will talk knows where he has gone. We are keeping watch from the gate lodge so if he comes back into the village from the south we will know it. What of the constables?"

"I have talked with them and they are still suspicious of Massengill. They say they are watching him, but I don't believe they know where he is. They are an incompetent lot. Massengill is up to mischief. I have made the decision. If we are not to be completely undone we must move the arms. One way or another Massengill or the constabulary will be in Croome Forest, and when they get in we are sure to be found out unless they are complete buffoons, and while the constables may be fools, Massengill is no fool. Smith, what is the situation with the arms?"

"It is this: we have 800 long guns, some rifled, we have bayonets for most; we have near two hundred pistols; we have near a ton of balls of sizes for our weapons; we have two score of barrels of powder, we have cartridge boxes and belts for two hundred or more men. There are some things, mostly the powder, in the warehouse at the wharf and the rest are scattered over barns and sheds."

"Three years of work! We must preserve it!"

"Yes, with God's help," agreed Smith.

"What is your plan?"

"Whether we have the time to make it work, I do not know, but there is a chance for us to get most, and perhaps all, out. We are blessed by God, who is on our side, that there is a barge alongside the pier that is empty 'cept for a few logs. We have sixteen men and we can command from the farmers all the horses and wagons we can use. At this point it is of no matter whether they think something improper is going on. We must load all we can onto the barge and set it in the current; we can pole it down the river, but what happens to it then must be up to you, Berrigan."

"Understood. I will leave immediately for Ballshannon. It may be that there or in Donegal we can find a place for storage. Terrance, you send a message immediately to O'Day and see if a ship can come to Ballshannon or Donegal; tell him it is desperate. Jonas, what is your plan for loading?"

"Of the sixteen men, two must stay at the gate lodge to keep all out and to warn us if anyone has been able to enter—and to keep the farmers in. I will be sure that they will be ready to shoot if necessary. I will set two crews of four to loading wagons and bringing arms to the pier, six will be at the pier to help unload wagons and move the stuff onto the barge. I will supervise this and I suggest that O'Sullivan spend his time patrolling other gates to the estate and keeping fear in the hearts of the farmers so none try to get out. Is this good?"

"It is a plan that can work. How long do you think it will take to load?"

"I'm not sure, but I think we will need three days to do all—maybe more."

"Get the message sent to Belfast and put all into operation. I will be off to Ballshannon. I will be back tomorrow."

"God speed you."

CHAPTER 43

Michael O'Day's counting room was impressive. A large outer office had desks for as many as eight clerks. There were many cabinets for storage of papers and in the back were two large offices, one for O'Day's chief clerk, Thomas Doyle, and the other for O'Day, himself. Clara arrived at O'Day's office in a state of real fear. This was either going to work or it was going to be a disaster. There could be no in between and she feared the worst. The clerk nearest the door rose to greet her and she gave her name and asked to see the chief clerk. She was told to wait, but quickly the clerk was back and said Mr. Doyle would see her immediately. She was ushered to the office and found Doyle standing to receive her. That was a surprise, but a pleasant one. "Mr. Doyle, I work with a friend of Mr. O'Day's, who is known as Lady B. Do you understand who I am?"

"I do know who you are and I am aware of Mr. O'Day's interest in Lady B. Mr. O'Day is not here."

"I understand, and that is what I have come to talk about with you. Are you aware that Mr. O'Day has left the city with Lady B?"

"My God! With Lady B? This is the answer! I was not aware of it. Are you sure of this?"

"I am sure. I was there when he came for her. I saw them leave. They left quickly and did not tell me where they would be going, and that is what I wish to ask you. Do you know where they have gone?"

Doyle hesitated, but he answered her, "I know only that Mr. O'Day ordered his brig *Ann Elizabeth* to be made ready to cast off and that he did board the *Ann Elizabeth* with a woman in his company. The ship left, but I do not know the destination. It is a ship that could go anywhere in the world." Clara felt a surge of relief. Doyle did not know what had happened and he was not hostile. Doyle wanted to know what she knew. She was going to be able to make her story work.

"Mr. Doyle, I think we must work together to serve the interests of our employers. It may be that you know how partial Mr. O'Day has been to Lady B. She is a woman of great beauty and accomplishment. She can charm any man she meets, and she does. That is her business—as you know. I have not only seen Mr. O'Day's partiality to her, I have also witnessed, and she has told me of, her deep respect for him and in fact her love for him."

"Love, you say? Is there love in her business?"

"There is no love in the business. I know what you think: how could a courtesan fall in love? But even though we sell ourselves, we do not sell our hearts, and we do have hearts. We can love, and she loves him—and he loves her. That is why he came to take her away. He is so besotted with her that he had to have her. He could not stand the thought of not having her as his own, but he also could not bring himself to marry a woman—of her type—for all to see, so the solution he decided upon was to take her away, marry her , and start their lives anew, away from prying eyes and insulting tongues."

Doyle was excited. He had felt that O'Day's departure was caused by some matter of great depth and importance—more important, and more dangerous for all concerned than an elopement, but when Clara presented this possibility, he realized it could work. "My God! It is incredible, but nevertheless, what you say makes sense. I know that he visited her two or three times each week. That is an inordinate amount of time to spend with a woman who is nothing more than a paid pleasure partner." He hastily added, "I mean no disrespect." Clara nodded and Doyle went on, "He ordered his trunks taken to the ship. He may have enough in cash there for a new start anywhere, but he can also communicate with me to request money as he needs it. I can keep the businesses here going and can send him money as he requires. This does seem possible."

"Thanks be to God that he has planned so well. We must counsel together to determine how to reveal this situation. It is important for them and for your businesses and for mine as well."

"Yes, we must." Doyle was emphatic and Clara was ecstatic. It was working just as she had hoped. What could have been a disaster that would have brought her down to nothing was working out as a partnership that would serve everyone. She wanted to cry, but she didn't. Clara and Doyle agreed on a plan to keep silent for a few days unless their hand was forced in some way and then let the story out to a few selected people who, of course, would spread it everywhere. When any official notice was paid and Doyle was questioned he would have O'Day's power of attorney, one that he would prepare and sign himself, ready to show anyone who asked. He would also prepare a similar document for Clara with a forgery of Bea's signature that he would create from a copy of Bea's signature that Clara would furnish. This was nothing new to Doyle. He had forged many documents using Michael O'Day's signature and others as well. O'Day had not been above bending the law when absolutely necessary and Doyle was his trusted accomplice in all business transactions. Doyle could keep the businesses going and Clara felt she could keep Lady B's establishment going as well, and working together they would be stronger than working separately.

Clara left delighted with her day's work, but she had more work to do. As she was driven back to the house, she began to plan. The only other people who realized that what had happened was not the simple elopement of a besotted lover and the object of his affection were the maid, Laura Doss, and Lady Conconnon. Laura would be easy to deal with. Clara now had almost complete control over Laura's life; she was the one who could ensure that Laura kept her relatively easy and very fulfilling job, or she could throw Laura out onto the street with nothing and Laura's only option would be to work in one of the rough brothels in the city or offer herself on the streets. It would only take a few words to ensure that Laura stayed quiet and Clara would take care of that before the day was over.

Lady Conconnon was another matter. Clara had no control over her, but Clara had an idea that she was sure would gain her the control she must have. Until yesterday Lady Conconnon had been absolutely thrilled to have B and Clara to help her realize her sexual dreams and now that B was gone, Clara was all Lady Conconnon had left. Clara knew from much pillow talk that Lady C, as she now started to think of her, had been at loss for years to find the woman of her dreams and when the word drifted to her about B she made contact as soon as she could and was ecstatic when she found what she had sought for so long. Up until now, the relationship, while highly satisfying, had been a commercial arrangement, but Clara was going to change that. She was going to fall in love with Lady C. It would be natural; she had lost Bea, the love of her life, and she would be desperate to have someone else to fill that role, even if incompletely. Lady C would understand and would be flattered when Clara made it clear to her that she had fallen in love with her. Clara would also make it clear that while she might take money from others, she wanted none from Lady C, only her love.

It would be a simple matter to make Lady C fall in love with her. Clara knew she had all the wiles and the charms needed to make it happen. She had done it with Bea, hadn't she? But she couldn't wait until Lady C's next scheduled visit on Friday. She had to bring Lady Conconnon under control as soon as possible so she would stay quiet about the real nature of the situation. She would send a message and arrange a meeting somewhere today.

All the pieces were coming together so beautifully. Only five years ago she had been a lady's maid, in service with nothing to look forward to in life but continuing to serve her lady until one or the other died. It was better than many of the alternatives for her life, but it was little enough. But now, now, she was the owner, at least according to the piece of paper she was to get from Doyle, of the most elegant brothel in Ireland's second city and she probably was going to become the petted darling of the wife of a knight. Even two days ago she had never dreamed that such a thing might be possible, but here it was. She was sure it would work. If Bea came back she would work out a reasonable agreement with her about ownership—and about who owned Lady C. And if Bea did not come back, Clara was set up for life.

Thomas Doyle was just as relieved as Clara. He feared the constables. Something was wrong or they would not have been after O'Day, but the elopement with Lady B, who was just as well known to the constables as was Michael O'Day, may have been the true reason why O'Day had left. In any event, it was a wonderful coincidence and he could use it to either satisfy the constabulary or, at the very least, to confuse the situation. A disaster for O'Day was a disaster for him and he wanted to ward off disaster at any cost. He realized he should get this information to the Chief Constable who could check it with Clara. This was good. Clara clearly knew nothing else about O'Day's activities so she could not harm the situation, whatever it was; Clara could only be a help. Doyle set about the tasks he needed to take care of.

CHAPTER 44

In the late afternoon of the 30th Captain Ievers returned to his home after a day of scouring the countryside. He was pleased to learn that his good wife, as he called her, had made arrangements for all of the troops to be quartered about the farm and that Massengill was well settled in the mansion. He went into the library where Massengill met him with a piece of paper in his hand. Massengill flourished it and said, "My list."

"Excellent, Captain. I have much good to tell you."

"Speak, I am all ears."

"First, I can say that the constables are keeping watch for you. They do not know where you are so they are watching the roads into Croome Court. Next, I can tell you that two of Berrigan's men have been in the village asking about you. They were none too subtle so it is clear that Berrigan is on the hunt for you. We must keep his men away from you; it is good that you came here early and have not strayed."

"That is as we have expected. It is good that you convinced me to stay hidden. None has any idea that I am here?"

"I think not. We are safe for now."

"Capital. What news of your labors?"

"Good news. I have two recruits from the farmers at North Hall. They are anxious to do anything to help rescue Lady Amanda, and they are good men. Both come with long guns, and as much ball and powder as they can round up. They are warned to be quiet about what they are doing. They will come here to stay tomorrow morning. Next, I have an unexpected recruit—two of them. James Walsh met me on the road and asked my business. I was careful with him, but soon realized that he was on our side. He is besotted with Lady Amanda. That has always been clear in spite of all his dalliances, and there have been a number. We have long known that he has been much taken with his brother's widow, and he begged me to help him find her. I have let him on our plan and he, too, will be here tomorrow along with his farmer Kennedy. He will bring a fair armory, all the weapons, shot, and powder he and Kennedy can raise on their place.

"Lastly, I went to see Atwood Corry at Corry Hall. Atwood is at an age that he cannot join a fight, but I knew he could be trusted to be on our side, and so it proved to be. He has rounded up two of his farmers, Lynch and Murray, who will serve with us. They, too, will arrive in the morning with all the weapons, shot, and powder they can round up at Corry Hall."

Massengill thought about what he had heard. "Capital work, Captain. If my arithmetic is right we now have eighteen men, all armed, and some extra weapons beside. Ten of them are prime, tried fighting men and the others are men we can work with and can trust."

"I think that is the right arithmetic and the right analysis of our forces. I think we can do our work with this many men, but it would be good to have more if they can be found. Do you agree?"

"I do. Think on where we might find more men. In addition, what we still need is training and more shot and powder. I fear we may use a lot."

"You can begin training them tomorrow when all are arrived and I will go out in search of more shot and powder. I fear it may be difficult to find what we need and get it here without arousing suspicion, but I will do it somehow."

Massengill was well pleased. "Good. I will set the men who are fighters to training those who are not. We will need to fire the weapons, so we will use powder and shot, making your work tomorrow all the more important. We should plan to execute our mission the day after tomorrow."

"Agreed," said Captain Ievers. And they felt the need to shake hands to seal this agreement that promised to send men into danger, and perhaps to death.

CHAPTER 45

The afternoon coach on the 31st brought a second message from the Dublin Constabulary. They had interviewed the girls at the brothel and had heard similar stories from all the girls, stories that would be of interest to the constables in Croome Court. The letter from the Dublin Constabulary read as follows:

Gentlemen:

We have examined the situation of the brothel on Fenton Lane that you have brought to our attention and have examined the girls who work there. Our findings are as follows: The girls have been recruited, mostly in villages and small towns, with the understanding that they were to go to Dublin to take jobs in service in the homes of well to do families. They were to work as parlor maids or cook's helpers, but would have the opportunity to rise to positions such as lady's maid, assistant cook, or even cook or housekeeper if they did well and invested the necessary years. The girls were placed on coaches by their recruiters, who tended to be men of moderate, but acceptable, standing in their communities. Their parents knew all and approved.

When the girls arrived in Dublin they were taken to a respectable rooming house where they would meet two or three other girls on the same errand, and were told they would be given instructions while there and would soon be taken to the homes where they would work. While they were waiting, each girl was instructed to write six letters home to let their parents know they were well and what they were doing. They would write the letters now and post them from time to time when they thought it appropriate—that way they would not have to take time off from their work later on to write the letters. Some sample letters, numbered 1 through 6, were available so the girls could see what their parents might want to know, and for the most part they simply copied the letters with a few changes that fit their situation and that were appropriate to the recipients.

The girls would spend half the morning writing and then would have a tea break and would be given instruction in domestic duties by a woman who acted as their guide in all that they were doing. After lunch they would write again for half the afternoon and then have tea and another instruction period followed by dinner. The food was decent and the accommodation was relatively clean and satisfactory. For the girls who either could not write at all or whose ability was so limited they were afraid to try the letters, there was help. It came either from other girls who were good hands or from their helpful lady guide. These letters would be signed by the girl for whom it was written, sometimes with the notation that her ideas had been copied out by another so they could be more easily read.

After two days the letter writing was completed and the instructions they had received made them feel quite accomplished and ready to start their work. They were told that on the morning of the next day each would be taken to their work, and the next morning after breakfast all had their belongings packed and were ready to go. Each girl was taken separately. They were driven to another place in the city, they knew not where it was, but there seemed to be several such places because the girls did not see each other again on this day—nor did they hear each other.

Upon arrival at the new address the girls were told to put their things, including their letters, on a convenient table and were ushered into another room. Here everything changed and the horror of what they were in for began. There would usually be three or four men in the room. The door would be closed behind them and they would be surrounded. First it was pawing and fondling, then they were stripped and raped—on the floor. This went on for half the day with each man taking a turn two or even three times over the hours. Some of the girls were gagged, some had their hands tied, most were slapped or hit repeatedly to quiet them or make them compliant. There was no escape. There was no help. During the ordeal they were told that their dream of a position in service was just that; the reality was that they were going to work in a brothel until they were dead or so worn or diseased that they were useless.

The blows to their bodies and their wills were crushing and most of the girls were broken, realizing that they were ruined, by the mid day. Those were ready to do what they were told, but others held out, some for more than a day before they gave in. All were made to understand that henceforth they would live in the brothel and that they would be watched all the time. They could not escape, and even if they did they could never go home because they were now such damaged goods that they would never be accepted by their families or any man they might hope to marry. Their other alternative would be to walk the streets of Dublin, offering themselves there. The brothel was a far superior alternative; at least there they would have a level of protection and a place to stay. They were, after all, valuable property for the brothel owner, who would take care of them in a fashion.

On occasion a girl would escape, almost always to be found and returned having suffered a beating that was so shocking that there would be no other escape tries for a long time thereafter. After a time, most of the girls, like Ailis Bannon, came to believe that there was truly no way out and that they might as well embrace their situation and live with it. When a girl was deemed to have reached this point in her "development" she was allowed to leave the brothel on occasion. She would be back.

The friendly lady guide, who knew where each girl had come from, kept the letters and sent them off with a longer and longer interval between each one. The letters would keep coming to their families for about three years, during which time the families had become satisfied with their daughters' situations and the wait between letters would stretch on so long that there would finally be no sense of danger when no letter arrived, only the feeling that she had moved on beyond her family back in the village. If any relatives ever got to Dublin, the address at which they thought their daughter would be found proved to be in error. The homeowner was sorry, there must have been a mistake; they could not help. Thus the procurers in the villages were protected and the girls' families were lulled.

We remain, yours most respectfully,
(signed) A. Alwyn, Chief Constable

This information made it easy to see how John Barber had thrived and how the Seymours—for now there seemed no doubt of their complicity—had escaped notice; the only question being whether the Seymours were the kingpins of the whole system or whether they occupied a somewhat lower rank in the enterprise. The system was devilishly devised and horribly effective.

"So where does this information leave us, Constable Supervisor?" asked Quirke.

"I think we can be sure that the murders of the Seymours and Barber were related, and we know why they were killed and who killed them, so that matter is closed. That case is solved, but we still do not know why the other crimes happened and at this time we have no reason to believe they were related to the Seymour killings. It appears that the best information we have on the other crimes is Berrigan's information that something outside the law is happening at Croome Forest and that Massengill is behind it. We must find Massengill and continue to allow him to roam freely and to watch him. We can hope that the information we receive from Belfast will shed much additional light on the situation."

CHAPTER 46

On the night of the 31st all continued as well at Lady B's as it had been on the 29th and 30th. Clara was greatly relieved and was actually beginning to relax. The fake transition was difficult enough, but doing it without four of her men had made the situation very tense, and every day without incident was a weight off Clara's shoulders. Near four AM, when the House had closed and all was secure, she left and was driven home by the House's driver. He dropped her at the door of the home and watched as she entered. She closed the door behind her and he drove off. Clara called, "Laura, I 'm here," and walked into the parlor where Laura would bring her a cup of tea and some biscuits before bed.

Everything fell apart when she opened the parlor door. There was no tea and there were no biscuits, but Laura was there, gagged and tied to an armchair. Her eyes were wide open and swimming with fear. Two men sat near her, one on the settee and one on a chair. They were heavy built men, both with short brown hair and rough clothes, and they looks so much alike that it would be easy to believe they were brothers. "Ah, Madame Clara, you have returned to our little party. Do not try to leave. As you can see, we have made your maid comfortable. We need to talk with you, so let us go up the stairs. The young lady will be happy to wait here for us."

Clara was struck dumb. Of all the problems she had envisioned, this was not one. Was it robbery? Before she could get her wits about her the two men were up, each grabbed one of her arms, they spun her around and marched her out of the room and up the steps. By the time they were on the stairs she was able to speak, "What is this? What do you want? If it is money, it can be had."

"We will speak to you." They went into the first door they came to, which was the bedroom she had shared with Bea. One of the men gave her a hard slap, pushed her into a chair and said, "Now we will talk. You and that whore of yours, Lady B, have caused a disaster. You know that Michael O'Day has fled Ireland and that your whore is with him?"

"Yes, I know what happened, but I had nothing to do with their affair. They are lovers; they eloped. I don't know where they have gone or why, except for love. Please believe me, I promise it."

"O'Day did not leave for love of a whore. He's not such a fool. He left because his life was forfeit if he stayed. Your Lady B betrayed him, and because she betrayed him he is gone and a great movement is ruined. Men will die, families will be ripped apart, and all because of her. She has got away, but here you are, and as she cannot be made to pay, you will be."

"Please, I will do anything. I will pay you what you want."

"Do you know Jimmie Kelley?"

"I know who he is."

"Well, it could be said he has been your competition, but from now he will be the proprietor of Lady B's and you will not be needed."

"That's not right! Lady B has given the House to me! I was not part of what happened! I have no idea what Bea may have done. I am innocent."

"You are not innocent. You sent your men on a certain errand to Croome Court in County Cavan, did you not? We know you did, and that was a move against us. You are not innocent! We work for Jimmie Kelley at his houses and in other affairs he has and you have interfered in those other affairs. In truth, we don't care whether you are innocent or not. He has sent us here to take over Lady B's and that we will do, over your dead body."

"No! You don't mean it. I have done nothing! I didn't know! I will work with you," she begged, horror struck.

"Oh but you have done something missy. You have done too much. You have been a high class whore, but now you are going to be a dead whore." They pulled her up off the bed and stood her up. One of the men took a length of rope from under his coat, expertly flung a loop of it over Clara's head, held one end and flipped the other to his companion.

Clara screamed, "God no!", but it was no use. They charged away from her in opposite directions and when the rope came tight Clara's throat was crushed; she made a gasping sound that was followed instantly by a loud crack as her neck was broken. They dropped her to the floor. The rope man retrieved his length of rope and remarked, "Fine that she called upon the Lord in her last words. Do you think it will be enough to get a whore past Saint Peter?"

"Only if she has rendered some fine service over the years to the Fathers at the Cathedral, or mayhap to the Bishop himself. I doubt she has done sufficient. I say she burns." They went down stairs and into the parlor. Rope Man went in first, his face wreathed in a broad smile. "Now then, lass, we can let you go." Laura was so relieved she could hardly move. They took off her gag, untied her, and helped her to her feet. She was trembling. Rope Man held her hands and continued to beam the smile at her. Laura could feel life flowing back into her. It was going to be all right, they were going to let her go. She was going to live. The other man stepped behind her, grabbed her by the hair and yanked her head back so hard and so quickly that her neck broke before she had time to realize that she was being murdered. They dropped her body to the floor. There was no blood so the fine Axminster carpet onto which she fell suffered not at all. "Shame of a waste. A right pert piece, if I do say so myself. Still nice and warm and soft."

"True, but I'm put off from screwing a girl whose head is at such an angle to her body. It's truly off-puttin'."

"Oh, off-puttin' it is, if you say."

"I do say. Anyhow, we need to leave—now. Let us go out the back. We'll leave the front door unlocked so the plod can get in easily if they ever find out something has happened here. It's a good night's work for Jimmie Kelley." They left an elegant home, beautifully furnished, neat and polished. The only jarring note was the two dead women. Rope man and his companion slipped out the back door into the dying night, closing the door carefully after themselves.

CHAPTER 47

On the morning of the 31st Captain Ievers left to search for more shot and ball. He was expected back in the late afternoon, but by nine AM he was back. "Captain Massengill, I have been told that there are four rough looking men, strangers, at the inn asking for you."

"Do you know anything about them?"

"Only that they say they were sent from Belfast by 'Miss Clara' and told to find you and help you protect Lady Amanda."

"Most curious. The woman I was visited by and who warned me Lady Amanda was in danger was from Belfast and I can tell you that she was Lady Amanda's sister-in-law, Lady Beatrice Bullen. She begged me not to reveal her name, and I ask you to keep it close, but there may be some connection with Miss Clara."

Ievers knew, "Yes! Lady Beatrice's ladies maid was named Clara. It could be the same woman."

"Four rough men could be of real help to us. I think we should find out who they are and whether they are truly on the side of Lady Amanda. But how? We cannot risk being seen with them. We must find a way to get them here so we can examine them."

"Let me think on it." Captain Ievers sat for only a moment and then said, "I have it. James Walsh. No one knows he is in with us and everyone knows that he is Lady Amanda's closest kin and virtually her lover. No one would be more likely to take them in without suspicion, and he could spirit them here."

"Excellent."

"I will go back out and try to find him along the road between here and the Walsh place. He can then go into the village, say he had heard of them and take the men to Green Fields where they can be hidden in a farm wagon and brought here. If they are kept under cover in the wagon, which will be needful, they will not know where they are and they can be taken away if they are not to our liking."

"A perfect plan, Captain. Perfect."

"I will launch it now." And he was gone. Later that morning the farmers from North Hall arrived and a wagon driven by Walsh's farmer, Kennedy, arrived. It carried a load of arms, shot, and powder as well. By noon the two farmers from Corry Hall had arrived with their weapons and ammunition. In mid afternoon, Milton Ievers was still not back but James Walsh arrived driving a wagon that appeared to be filled with potted plants that, if he were asked, he was ready to say he was donating from his garden to Mrs. Ievers. It turned out that he had not been questioned along the way and had had no reason to tell that story. The four men who were under a tarpaulin in the wagon were not noticed by anyone.

When Massengill heard of their arrival he came out and Walsh presented them, "Captain Massengill, these are the men who were at the inn seeking for you. I have examined them closely and I believe they might be of use to us, so here they are. You may hear their story and if it don't suit, they can be ejected."

"Very good, James. Many thanks for this work and for joining us. You add much to us. Men, your story."

"Sar, I am Henry Rider, and these men with me is Niall O'Malley, Jarrod Whaley, and Padraig White. We all works for Lady B and her accompaniment, Miss Clara, who is lately now in charge. You may not know that Lady B keeps a house—it could be called a house of pleasure—in Belfast. She caters to the higher of society and has girls of the top class. We is in the line of door keepers, keepers of the peace, assistants to customers which has a need for help getting home after an evening, and any work what Lady B, or now Miss Clara, calls us out to do. We are men who can fight, sar, and we are looking to fight on your behalf. Miss Clara has told us that a lady most dear to her and Lady B, the Lady Amanda Walsh, has befallen with difficult times and needs help. We be here to help at your command, sar, as she has ordered."

"Most interesting." Massengill described Lady Beatrice as he remembered her appearance from years ago and asked if Lady B fit this description. He was told that she did. He asked if Lady B had made a trip recently and he was told that, "she has done made two trips near back to back. First she went off in a coach and stayed for two days and then, hardly was she back when she run off and eloped with Mr. Michael O'Day."

"O'Day, you say?"

"Yes sar, Mr. Michael O'Day was one of the loyal customers of our house and favored totally Lady B herself. Mr. O'Day is a gentleman of business in Belfast, a rich man. He has fallen in love with Lady B, and she with him, and they has eloped on a ship to start a new life. Very romantic, sar." Massengill, Walsh, and Ievers exchanged glances.

"Very good, men. I will have a talk with Captain Ievers and Mr. Walsh and we will tell you how you can be of service to us. You may wait here." The three went into the house, and Massengill turned to Ievers and Walsh, "Gentlemen, the man Michael O'Day that they name is the very man I found had known about the fire at North Hall so soon after it happened. His connection in Croome Court may be with the perpetrators. These men may mean us harm."

"It is possible", said Walsh, "but I know that the name of the woman who sent them, Clara, is the name of the ladies maid of Lady Beatrice Bullen, and Lady Beatrice means Lady Amanda no harm. Of that you can be sure."

"Well said," agreed Massengill, "and I am sure that the unknown woman who gave me the information about O'Day was actually Lady Beatrice. Upon consideration, I believe you are right and these men are truly on our side. Let us take them in to our service, but I will have Otis keep a close watch on them. He will ferret out any disloyalty."

"Good. We'll do it. But, Captain", said Milton Ievers, hardly able to contain himself, "this is the juiciest news ever I have had! William Bullen's wife run off to Belfast to become the madam of a brothel! Wild beyond belief! I can see why the man shot himself. This is too much!"

"Good God yes," said Walsh, "It is hard to imagine."

"It is beyond belief, but it must be true. These men are simple fellows who would never make up such a story, nor is there any reason they should concoct such. We will believe it, but for the sake of Lady Amanda, who must not know this story herself, and for young Henry, we will keep it quiet. Captain," said Massengill, "you must not even tell Madam Ievers."

"Oh, God no. My good lady least of all, she would leak it like a sieve. You are right. We must keep it quiet."

"Otis, tell the men they are enlisted and find them accommodation. Tell them that on pain of dismissal or worse they are to keep the story they have told us close. No one is to hear it. Otis, your mouth will be shut about this."

"Aye, cap'm."

"Now we are twenty-two, a number I think will be sufficient. We have done some training today and tomorrow we will continue, with the new men as well. On the day after we will go."

CHAPTER 48

On the morning after Clara and Laura were murdered, Jimmie Kelley continued to consolidate his position in Belfast. In Kelley's string of brothels that catered to the lower class of clients very few of his girls were still girls. Most had been in the trade for too many years, even though very few of them were older than thirty years of age. They were worn, not from years, but from their trade, and most were only the shell of what they had been when they were attractive, but they were female and where they worked that was what counted.

Jimmy had been in businesses of one kind or another in Belfast for almost thirty years. His businesses were all outside of respectability and outside the law, and his sex trade businesses all depended on the oppression and fleecing of the poor. He never took much, but he took what little he could get time after time after time and made good money doing it. He had long wanted to upgrade his activities, to be able to work with a clientele that had real money and to get his hands on that money in large amounts. It not only would be remunerative, it would be a source of respect and it would be a stepping stone to more and more of the same.

Jimmie knew why Michael O'Day and Lady B had fled. He knew O'Day well, and had had a long and close association with him, an association that, unfortunately for Jimmie, had never included being welcomed into any of O'Day's many legitimate businesses. Jimmie and O'Day were linked in a patriotic endeavor that included an important project in the village of Croome Court in County Cavan, and when the request had come from the Croome Court constabulary for information about Michael O'Day and his activities in Cavan, Jimmie had been told of the inquiry and the constables move to take O'Day for questioning almost as soon as O'Day, himself, had found out about it. . Jimmie had been told about O'Day merely as a courtesy from an informant in the constabulary who was one of the large number of paid contacts Kelley had in that organization.

Kelley's name had not been mentioned in connection with Cavan, so for now at least, he was in the clear. He did not know what the constables knew about O'Day's connection in County Cavan, but he did know that if their knowledge went deep enough O'Day faced disaster. O'Day had known the same, and rather than run the risk of assuming the constabulary knew so little that he would get off without a scratch and perhaps even be able to have the constables called on the carpet, only to find out when tried his move that he had been wrong and he was trapped, he had decided the worst was known and he had fled. That, of course, was only going to make whatever matter there was against him look all the worse. He was gone for good and Lady B was gone with him.

Lady B had had a phenomenal rise in Belfast's netherworld, a rise that both angered Kelley and made him jealous of her. He had never had the polish to pull off what Bea had pulled off, but he did think that now that her house was up and running so successfully, he would be able to carry it on without her. Getting rid of her earlier would have been easy enough for Kelley, but the problem with this was that she was a favorite of O'Day, and Kelley knew he dared not risk any move as long as O'Day was a regular at Lady B's and was so enamored of B herself. But now, with the two of them gone, that was all taken care of and the only thing of any importance that had stood between him and taking over Lady B's operation was her assistant, confidant, and bed mate, Clara Rohan. Jimmie had made quick work of Clara and now, on the first of September in the year 1814, he was going to march into Lady B's house, along with some of his rough boys, assemble the staff, and announce that there was a new owner and that he was now in charge. Clara, who had been given ownership by Lady B and who had recently suffered a most unfortunate accident which they would soon read about in the newspaper, had seen fit to pass that ownership on to him. A woman of Lady B's standing would be taking over the day to day operation of the house. He hoped none of the loyal staff would have any problem with this, but if anyone had a question or a problem they should simply come to him to discuss it. One of his boys would be glad to make an appointment with him for anyone with a grievance. He was sure they would be able to work it out.

Even though that meeting had gone smoothly, there still was the problem of finding a woman of Lady B's standing. Jimmie had to have a woman with a veneer of class and beauty to run the place and none of the women who worked for him had what it would take. He had to find someone, and he thought he knew the way to do it. He had drug clients among the upper class and one of those was a woman who, while she would never have worked at such a place, had firsthand knowledge of women who sold themselves. His mark was Lady Conconnon, elegant in the extreme, unhappily married and a user first of laudanum and then opium itself to dull the days. During the last year Lady Conconnon had reduced her drug purchases from Jimmie because she had discovered a new drug, Lady B and Clara. B's sudden departure and Clara's death would do two things, strike fear into Lady Conconnon and bring her back to opium. Both would play nicely into Jimmie's hands. Lady C would know someone who for enough money, and there would be money enough, would take on the job at Jimmie's new house of pleasure. The woman she would come up with would not be an aristocrat, not even one fallen on hard times, but would be one close to the upper class, a lady's maid disgraced, a governess who had been impregnated by the master, perhaps even a senior parlor maid who had done wrong. These women would have the polish he needed, and they would need a place. They were out there, and Lady C would know of one, if not several. Gossip about these happenings below stairs flowed through the parlors upstairs just as it did through the servants' halls downstairs. One woman was all he needed, and through Lady C he was sure he could find her. Everything seemed to Jimmie Kelley to be falling into place perfectly.

CHAPTER 49

Berrigan's men were hard at work. Two wagons, each with a crew of four men, were at barns on the place loading long guns out of hay lofts and storage areas onto the wagons. Each wagon could carry about forty guns along with its crew and it was taking about an hour to load, around thirty minutes for the drive, another three quarters of an hour for unloading on the pier and another half hour ride back to the barn. This was two hours and forty-five minutes per load. It was going to take about twenty loads, or ten loads per wagon to get all the guns to the waterfront, so if each crew worked twelve hours a day they could each carry four loads and have some time to eat meals and then collapse into bed for a much needed sleep. This meant it would take about two and one-half days to get all the guns on the barge. When the loading of the swords, pistols, and belts was added in, it came to close to three days, just as Jonas Smith had estimated.

This still left the powder to load. The six men on the pier could get a wagon load of long guns from the pier to the barge in less time than it took for another wagon to appear so they had some time to load powder barrels from the waterfront warehouse onto the barge between wagon loads. They might get all the long guns, which were the most valuable items, onto the barge, but unless they had more than three days they were not going to get everything out, and if they had less than three days they would be lucky to escape with the bulk of their stash. Since no one, including the constabulary, could find Massengill, there appeared to be nothing else they could do in Croome Court to slow down whatever attack was coming, so their only option was to work as hard as they could and pray that there would be time.

While Berrigan's men were doing their best, Massengill's men were doing their best as well. They were divided into three groups. Bowyer, Massengill's writer, and Cheshire, his valet, were men who had seen much fighting at sea and were hardened to it, but they were not fighters themselves. During combat at sea their role had been to help the ship's Doctor tend to the wounded, so for the action at Croome Forest they were to have a special and very important job: they would be the powder monkeys. No fighting man would be able to carry with him all the balls and powder that he would need if the fighting was as prolonged as Massengill expected it would be, so Bowyer and Cheshire were assigned to a middling sized wagon that would be pulled by two horses. They were spending their time dividing the balls into groups of different calibers, placing them in wooden boxes that had been taken from the hen house, labeling the boxes as to caliber and placing all neatly in the wagon bed in order of caliber. The two were also filling powder flasks and laying them out for each shooter to pick up his own flasks and were dividing the rest of the powder into flask-sized cloth bags that they tied with a string and laid out to carry to shooters as they were needed. This was a full day's work and went on into the second day.

When they had finished, Massengill inspected the powder wagon. There was fully enough powder, but he was concerned that there might not be enough balls of some calibers. It had proven too dangerous for Captain Ievers to be scouring the whole neighborhood for powder and ball because someone would have gotten the drift of what was happening and the constables would have been told—or Berrigan's men would have been told. After giving up on getting ammunition in the neighborhood, Ievers had gone back to scour North Hall, Corry Hall and Green Fields for every scrap of powder and every ball that could be found. There was nothing else to be done, so they had to go with what they had got.

The other men had been divided into two groups of ten each. There were eight hardened fighting men and four had been assigned to each group. Massengill, Seargent Watterson and two of Massengill's boat crew were assigned to one, Captain Ievers, Massengill's coxswain, and the other two of Massengill's boat crew to the other. Each group was divided into two squads consisting of two battle- seasoned men and three volunteers. The seasoned men were talking the non-warriors through what they could expect during the coming fight and coaching them on how to follow orders and to react to the combat situation. All were good shots, so it was decided not to waste precious ammunition by any practice shooting. This would also remove the risk of a traveler on the road hearing the firing and putting two and two together to make a warning to the constables that something was going on.

A hay wagon was got for each group. The wagons were large enough to hold all of the men and their weapons and they had the makings of conveyances that would be as safe as possible. The wagons had high sides to hold large loads of hay, but the sides were an open framework and this would not do. Four of Captain Ievers' farm hands who were not going to fight were set to work sawing thick boards and nailing them into place to close up the gaps in the sides and ends of the wagons. This would allow the men to be hidden from view, under a topping of hay, while they were moving from Ievers Court to the village gate of Croome Forest, and the solid sides would provide some protection from gunfire if the men were surprised by hidden gunmen as they were moving through Croome Forest. The wagons could not provide perfect cover, however, because once the fight was joined, there might be some cover while behind the wagons but most of the time the fighters would be out of the wagons, on the move, and exposed to fire.

By the end of the day Both Massengill and Ievers felt their men were as ready as they were going to be. All had been given the opportunity to back out of the fighting, but none had backed out and most had expressed outrage that they would even be asked if they wanted to. Everyone set to cleaning his weapon and ensuring that his kit was ready. They were fed a good meal by Mrs. Ievers and her cook and several of the farm wives, and by nine o'clock they were settled in to sleep if they could. Reveille would be at four in the morning. They would have breakfast, load up and head for the village gate of Croome Court which they planned to get to soon after sunrise. Massengill wanted a good long day to get the job done. He also hoped that an early beginning might catch Berrigan's men before they were ready for a fight.

CHAPTER 50

September second gave promise to be dry, just as the past week had been. This was good; Massengill did not want to have to fight in mud. The early morning unfolded as planned and by a quarter after the hour of five each man was ready, had his canteen of water, and there was a cask of water in each wagon along with a batch of potato cakes and ample butter. Each wagon was equipped with two pickaxes, two heavy hammers, a wrecking bar and a bull point. Each of the two large wagons had an extra horse tethered behind it. All was ready. The men got aboard and they moved onto the road, two hay wagons that seemed to be loaded with hay and a smaller wagon with two men up carrying a load that was covered by a tarp. For this part of the journey all of the men in sight were farmers from Ievers Court and Corry Hall, men who might be expected to be driving wagons into the village in the early morning. The ride into the village took about forty-five minutes so at six AM they were approaching the village gate of Croome Forest, just as scheduled, and so far all was well.

As they entered the village Sergeant Watterson, who was driving the first wagon, began to tell the hidden Massengill in a low, calm voice as if he were talking to the man seated next to him, what village landmarks they were passing. Tension was rising because the first test was coming soon: would they get through the gate without a fight? When they were about twenty yards from the gate, a voice from somewhere north of the gate yelled out, "Wagons approaching the gate!" It was one of the constables. So sure were they that Massengill was the perpetrator and Berrigan was the innocent victim that they were keeping a day and night watch on the gate to make sure Massengill did not attack Berrigan, and now they were afraid it was happening.

The call elicited a jumble of cries and questions from the area of the constable's office and it called to action Berrigan's two guards at the gate lodge. They came out with pistols at the ready. "Now," shouted Watterson in the agreed upon signal for action. Hay flew and soon there were twenty men visible in the wagons with guns everywhere. The two gate guards fired their pistols and were answered with a fusillade of balls. Both were hit and down. No one on the wagons was hit. Two men were out of the wagons, one with a sledge hammer and the other with a bull point. They went to the gate ready to smash the lock, but the tools were not needed; the gate wasn't locked. They opened the gates, the wagons moved ahead and the two jumped aboard their wagon as it passed. At that moment gunfire sounded from up the High Street. The constables were firing on the wagons.

"Down, men! Move it! Move it!" shouted Massengill and they picked up speed until the horses were going as fast as they could. Shots continued to ring out behind them, but there were no real marksmen among the constables and they were too far away for accuracy so the only hit was to part of the frame of the second wagon. They kept going at speed and within a minute were around a bend and had trees between them and the gate.

The constables and their volunteers were all tumbling out of the constable's office and pounding down the street to the gate. By the time they got there the wagons were rounding the bend and going out of sight. There was no catching them on foot, so everyone clustered around the two guards. One was killed, but the other was struck in the leg and, although in great pain, was very much alive and moaning. "You two," yelled the Constable Supervisor, "Bring the litter from the office and take this man to the apothecary. Send for the doctor! They have got in, but the bastards won't get out. We are going to guard this gate with our lives. I want six men here. Quirke, organize it and meet me back at the office." With that he left for the office and the constables settled into a defensive position. The Constable Supervisor had seen the strength of Massengill's force and he was not about to engage it. They would save the gate and hope that Berrigan had a force inside that was sufficient to stop Massengill.

A quarter of a mile down the drive the horses were slowed to a walk and the attack force proceed on at that pace. There was no wind, and strangely, there was no bird song. The only sounds were the thudding of hooves and the rattle of the wagons. It was an eerie stillness, as if they were the only ones there, but they knew they were not. Massengill's men had no idea what to expect, nor did they know from what direction the enemy might come. From the gate it was a mile in to the mansion, and the stables, ménage, linen hall, and kitchen garden were all well behind the house, not connected with it as they normally would be. They expected to encounter some force before they got to the house and everyone was at the ready with eyes peeled in all directions.

CHAPTER 51

Berrigan had returned to Croome Forest from his trip to the coast. There was no ship at Ballshannon that could take their cargo, but he had located a warehouse. It was better than nothing, but little better because they were going to be pursued and likely places downstream would eventually be searched. They could only hope the message to O'Day would get through and he would quickly get a ship to the mouth of the Erne. Berrigan's men had continued to load the barge. They worked as long as the men could keep on and he had let them quit as darkness fell and sleep until five in the morning. Berrigan and the two lieutenants had split the night hours between themselves and had kept a watch at a point about one hundred yards west of the intersection at which the road to the waterfront met the main drive to the house. It was this intersection that the Massengill force was now approaching.

None of the attackers had good knowledge of the Croome Forest estate. Walsh and Captain Ievers had both been to social events at the mansion, but had never explored the entire property. Massengill had visited as a boy, but his visits were limited to the mansion and the nearby ménage, and had been more than twenty years before. None of the others had ever been on the estate, so given their lack of knowledge they had decided to take the right fork at the intersection and head for the mansion.

Terrance O'Sullivan, Berrigan's most vicious lieutenant, had the watch at the intersection and he heard the gunfire at the gate. He knew trouble had arrived and he mounted his horse but waited to see what force was coming against them. He saw the two large wagons followed by a smaller wagon as they headed toward the intersection and he turned his horse to the west and started at a gallop for the waterfront, but before he did so he made a mistake. O'Sullivan had a bloodthirsty nature and he couldn't resist firing a shot at the attacking force. From a hundred yards away the shot did no harm, but it did alert the Massengill force as to the location of the enemy. If O'Sullivan had not fired his shot and had kept quiet, the attackers might have missed seeing him and would have continued toward the mansion where they had expected to be confronted. Instead, following the direction from which the shot had come, they turned toward the waterfront.

The waterfront was a mile down the road and a man on horseback at a full out gallop could cover the distance far more quickly than heavily loaded wagons so O'Sullivan was able to raise the alarm and get Berrigan's force on a defensive line well before the attackers arrived, but if he had not fired the shot they would have had a half hour or more of additional time to get ready. As it was, they had plenty of weapons and ammunition so that was not a problem but they were torn between forming a good defensive position and continuing to load the barge. They were hampered by the fact that they could not get word to the two loading parties at the barns so those men could come back to the waterfront to add to the defending force. The best they could do was fall in behind a pile of logs and wait. Of the sixteen men Berrigan and his lieutenants had, two were hors de combat at the gate and both wagon crews of four were already at distant locations loading. This left only nine men to hold off their attackers at the waterfront.

The two wagon crews heard the fusillade of shots at the gate and O'Sullivan's later shot and they knew that the feared attack had begun. The crew that was at the south barn took counsel among themselves and decided that they were too far from the waterfront to get there in time to join a defensive line. They would probably be overwhelmed trying to break through the attackers to get into the waterfront area and there was no use in that. Their best bet, for themselves and for the cause, was to escape. They had a wagon partially loaded with long guns, pistols and shot, all of which would be useful to the cause someday even if Berrigan were overrun, and if they fled they would live to fight another day, so they turned their wagon south and headed for the mill gate of the estate. Outside the gate, they would head south and would make their way to Dublin where they would join their confederates, many of whom were known to be in that area.

The other crew was at a shed to the north and there was no easy way out for them. It may have been this, or it may have been that they were made of sterner stuff, but for whatever reason, they headed for the waterfront where they could join the fight.

The road that Massengill's force was taking from the village gate to the waterfront passed through a wooded area until about fifty yards before the warehouse it then crossed an open field that was used for storage of logs awaiting shipment. There were some logs in the field that could provide cover for the attackers, but Berrigan's force was fortunate that there would not be deep woods as a cover right up to the waterfront. They had more than ten minutes after they took their positions before the wagons arrived at the end of the woods. Given the strength of the attacking force that O'Sullivan had reported, Berrigan felt that escape was their only option. They would have to make the barge ready to leave, hold the attackers off as long as they could, get the barge under way, and hope for a miracle. He sent three men, and Smith as their leader, to hunt up poles they could use to pole the barge and to single up the lines in preparation for a quick getaway. Berrigan and the other four were behind a pile of logs, waiting.

As his force approached the end of the woods, Massengill called a halt. He felt there was no hurry and he wanted time to survey the situation and develop his tactics for the fight. No shots were being fired at them and he could see no one except for a group of men working on a barge that was alongside the pier. It looked as if the waterfront was lightly defended. He and Ievers talked and decided to detail two of their squads, the ones led by themselves, to carry out a frontal assault, moving forward from log pile to log pile; the other two squads would be sent to circle the clearing, staying in the woods until they got to the river front and then attack across the clearing from the north and south. This would put the major force close together in the front and would allow the other two forces to split the enemy fire and confuse the battlefront for Berigan's men.

They briefed the men, and the two flanking forces moved off to take their positions at the north and south ends of the clearing. The signal to begin battle was to be a shot fired by Massengill after the two frontal assault squads had made their run for the first log pile, and had hopefully gotten behind that cover. The circling squads were to be given ten minutes to gain their positions before the starting shot. One man in each squad was assigned to count slowly to six hundred. When he got to that number they should be in position, but they should expect fighting to begin whether they were in position or not. If there was any other gunfire from the enemy, that would become the signal to start the attack.

As it turned out, the battle began, not with firing from the center, but with firing from the north. The north circling squad and Berrigan's wagon crew from the north came together unexpectedly and both sides tumbled into a confused action. Each side had guns loaded and at the ready and when they came upon each other firing began immediately. They were close together, no more than twenty yards apart when they saw each other, so accurate fire was possible. One of the first shots from the wagon crew hit and killed James Walsh, who was in the lead. At almost the same time two men in the wagon crew were hit and were down. The remaining two men in the wagon crew were more exposed on the road than the attackers who were in the woods and they were soon shot down. No one gave up and the only ones captured were two of the wagon crew who were wounded. The Walsh squad determined that their leader was dead and that all the wagon crew was beyond further combat, picked up all the arms, commandeered the wagon and headed for the waterfront.

Everyone else heard the firing from the north and the battle was joined at the front. The Massengill and Ievers squads unloaded a round of fire toward the warehouse and the barge and then began running for the cover of the first pile of logs. Berrigan's crew then opened their fire, having good targets. One shot of that fusillade hit Captain Ievers. He went down, but his men went on to the log pile. All of the rest of the attackers made it to the logs. A brief quiet fell over the battlefield while every shooter reloaded his weapon. There was no continuous roar of fire. There were so few men fighting that a quiet would descend each time the two sides were reloading after a volley and then all would fire again. This gave the battle a statico quality that was strange to the seamen who were used to the nearly continuous roar of cannon and rifle fire during a battle at sea. Massengill yelled, "Sharpshooters, aim for the barge crew," and all of the military men did so. The result was a man down on the barge and a ragged volley of return fire from Berrigan's men. By this time, only about four minutes into the fighting, two things happened, the south squad of attackers was in place and was firing into Berrigan's right flank, and Smith yelled at the top of his lungs, "Casting off!"

Massengill's front line poured another round of shots toward the defenders, whose positions were now known, and after Berrigan's men had unleashed another round at the attackers, Berrigan shouted, "To the barge!" He and his four men headed for the barge, and as they ran Massengill's squads, now joined by the north squad, fired another volley at the defenders, who were now in the open. Two went down but the other three made it to the barge. The barge was cast loose, two men with poles pushed with all they had, and it began to move. Berrigan, and Smith resumed firing at the attackers and Massengill's men concentrated on firing at the men on the barge. Berrigan was hit and fell into the water; the barge crept on without him.

Massengill's men poured in another round of fire and the air was rent by the largest explosion the landsmen had ever heard. The military men knew what had happened, a ball had hit one of the barrels of gunpowder on the barge and it had exploded, causing all the other powder on the barge to explode as well. The area was already wreathed in smoke, but the explosion created a blast of fire and a huge ball of smoke that covered the entire battle area. The heat and force of the blast were felt by all the men on shore and the sound deafened everyone. When the smoke cleared, the barge was nothing more than floating debris and parts of the barge and the men on board were scattered over the entire battle area. The fight was over, less than ten minutes after it began.

CHAPTER 52

In Croome Court the firing at the Croome Forest gate had alerted almost the entire village and people began coming out onto the streets, walking furtively and keeping close to buildings. They wanted to be in on what was happening, but they didn't want to be exposed to gunfire. After a few minutes it became clear that fighting in the village had ended and knots of people began congregating to wait for what would happen next. The next thing that happened was disappointing; there was only the one shot fired by O'Sullivan, and then for a long time there was nothing. The crowd was beginning to get restless and a few drifted away, mostly into the taproom at My Lord's Wood. They could wait in comfort there with a pint and come back out when need be. The Constable Supervisor decided to move all his men to the gate lodges. They brought with them all the weapons they had and all the ammunition they could lay hands on

The silence lasted for almost thirty minutes and then the firing began in earnest. Everyone was back on the streets, keeping a respectful distance from the gate lodge, but hoping to be in on whatever was happening. The constables were beginning to worry. There was a lot of shooting going on in Croome Forest and it might well spill over into the gate lodge area, and if it did they were going to be in the thick of something bigger than they had bargained for or had ever had to face before. Then came the explosion. Even in the village, more than a mile away from the site, the explosion was the most incredible sound anyone present had ever heard. Soon they could see a haze of smoke drifting over the treetops. It was stunning. No one could imagine what had happened and the speculation on what would happen next ran wild. People started to desert the street. But, then, everything went silent again. They were left to wonder.

CHAPTER 53

Some of the men on the battlefield were knocked down by the blast. Every one of them was stunned. Massengill's force spent a minute recovering their wits and then they waited. There was nothing. Not a sound. No breeze brushing the trees, no bird sounds, nothing. It was an unsettling feeling, but gradually it sunk in that every man who had gotten onto the barge was dead and the fight was over. They had won. Massengill hallooed his men together. Eighteen men answered the call. Sergeant Watterson, who had led the north squad, reported that James Walsh had been killed in the first skirmish. There was shock all around. Ievers' farmer, Duffy, who had been in Ievers' squad reported that the Captain was down and Massengill sent him and three other men to search for him. Womack and Lynch of Corry Hall were the other unaccounted for men. The rest of the men were sent to search the battlefield for them.

Within five minutes men were back with Captain Ievers body. He had been shot through the head. Lynch was found with a wound in his arm, something that was not likely to be fatal but that might make him incapable of doing hard farm work. Womack was quickly found as well. He had been shot in the abdomen and was barely conscious, but he was not dead—yet. The searchers also found the two men of Berrigan's who had been shot during the run to the barge and had wounds that they might survive. In only a few minutes more Watterson and his squad came back with the wagon they had captured carrying the body of James Walsh and the wounded and dead men from Berrigan's force. There were two dead from the attacking party and two dead—whose bodies could be identified—from the Berrigan force and six wounded.

The first thought was for the wounded. Wounds were stuffed with rags to stop blood from flowing and they were loaded onto the two large wagons along with the bodies of James Walsh, Captain Ievers, and Berrigan's two dead. Bowyer and Cheshire were put aboard to tend the wounded as best they could and the drivers were told to get to the doctor in the village as quickly as they could. At the last minute, Massengill called to them to have a white shirts ready to wave as they approached the gate. The constabulary would probably be there ready to shoot, and they would be more likely to shoot at Massengill's men than they would to shoot at Berrigan's men. The wagons would need to show themselves surrendering. Hopefully they could explain enough of what had happened to convince the lawmen to let them out without a fight.

The rest of the men still had business to tend to. Lady Amanda had not been found. There were no prisoners who had not been wounded and the wounded were gone, so there was no one to question. They would have to find her themselves. There was another problem as well: they had no idea whether there were any more of Berrigan's men on the estate, so as they searched for Lady Amanda they were also going to have to keep a careful watch for other enemies. Every man they saw could be an enemy, and they could be hidden anywhere. As many as could piled into the ammunition wagon and the captured wagon and they headed toward the mansion at a slow trot. The other men began to walk.

Within three quarters of an hour the wagons were approaching the mansion and everyone aboard was alert for danger. All weapons were loaded and ready. Massengill decided that it was likely that Lady Amanda was being held in the area of the stables and the linen hall, or that if not, there would be someone there who would know where she was, so they passed by the mansion and rolled up to the gate of the stable yard. There they got off the wagons and began a careful walk into the yard. Although there seemed to be no one about, Massengill told off four men to stand in the middle of the yard looking in all directions and ready to shoot if anyone showed his face in a menacing way. The others, including Massengill, started searching stall by stall and room by room. In addition to looking for her, they were calling to Amanda and hoping for a reply. They had searched all the stalls and were starting to check the rooms in the wing that held the linen hall when one of the men heard a voice and shouted, "Someone this way, cap'm!" Massengill and several of the others headed for him and Massengill called, "Amanda! Is that you? Keep calling." She did, and they followed her voice to a stout door. It was locked. "Lady Amanda, is that you?"

"It is I. Who is there and what do you want? What is happening?"

"It is John Massengill and a crew. We are here to take you home. We have fought Padraig Berrigan and his men and have won. You are safe. We will have you out soon. Otis, find something to break this lock."

"Aye cap'm." Otis was back in less than a minute with a pickaxe which he used to rip the lock and hasp out of the door frame. The door started to swing open on its own, and suddenly Amanda called out, "Wait! Not yet, not until I tell you." Everything stopped. Massengill pushed the door shut and held it. "I am not presentable. I must prepare myself. You will wait." They looked at each other and grinned, and they waited. When Amanda indicated that she was ready Massengill opened the door. She flinched a bit at the bright morning light and stepped out. Massengill gave her his hand; he could see that she was not steady, and even though she had prepared herself, she did not look well. Her clothes were much wrinkled and were dirty. She was dirty, and her hair, which she clearly had tried to put up, was dirty and disheveled. Amanda had never presented herself to anyone in such a state. "John Massengill, they have told me that I am in danger because of you. Have you done something wrong? What has happened?"

Massengill assured her that he had done nothing wrong and had been the target of the same men who had abducted her and he reassured her once again that she was rescued and was going home. He would explain everything.

Chapter 54

When the sound of the approaching wagons was heard at the gate lodge, the constables girded themselves for battle. They had been glad to stay out of the fight in the estate, but they did have a duty to safeguard the public in the village, so they were ready to stand fast. The sound increased and tension mounted. Dust could be seen wafting above the trees. When the first wagon came into view guns were being raised, but Quirke saw Bowyer madly waving his white shirt and shouted, "Hold your fire, men, they are surrendering." Sergeant Watterson was driving the first wagon and he slowed to a walk as he approached the cluster of constables. "We've wounded aboard. We must get to the doctor without delay." He kept the wagon moving, turning north on the High Street toward the doctor's office.

"What's happened, man?" shouted the Constable Supervisor.

"Berrigan had a plot. We've fought them and won. Captain Massengill is gone to find Lady Amanda Walsh. Berrigan and his crew are dead in the blast except for four wounded we have. We've dead, as well." He kept moving up the street and it was clear he was not going to stop until he got to the doctor's office so the constables began to run along with him. The wagons stopped at the doctor's office and the wounded were unloaded and taken in.

"Who is killed?" asked Quirke.

"It's my own Captain, Milton Ievers," responded Watterson, "and Mr. James Walsh of Green Fields. We have done lost two fine ones. This is disaster."

"Disaster it is. My God, sergeant, tell us all you know."

"I know little more than I has already told you. Berrigan and his men were at the waterfront where the logs are loaded out. They had a barge alongside and it was loaded with guns and gunpowder. They were trying to get it under way when we got there and some fired on us while the others was readying the barge to go. They was just in the stream when one of our balls struck a powder barrel and set it off. The whole barge blew to smithereens. All aboard died. Their wounded we have brought are ones who was shot on the ground before they could get to the barge. We've scoured the field and all ours is accounted for, dead or alive. Lady Amanda was nowhere to be seen, so when we finished scouring of the battlefield Captain Massengill and a crew drove off toward the mansion to try and find her. We don't know whether there are others of Berrigan's men still on the place and ready to fight."

"What of Massengill," asked the Constable Supervisor.

"Why, man, he has led everything. He and Captain Ievers determined that Berrigan was up to something rotten at Croome Forest and that Berrigan's men was the likely ones to have taken Lady Amanda, and he was determined to get to the bottom of it and to save the Lady. He is on your side, Constable. He has done all in spite of you, and you are in his debt and in the debt of my Captain, God bless his soul."

The doctor and the apothecary, assisted by Bowyer and Cheshire, were soon able to say that all of the wounded should survive except for Womack, whose wound was to vital parts and who might not pull through. The constables were beginning to believe that Massengill was on their side and that Berrigan was the culprit, but they weren't sure, so they waited. Sergeant Watterson commandeered a horse and rode off to bring the tragic news in person to the widow Ievers. The village was in frenzy. People had poured onto the high street when it became clear that the arrival of the wagons was not going to cause gunfire, and they crowded around the doctor's office to find out what had happened. Watterson's message spread through the crowd and a hubbub developed with people calling for the constables to go in to Croome Forest and help Massengill's crew, others praising Massengill and his force, and others mocking the constables for their inaction and incompetence. Still, the constables did nothing. Like everyone else, they waited to see what would happen next.

CHAPTER 55

When Amanda was able to leave her cell she was dazzled by the sunlight, hungry, thirsty, and weak and unstable on her feet, but the only thing on her mind was Henry. "John, you must take me to my boy. He must be suffering terribly because of all this."

"I will get you to Green Fields immediately, but I can tell you now that Henry is well. James Walsh has been with us and when he came from Green Fields he brought the latest report on the boy. Henry thinks you are merely in seclusion, suffering from the shock of the fire. Everyone has been careful to shield him." Massengill decided to leave the news of James' death for a better time.

"Oh, I'm so glad. But we must go to him."

"We will. Otis, search out a suitable carriage for Lady Amanda." Otis was off immediately and came back within two minutes, "We has a phaeton, and there is only a few of horses, but enough for it and for a wagon, which we has found to take the all of us. We will harness up and be ready to go directly." The farmers among the crew were already busy harnessing horses to the phaeton and wagon and within five minutes they were loaded up and along with the ammunition wagon and Berrigan's wagon were on the way to the village. Massengill drove the phaeton with Amanda beside him and the wagons followed.

"Captain, I am a most awful mess. I am ashamed that you are seeing me in this state. I am dirty, I am unkempt, I even smell bad, I have never been so horrible, and now I am to be paraded through the village! I apologize for my appearance. I wish I could hide!"

"My Lady, you are a sight for sore eyes. I cannot tell you how glad I am to see you, nor do I have the words to tell you how beautiful you look, in spite of the treatment you have endured. To see you is a dream come true. Fear nothing; you will be welcomed in the village as a returning princess.

"My Lady, I do have sad news for you. Two of our number have been wounded in the fight and I am sorry to say that we are two killed. Captain Ievers fell leading his squad in the charge—"

"Oh, how horrible. The dear man. He has been a love always. Oh God—"

"It is a true tragedy. He was a brave man who rallied immediately to your cause. As a King's officer, he knew how to fight and was in the very front of the charge. We did our preparation and training at Ievers Court, and he and his lady gave all possible support. He put himself in danger to save you. There was nothing more fair than his efforts in your behalf. It is a measure of everyone's love and respect for you."

"I hate it that he should have died for me." Tears were running down her cheeks.

"Fighting men risk their lives for causes they believe in, and he believed in succoring you and in stopping Berrigan. "

"What was it that Berrigan was doing, and why did he want me?"

"I do not know all the answers, but he was on a desperate errand, one that was worth lives. When I have a chance to interrogate his remaining men I hope to unravel the whole story. Until then do not concern yourself; I will tell you the story when I am sure of it. I have one more thing of importance to tell you. A man who loved and respected you greatly has died as well."

He paused for a second, collecting himself, "James Walsh was killed in the first skirmish. He died doing everything he could for you. When he was told by Captain Ievers what we were doing, he immediately volunteered. He made clear his love for you and his resolve to do anything he could for you."

"Oh, God! James! I have always known of his infatuation with me, but I have always thought I was merely one of many women for him and wanted none of that. I have not treated him well, and now he had died for me. What misery! What tragedy!"

"It may be that he was not worthy of you over the years. In fact, he told us that he felt he had contributed to your troubles by telling Lady Susan Seymour about my visit to you after Lachlan Edwards' death. Somehow, she thought I had told you something that was dangerous and James feels—felt—she was in touch with Berrigan and began the process that resulted in the fire and your abduction. He told us that when he realized this it changed his life. He realized that of all things or people in the world you were the most important to him and he resolved to forgo all else, and all other women, and do everything he could to save you and convince you of his true love."

"Oh, poor James. Poor James. The disasters that have befallen this community are beyond belief."

"Let us dwell on the facts that Berrigan is stopped and you are saved. That is enough good news to push away the bad.

"I will tell you one other bit of shocking news. It seems there is all too much of it. Lady Susan Seymour, Sir William Seymour and innkeeper John Barber are all dead."

"Incredible! How can it be?"

"I hate even to speak of this to you, but it seems that the three of them were part of a large ring of white slavers. They were abducting young girls and forcing them into prostitution in Dublin and possibly in other cities. A local boy, Niall Bannon, while in Dublin stumbled onto the fact that his own sister had been a victim of the ring and he and his father took revenge upon the three, shooting them to death during a meeting that was being held by the constabulary at the inn."

"This is beyond belief. I am overwhelmed by all this. It is simply too much."

They fell silent, and moving at a brisk walk within fifteen minutes they were approaching the gate. Since they had heard no firing when the two wagons had left they felt they would not face gunfire when they went out, but, still, Massengill slowed and moved with caution. Although almost all the constables had followed the wagons to the doctor's office there were still two at the gate. They were armed, but as soon as they were in sight Massengill began waving his bandanna in what he hoped would be seen as a friendly gesture. The constables saw him, but more important, they could see a woman beside him and they knew he was bringing Lady Amanda. They waved him on and gave a shout up the High Street that the Lady had been found and was coming. The crowd, including the rest of the constables, did an about face and started moving toward the gate, eager to see Amanda. When Massengill reached the first constables he called, "The Lady Amanda is here safe, we have won the day. Berrigan and his forces are destroyed." Amanda waved to the crowd and Massengill and the wagons behind continued on up the street. As soon as they came abreast of people on the street cheering and clapping began; it followed them to where the Constable Supervisor and Quirke were standing and continued while Massengill stopped and the law men greeted Lady Amanda and showered Massengill with questions.

The constables told him what Watterson had told them and were disappointed to find that Massengill could add nothing except for the fact that they had encountered no other armed men after the battle at the waterfront and the obvious fact that Lady Amanda had been found. He explained that Lady Amanda needed to see her ward, Henry, and that she needed rest and 'much coddling'. They would go to Green Fields where Massengill would deliver Lady Amanda and would bring the sad news of James Walsh's death. Massengill told the constables he would return to describe to them in detail what had happened at Croome Forest. He inquired after the wounded, and found that Watterson had gone on to Ievers Court to bring the news of Captain Ievers' death. He rallied his crew and thanked the men for their brave and successful day's work, gave orders to Otis to see that the men were able to return to their homes or places of lodging, and set off with Lady Amanda for Green Fields.

CHAPTER 56

Massengill and Amanda arrived at Green Fields before any news of her rescue had reached the place so her appearance was both astonishing and wonderful. Massengill stopped the phaeton in front of the door and helped Amanda down. There was a boy to take charge of the horses. They had hardly knocked at the door when it was opened and, Martin, the butler, was immediately almost beside himself with delight. "We will see Mr. Walsh, Martin," said Lady Amanda.

Martin gleefully lead the way to the parlor, opened the door and announced as if nothing more interesting than the visit of a neighbor from down the road were happening, "Lady Amanda Walsh to see you, Sir."

It was fortunate that William Walsh was seated on the settee and not on a chair, because he sat bolt upright with such force that a chair would have surely been overturned. The settee, itself, lost its moorings and leaped back a good six inches. "God almighty, child, you are delivered! Come here to me, dearest one."

They embraced, but Amanda quickly drew back, "I am in such a state that you should not soil yourself with me, father."

"You are in a perfect state, my precious girl. Martin, get young Henry and spread the word that our prodigal one had returned home! We will partake the fatted calf for sure. By God, dear Amanda, you must be famished for decent food. Where have you been? Who has taken you?"

By now, running feet could be heard and within seconds the entire household fell on her in joy, dogs and all. Massengill watched with pleasure but with great sadness, knowing that he was going to have to break the news of his son's death to William Walsh. Amanda wrapped Henry into her arms and gave him a great kiss. They talked, but very soon Amanda looked up and said, "Anna, you must make me a bath as quickly as you can. I can't wait to get this filth off me. Find me fresh clothes and burn these things!"

Amanda and Anna left, and Henry was taken by his nanny to clean himself and be prepared for a long talk with his auntie. Massengill and William Walsh were left alone. "Massengill, tell me everything."

"Mr. Walsh it has been a great adventure. Quickly, I can tell you that Berrigan was up to no good at Croome Forest, just as we surmised. It was he who had Lady Amanda. I am sure that he and his men were the spawn of the men of 1798 and were amassing arms for another try at rebellion. They are stopped and Berrigan is dead."

"And what of my son?"

Massengill girded himself once more to deliver the devastating message, "I must now tell you tragic news. James fell in the battle. He gave his life most nobly, in the front of an encounter with Berrigan's men. Captain Ievers also lost his life. One of my men, Womack, is wounded, mortally I am afraid, and one of Mr. Corry's farmers, Lynch, is wounded as well, although with luck and by the grace of God his wound should not be fatal."

The old man's face crumpled, "James! My God, the boy wasted his whole life. I watched it happen and could do nothing to stop him. And now this."

"I can tell you, that whatever the story of his past may have been, he died with the greatest of honor. You can be proud. He was ready to do anything to succor Lady Amanda, and he did all."

"Amanda—yes. He was besotted with her almost from the minute she married Thomas, and when the news of Thomas' death came, James wanted her more than anything in the world. But she knew him well by that time. Knew all his faults all too well and wanted no part of him as a husband. He never slacked in his love for her, but he had many a dalliance during the years she put him off, and she knew enough of what was going on to keep her firm in refusing his attentions."

"He changed. He felt he had harmed her by not being of enough help to me when I was in the hands of the constabulary and that that omission had led to her abduction. His need to atone for this by helping to save her had overcome all else in his life. He had only the most noble motives and he was ready to give his life if need be for her."

William Walsh gave a great sigh, almost a moan, "I take comfort in that. I have never known what would become of James. I will tell you I feared the worst after my death. James was on a path to gamble or fritter the estate away. Now, at least, that will not happen. What will happen is that my godson, young Henry Bullen, will inherit Green Fields and his auntie, my sweet and beloved Amanda, will never lack for anything though she might live to one hundred years. That I can promise."

"Noble, indeed. James' remains are at the doctor's surgery. I will make arrangements with the undertaker for a coffin of the finest kind and I will be sure the rector is notified."

"Do that for me. My thanks. We will devote ourselves to giving every comfort to Amanda. You will tell me all the details of this amazing series of events when time permits. Once again, Captain, my warmest thanks for all you have done. By God, you have done well for me, for Amanda, for Croome Court, and for all of the British Empire. What a stroke you have made! Go with God who will guard your every step."

CHAPTER 57

Massengill drove the phaeton back into Croome Court and pulled up before the constable's office. He tethered the horses and went in where he found the Constable Supervisor, Quirke, and Monaghan's Chief Constable, seated around Quirke's desk. After calming the crowd, posting two men to keep a guard at the gate to Croome Forest and checking on the wounded, they had been waiting for him. "Captain, we are glad to see you. It seems we owe you our most profound apology, and we offer it most sincerely."

"Thank you, Constable Supervisor, I will say that you have given me a hard time, but I know you have done your duty as you saw it. I cannot fault you for that. Your apology is accepted—with pleasure."

"Captain Massengill, in addition to the great work you have done here, we have this day by the Monaghan coach received a communication from the Port Captain at Belfast in response to a request we had made of him for information about you. We can say that we are much impressed with the information he has sent us."

"I have the pleasure of knowing Captain Vantrease. I met with him not a week ago when I was in Belfast. We served together in *Elephant*, years ago. I trust he gave you a good report of me," said Massengill with a smile, "and I trust he has backed up his statements with enough documentation to convince you that my old friend is not simply covering his old friend's indiscretions with a story made to order."

"Captain, we can assure you that there is much proof of what he has told us. The very tone of his personal communication is so open and frank that we would not doubt it even if there were no other documents to back up what he has said. His history of your years at sea and the manner in which you have made your fortune was a wonderful tale. He was able to loan to us two articles clipped from *The Times* of London that reported some of your victories and the resulting prize money. To say that your story is impressive would be to say all too little. We wish you joy of your success.

"We will be frank to say that we had many questions about you. The recent events began immediately after your arrival after an absence of many years; that in itself was curious. The facts early on seemed to point to you. You had with you a crew of rough men who looked as if they could have carried out any number of crimes. Then we felt you were absolved of guilt, but then—and we must presume you do not know this—Berrigan brought us proof that you were the owner of Croome Forest and a tale that you were behind nefarious deeds there. We were astonished that a man of your background and story could have honestly amassed a fortune that would have allowed him to buy such and estate, and this made us think you might have been in league with the Seymours and had made your fortune in their dastardly businesses. It seemed possible that having returned home, you were in the process of silencing all who knew of your past, including Lady Amanda, to whom you had inadvertently revealed your secrets. There have been so many things…"

"I can see how it seemed to you," responded Massengill, "and I can wonder that all might have been better if I had come to the village announcing my ownership of Croome Forest, but I had thought it better to move slowly on that matter. A mistake,

I now believe. I am sure I need not tell you that bringing any harm to Lady Amanda is the last thought I would have."

"We understand. There is much else that we still do not understand. Do you know the full nature of what Berrigan was doing?"

"I do not, but I have my suspicion. The explosion that you no doubt heard even here—"

"We did. It was like nothing ever heard before in Croome Court," broke in Quirke.

"Yes. The explosion was caused when one of our balls hit a barrel of gunpowder that was on the deck of the barge on which Berrigan and his men were trying to escape down the river. The barge and all on it were completely destroyed by the blast, but before it happened we had been able to see that the barge was loaded with guns and many barrels of powder. There must have been hundreds of weapons of different types, muskets, rifles, pistols, and bayonets were all in the mix. Such an armory, in my opinion could have had only one purpose: rebellion. I think they were part of a rising planned against the King. That can only be a supposition, but I hope we may be able to find more from their survivors. Are any able to talk?"

"One, at least, appears able to be interrogated."

"And you have not spoken with him?"

"No, Captain, we felt obliged to wait for your return. You are the man of the hour; you know more than anyone else of these doings and you can best be the interrogator."

"Where is the man?"

"He is at the doctor's surgery. Let us go now." Quirke led the way to the surgery where the six wounded men remained. Four were bandaged and still weak but were seated or walking. Berrigan's men would be moved to the inn and kept under guard and Lynch, the farmer from Corry Hall, would be returned home. The other two, one of Berrigan's men and Womack were in dire straits. Both were still alive but both had wounds that were expected almost invariably to be fatal. Bowyer and Cheshire were still there, assisting the doctor and, along with one of the constables, making sure that none of Berrigan's men made a run for freedom.

Massengill spoke with Bowyer and Cheshire and spent some time with Womack while the constables waited. Womack was barely conscious, but he did know that his Captain was tending to him. Each thanked the other for his service during the day and pledged eternal respect and love. Massengill had seen many such wounds and knew that Womack had only a slight chance to live. He knew that Womack probably knew it as well. "I am going to interrogate one of the enemy's men. We will find out their story. Stay at rest; I will be back."

"Aye cap'm."

The constables and Massengill turned their attention to the least wounded of Berrigan's men, whose name proved to be Nolan. Nolan had a wound to his right arm that was painful, but that with any luck at all he would survive easily. He was not cooperative. "I've no desire to talk to King's men. You have took over our country; I want none of you."

"Nolan, how long have you worked with Berrigan?"

"These three years. All on the work at Croome Forest."

"And what was your goal?"

"Find it for yourself."

"For the sake of Lady Amanda Walsh we need to know why she was taken. Were you a part of that?"

"She knew what you knew, Captain. All had to be silenced."

"And that included the attorney Edwards?"

"You talked to him as well."

"Good God, I have been the kiss of death for all I came near."

Constable Quirke broke in, "Nolan, tell us about Sir William and Lady Susan Seymour."

"They was not done in by us. They was done in by an aggrieved father whose girl had done been took by them. Barber, too."

"Were they associated with Berrigan?"

"They had nothin' to do with the cause. They was running their brothels and we was providin' rough men to keep order. They paid well and we needed the money."

"For the cause?"

"Find out for yourself."

Massengill took over. "What do you know of a man named Michael O'Day from Belfast?"

"I know nothin' about nobody in Belfast. I am from Longford and I know nothin' about Belfast. O'Day is no one to me."

"Tell us about the cause."

"Learn it for yourselves. I has nothin' more to say."

"Very well, but you will talk with us again."

Massengill said goodbye to Womack, for the last time, he feared, and told Bowyer and Cheshire to continue to help the doctor as he needed them and to reestablish themselves at the inn when the doctor could do without them. He and the constables returned to the constable's office.

CHAPTER 58

The fourth of September was another day of funerals, a train of funerals such as Croome Court had never seen and one that was not ready to end. The service for James Walsh was held at ten o'clock in the morning and the service for Captain Milton Ievers was held at two o'clock in the afternoon, both at the protestant chapel. Both had died in battle under the command of Massengill and it was his opinion that they deserved every honor that could be bestowed upon them. He was there in his dress uniform, wearing enough gold to impress everyone who saw him, and with his sword at his side. Cheshire had done him proud; he was resplendent. His remaining five men—one was keeping watch over Womack—were rigged out in their best uniforms, all cleaned and brushed and polished to the nines. At both of the funerals it was Massengill and his men who carried the coffins that held the mortal remains of fallen comrades.

They made a good show and it was much talked about in the village for long after that there had never been funerals with more style and gravity in living memory. Amanda was recovered almost to her normal bloom of beauty and she was present, dressed in a severe dark grey dress, one that belonged to the housekeeper at Green Fields and had been altered to fit her. It was not the perfect mourning costume, but it was the best that could be had in the circumstances. Amanda was mourning for both of the dead and was shaken by the realization that both had died in the fight to free her. She was comforted, but only in part, by the knowledge that their lives had been taken in a battle that had not only freed her but had broken the back of a rebellion that would have taken many more lives if it had not been snuffed out before it began in earnest. Massengill was relieved to see Amanda at all, and to see her in such good spirit and looks was a greater relief. He spoke to her and made arrangements to visit her at Green Fields to tell her what he knew.

Both of these funerals were the more solemn and moving because each of these men was the last of his line. Captain and Mrs. Ievers, though married for over thirty years, had no children, and James Walsh had never married and his only sibling, Thomas, had not fathered a child in the tragically short three weeks he had with his bride. All were already wondering what would happen at Ievers Court on the death of Mrs. Ievers, and only a few knew the plans for the future of Green Fields that William Walsh had made.

On that same day late in the evening Womack died. He had endured two hard days of suffering. His wound continued to bleed and would not close and he became weaker and weaker, losing consciousness early on the second day. Either Massengill or one of his fellows was with him all the time, even after he lost consciousness. It was Douglass who had the watch when he breathed his last at eight PM on the second evening. Massengill and the rest of his crew were living at the inn and they were dining together when Douglass brought the news. The death had been expected; the only question had been how long before it came. Womack had been with Massengill and the rest of the crew for eight years. He was a sturdy and tall fellow of modest intelligence but unlimited devotion to his captain and all were agreed that a better seaman had never lived. Every tie to his family had long been lost so Womack's only kin were his crew. Massengill found it both remarkable and wonderful that Womack's death caused almost as much pain in the village as it did among his fellows. Every man who had taken part in the fight and the rescue at Croome Forest had been taken to heart by virtually the entire population and Womack's case, along with the case of their other wounded man, a man from the village whom they all knew, had been followed on an almost hour by hour basis until he died.

Massengill declared that since Womack had died wresting Croome Forest away from the traitors to the crown who were ill using the place, he would be buried in the family burying ground on the estate. This was unusual, and perhaps even improper, but by this time Massengill's word was more than as good as law in Croome Court, and steps were taken to place his edict into effect.

CHAPTER 59

On the morning after the day of the funerals of Captain Ievers and James Walsh, John Massengill rode to Green Fields to see Amanda as the two of them had planned the day before. He was ushered into the drawing room and found her seated, and even though the weather was warm, wrapped in a large silk shawl. She offered her hand, he bowed over it, and she motioned him to a seat. "Tell me all."

"I'm afraid I do not yet know all, but I can tell you what I know, which is a lot. Berrigan and his men were the successors of the United Irishmen. They were determined to reignite the rebellion that failed in 1798 and were amassing a great store of weapons and ammunition with which to arm, it appears, as many as a thousand men. Croome Forest was found to be the perfect place for their activities: a large estate, much wooded, almost never accessed by the public, and owned by an ailing and inactive landlord. They had been amassing their goods for a number of years. The sale of the estate was a great problem for them because they knew that the new owner might be much more active than the Earl de Croome and that they were likely to be found out.

Lachlan Edwards was murdered and his records covering Croome Forest and my dealings were stolen because they feared that Edwards might know something of the goings on and would warn me of the situation and I would then be the catalyst for action against them. The fact that I became implicated as his killer was balm to their souls; my incarceration gave them time. My visit to you was most unfortunate for you because they feared that I did know something damaging to them and that I had told you."

"Which you had not done. There was nothing!"

"True. But their suspicion was more important than the actual fact. They found out about our visit by way of James Walsh and Lady Susan Seymour. It seems that Lady Susan and Sir William had for a number of years been operating a virtual empire of, ah—houses of ill repute."

"Yes, I know. Incredible! They were always thought odd, and she was a notorious bawd, but that they were doing such a thing is beyond belief."

"Most certainly, but, nevertheless, it is true. They were recruiting girls from country villages who thought they were going to the cities to get positions as domestic staff in the homes of the wealthy when, in fact, they were being conscripted into lives of unspeakable degradation. For such activities they needed security and that is where they joined forces with the United Irishmen. The Irishmen could provide rough men ready for any fight and the Seymours could provide payment that the Irishmen needed. It was a match made in hell.

"Amazingly, the deaths of the Seymours and John Barber had nothing to do with the rebellion. The Bannons, father and son, were merely avenging the degradation of their sister and daughter, Ailis, who was one of the unfortunate girls who was lured into destruction by Barber, who was the Seymours' agent in Croome Court."

"A fitting end for people of such evil natures. What will happen to the Bannons?"

"I do not know. It is not yet decided, but we can hope that they are shown some mercy. Their deed was foul, but it cleansed the earth of people still more foul. Perhaps they will be transported."

He paused for a moment and then continued, "after I was cleared of suspicion and released from custody Berrigan cunningly re-implicated me in the minds of the constabulary and, although I remained free, the constables were determined to keep a watch on me to try to determine what I was up to. By that time you had been abducted and it had become clear to me that something outside the law was going on at Croome Forest and that likely you were there. Because of you, I determined to get to the bottom of the case on my own, feeling that the constabulary were going to do nothing but wait for more information and then perhaps do nothing when the information had arrived. With the help of Captain Ievers I and my men were able to recruit a fine force of men from the neighborhood and we attacked. The battle was at the waterfront and Berrigan and almost all his men were killed, either from gunfire or in the explosion."

"I heard it all. The explosion was incredible. I've never heard anything like it before."

"It was dazzling," he agreed, "but I have to say that I have heard a good many like it before. We must put all this behind us. It will take us time to recover and return to a normal life, but we shall do it. Tomorrow at ten in the AM is the funeral of my man Womack, who died yesterday. I hope you will be able to attend at the chapel."

"Yes, yes, John—Captain—how terrible. Count on it. I will be there."

"It will be a pleasure to see you again. May I say that you are looking well and most fully recovered."

She gave him a warm smile, "You may, and I thank you. Until tomorrow."

CHAPTER 60

The time for Womack's funeral came and the turnout of mourners was the same as it had been for James Walsh and Captain Ievers. Massengill was once again in his dress uniform and Womack's fellow seamen were in their best dress. The rector of the protestant chapel read the service in the chapel, the coffin was placed on the wagon on which Womack had ridden into Croome Court, and a slow journey to the Croome Forest burial ground began. Massengill and his seamen walked behind the cart. The cortege moved at a walk and while there were carriages and wagons in the cortege there were also many in addition to the naval party who made the trip on foot. It was estimated by the rector that over a hundred people had come to see Womack laid to rest. Some had come because they thought it would be their only chance of a lifetime to get into the Croome Forest estate and see the mansion, even if only from the outside, but most were there to honor a man and his comrades who had brought to a close the greatest disaster in Croome Court's history. Massengill found it all to be most satisfying. He had lost a good man, but in almost twenty years at sea he had lost many good men, so he was as used to loss as a man could be. He took solace in the thought that Womack had died for a cause that was good in every way.

After the graveside service was ended Massengill, as the chief mourner, stayed to speak to those who wanted to express their condolences, and when the rector had left and the crowd had dwindled Amanda Walsh was among those who remained. Massengill approached her and said, "Lady Amanda, I have access to the mansion and would like to take you to show you the place if it would please you."

"I would be delighted, Captain."

"Excellent," he said, "Cheshire, take Henry and Miss Anna to see the linen hall where Lady Amanda was held captive. You will entertain them. Let it be so."

"Aye, Cap'm. Come, lad and Miss Anna, I'll show you where Cap'm Massengill rescued your auntie. It were a hot fight, it were, and I were there with 'em. I can tell you all about it. You'll see." Cheshire, Anna, and Henry headed toward the Linen Hall in the range of buildings behind the mansion house and Amanda gave Massengill a smile, took his arm and they began walking across the greensward to the front of the mansion. As they walked Amanda thought of Laurence. How he would love to bound across these meadows! If only a wolfhound were fit to be a mourner at a solemn funeral and burial he could have been with her now, enjoying a wonderful gallop.

The grasses were not high and the bright sunlight had dried the dew so the walking was pleasant. Amanda was conscious of Massengill's limp. One could have thought it was the rolling gate of a seaman whose land legs were not yet under him, but she knew better. She asked, "Have you been in the mansion before?" "Yes, one time. I came with my father a number of times when he met with the chief steward or the Earl and once I was invited into the ground floor. That was over twenty years ago, but I remember it well. It was magnificent beyond anything I had ever seen."

"It is magnificent. I have been to Croome Forest from time to time. We were invited to balls on the rare occasions upon which the Earl and Countess gave them and to tea from time to time. One would have to go many miles to find a place so fine, perhaps not in all of Cavan. I wonder what will happen to it."

"Time will tell, and you shall see."

"Yes, the time will come. I wish that whoever shall have it is a lover of gardens. I have always bewailed the lack of a garden. It is amazing to me that generations of Earls and Countesses have lived here and none has made a pleasure garden. The house sits so starkly, with nothing at all around it. Not a tree, not a bush, not a garden wall, just itself. It would be a good life's work to create a proper garden here."

"It does sit bare, but one could say that makes it all the more imposing. It crowns the ridge in true grandeur. I think the house has great dignity rising alone, but a proper garden would greatly add to the beauty of the estate."

"Grand it is, but the brick gives it warmth," she said. "A house of cut stone is magnificent, though a bit hard, but a house of brick can be impressive and at the same time inviting. More of a home. This mansion has that feeling of a home. Let us hope it becomes one once again." They reached the graveled drive and mounted the broad flight of stone steps leading up to the porch. On the porch Massengill pulled a key from his pocket and inserted it into the lock of the front door.

"You have a key!" Amanda exclaimed. "Oh, of course you would. You have captured this place and it is yours!"

"Captured it I have, and mine it is," he smiled. "Come in." They entered the stone floored entrance hall, a handsome room with walls painted a stone grey to match the marble floor. It had a twenty-foot high coved ceiling, a fireplace with carved marble mantle and niches above the doors where the marble busts of Roman emperors still sat in their places. They studied it with pleasure then Massengill opened the door to the dining room and they went in. It was all in white except for the grey painted background of the frieze below the cornice. It, too, had a high coved and coffered ceiling and there were Ionic pilasters around the walls. The long oval-ended dining table was still there as were the chairs and the mahogany sideboard. There was no plate on the sideboard, there were no candlesticks or candelabra, no dishes or flatware on the table. A light coating of dust was everywhere and the brass railing around the top of the sideboard was dull with tarnish, but the effect of the room and it furnishings remained striking.

"A wonderful room; grand for entertaining," said Amanda.

"Indeed it is," replied Massengill, "but I remember the ballroom as more handsome by far. Come, let us go."

"Yes, the ballroom is truly fine, I have warm memories of it and think I have never been in a room that was more elegant." They opened the door and walked slowly into the adjoining room. It was as they had remembered it. Twenty-five by thirty feet in size with a high flat ceiling that was covered in fine plaster work. There was a frieze with elegant plaster moldings below the cornice, raised carved wood surrounds around the three large windows, the doors, and the panels on the walls where paintings had hung. An elegant glass chandelier hung from the center of the ceiling and the room retained its furniture, arranged along the pale blue walls, although none of the accessories such as candle sticks, porcelain, or bric-a-brac remained. They looked in silence for a moment and, at the same time, turned to look at each other. Each knew what the other was thinking: It was evening, the chandelier was lit and there were candles everywhere casting light that was reflected by the window glass and the mirrors. The fire was lit. The room had a complement of elegantly dressed people, moving about and chatting lightly. Three musicians in the northeast corner were playing an introduction. Dancing was about to begin. Amanda had been in this room and had been part of the scene. Massengill could see it in his mind's eye. They smiled at each other.

The furniture was all in white cotton dust covers and Massengill pulled back the cover on the settee and dropped it to the floor. The settee was covered in peach colored silk and the visible wood was all gilded. It was an extremely elegant piece, and was just one of the full set of similar pieces arrayed along the walls that furnished the entire room's seating.

"Please, Lady Amanda, be seated."

"Captain, you must stop calling me 'Lady Amanda'. You know my name is Amanda, and you shall use it so from now on." She sat down and Massengill seated himself beside her.

"And you shall call me 'John', since my mother never had me christened 'Captain'."

She gave him a delighted smile and said, "It shall be so, John."

He thought for a moment and looked at her. "You know," he said, "I can see you as mistress of this place. You have everything Croome Forest needs: beauty, intelligence, wit, dignity, grace, accomplishment, and honor. You would fit this place admirably."

She laughed. "You compliment me and I thank you. But there is the one problem: to be mistress of this place I would have to be married to the master, and we do not know who the master of this place will be or even when he might arrive. And even if we knew those things there is no doubt that such a man would come with a wife already in place. I believe my elevation to mistress of Croome Forest must remain a dream of mine—and yours," she smiled, "   but only a pleasant dream."

"I do compliment you, Amanda, and it is my great pleasure to do so. I have traveled the world these twenty years and never in all the places I have been have I met any woman so fine as you. You are a delight. I would like to spend my whole life giving you compliment after compliment."

She looked down, not daring to look him in the face. "John, you are too kind." Amanda could hardly speak, "you embarrass me!"

"Never in life, my dear. You qualities allow you to accept any compliment without embarrassment. I do not wish to cause you embarrassment. But it is mine to tell you that I do know the name of the new owner of Croome Forest. He is, in fact, seated here with you." He paused. She looked at him in amazement. "I know this is hard for you to understand, but it is fact that through prize money amassed during my Navy years I have achieved wealth beyond anything I ever imagined, or even dreamed, and one month ago I purchased Croome Forest from the heirs of Lord de Croome.

"I came to the village to take up residence in my new home, never realizing what a task it would be. But now it is done. I know that I am only a son of the gentry and that I have lived a rough life among rough men for two decades. I have not the polish and elegance you have and am in no way your equal, but in spite of my deficiencies, it is my most ardent wish that you would do me the greatest of honor, the honor of becoming my wife. I am conscious just how bold it is of me to make such a request and I know you could not answer such a sudden request at this minute, but please—think on it. Please."

Amanda fixed a most loving look on him and said, "John—I am dazzled. I am astonished that you are the owner of Croome Forest and that you should have wanted to return to a simple place like Croome Court after a life of adventure—and one that made you a fortune. It is stunning that you return with such a fortune and that you have Croome Forest as your home.

"You do dazzle me," she paused. "It is hard to take this in. You can be the husband of any woman you choose, and I can hardly believe that you would choose me. I respect you, for you are a man who has made his own way in the world and has reached a height few have attained. Though you may not believe it, I have had a love for you since we first met at North Hall, but I thought I would never see you again and tried—but never succeeded—to put you out of my mind. Much has happened since then. You know the scandal and tragedy that have surrounded me. I have no fortune worthy of mention. I feel as if I would be more of a burden than a blessing to you, and my only desire would be to bless you. Can you really mean this proposal?"

"I mean it and, more than anything else in life I want it to be so. Please, make it so."

Amanda took his hand and smiled, "Let it be so."

THE END

CPSIA information can be obtained at www.ICGtesting.com
Printed in the USA
LVOW05s0737171014

409205LV00002B/4/P